THE CAULDRON, THE SPIT & THE FIRE

Over Five Hundred Years of Downhearth & Bargrate Cooking

By
Robert Deeley
with contributions from
Andrew Crawforth
David Pearsall
Tony Weston

Photography by
David Pearsall, Philip Drury and Michael Roberts

Edited by
Sara Roadnight
&
Catherine Aneja

Illustrated by
Sara Roadnight

Studio Artwork and Production
by
www.StunningMedia.co.uk

CONDITIONS OF SALE

This volume is sold subject to the condition that the designs, photographs and copyright are not for commercial reproduction without written permission from the designers and copyright holders.

All rights reserved. No part of this volume may be reproduced, stored in a retrieval system or transmitted in any form or by any means, electronic, mechanical or otherwise, without the prior written permission of the copyright owners and publishers.

The author has been a collector of cooking utensils and allied kitchenware for many years; his knowledge and expertise of all things culinary from downhearth to bargrate is extensive. While every care has been taken to ensure that the names, dates and uses of each item mentioned in this book are correct, the authors and the publishers will not be held responsible for any statement, date or description mentioned in the book.

Published by

© Michael.D.L Roberts 2011
Published by Gold Cockerel Books
ISBN 9780947870737

Acknowledgments

I would like to thank all those who have encouraged me to complete this book. I do not profess to be an academic or great expert, but this book reflects the interests and passions that have filled my life over many years and which I thought worth recording before my collection becomes dispersed.

I also want to thank all the people mentioned below, and any others whom I may have inadvertently forgotten: first, thank you to my wife whose tolerance and forbearance have allowed me to complete this three year project, and Andrew Crawforth for his contributions, patience and friendship, without whose help this book would never have been completed; his knowledge and taste are reflected in the diverse objects he collects and cherishes; also, David Pearsall who has supplied items from his collection for inclusion in the book, and whose mouth-watering and atmospheric photographs have helped to bring it to life, and Tony Weston for his expert contributions on spit jacks. Thank you as well to Sandy Andrew for her inspired and painstaking cooking and to Mandy Barnes for her help and common sense, the proof readers Michael Wakelin and Michael Golding for their time and encouragement; Roderick & Valentine Butler for their assistance and advice in preparing this book; the many people who have collected and saved antique culinary utensils over the years, my sister Francoise Daniel, and all the following who have been involved in various ways: Alan Jackson, Graham White, Anita and Bill Allan, John Tredant, Bruce Howard, John May the butcher and Mr. Gibson the fishmonger. Finally, a special thank you to Michael Roberts, Sara Roadnight and Catherine Aneja; I can't begin to thank them enough for the hours of help and encouragement they have given so freely; also Phil Drury whose great help with photography and computer skills have contributed so much to the finished book.

Also: Colin Morris, Jubilee Hall Antiques, Lechlade. John and Monica Douglas. Lee Materia and Alan Durham Smith, Durham House Antiques, Stow. Chris Walker. David Levi, Olympia Antiques Fair. Michael Finlay. Diana Crawforth-Hitchins. Peter Gibbons. Peter Denis, Winchcombe. Mark Newsum, Winchcombe. Roger Little, Harmic-Little Antiques. Philip Lucas. Philip Chaney. Stewart Hofgartner, Below Stairs Antiques, Hungerford. Nick Podmore, Jubilee Hall Antiques, Lechlade. Paul Eisler, Jubilee Hall Antiques, Lechlade. Robert Duff, Tudor House Antiques, Stow. Christopher Green. Hilary Fisher. Brian Eldridge. Terry Sparks, Durham House Antiques, Stow. Michael Gray, The Merchant's House, Marlborough. John Howard, Heritage Antiques, Woodstock.

I know there must be people I have forgotten. If so please forgive me, and many thanks to all of you.

Foreword

A delightful book. Not intended as a learned, academic exercise, as its context 'The Yeoman's Kitchen' indicates, however, it is an historically important work for it brings together and illustrates probably the most comprehensive private collections of antique period cooking utensils ever assembled, confirming the authors' almost obsessional pursuit of anything and everything culinary through the ages. Not only do we find out what sometimes strange and foreign objects were, but how they worked and still work, as the frequent, mouth-watering examples illustrated, (created and cooked by Sandy Andrew in period conditions) testify. I wish my mother-in-law cooked as well with all the available 21st century gadgetry!!

Robert Deeley leads us gently from the primitive cooking of the ancient cave dwellers, through the medieval kitchen gardens of monasteries, almost imperceptibly illustrating the evolution and ingenuity of yeoman utensil creativity through the 17th - 19th centuries in the ceaseless pursuit of culinary improvements.

It should not go unremarked that Robert was not only satisfied with collecting the mass of antique kitchenware - he had to make it work! Thus he decided he would source, within reason, his vegetables, herbs, fruit and flowers from his own garden, and his game, meat, fish, milk and honey from local organic producers, similarly his spices and flour. The results make for the most seductive and scrumptious photos within this delicious book - it is a very rare person who can produce, using only these antique articles, the huge variety of excellent food many of us have been privileged to share during the making of this wonderful book. Take a bow chef!!

A delightful and historically important addition to our understanding of our ancestors' kitchens.

Michael Golding,
Managing Director of Huntington Antiques, Stow-on-the-Wold, Oxfordshire;
former Chairman of Cotswold Antique Dealers Association;
Deputy Chairman of LAPADA.

Contents

Fire	1
The Evolution of Cooking with Fire	1
Downhearth	5
Skillets & Posnets	6
Cauldrons	10-15
Boiling, Seething & Simmering	11, 14
Brandreths	16
Trivets	17
Frying Pans	18-20
Griddles / Gridirons	21-22
Fire Dogs	23-24
Porte de Chimenee	25
Cob Irons & Curfew	26
Flesh Forks	27
Toasting & Cooking Forks	28-34
Curfews	35
Fire Tools	35-36
Fire Baskets	37
Bargrate	39
Bargrates	40-42
Fire Backs	43-44
Bargrate Attachments	45-46
Keeping Food & Plates Warm	47-50
Late Bargrate	51
Spits	52
Spits	52-74
Spit Racks	56
Dog Spits & Lark Spits	57-58
Fire Screens	59
Skewers	60
Dangle Spits	61
Bottle Jacks	62
Spit Jacks	63-68
Clockwork Spits	69
Smoke Jacks	70
Dog Spits	71-74

Cranes, Pot Hooks & Kettles	75
Kettle Tilts	76
Early Kettles	77
Kettles	79-80
Cranes	81-82
Pot Hooks	83
Dutch Ovens	85
Dutch Ovens	85-86, 88-89, 91
Marriott (Dutch) Oven	89
Bottle Jacks	90
Dutch Ovens & Hasteners	91
The Yeoman's Kitchen	93
Chopping Boards & Peel	94
Knives & Steels	95-96
Kitchen Treen	97-98
Kitchen Utensils	99-101
Clock	100
Ladles	102-103
Skimmers & Scummers	104-106
Kitchen Utensils	107
Miscellaneous Kitchen Items	108
Ale Mullers	109
Costrels	110
Basting/Glazing Pot & Bain Marie	111
Bed Warming Pans	112
Chestnut & Coffee Bean Roasters	113
Eggs	114
Sugar	115-116
Kitchen Storage	117
A Victorian Grocer's Ledger	119
Recipe Book	120
Settles	121
Traps & Vermin Control	123-124
Buckets	125
Cleaning & Hygiene	126
Repairs	128
A Typical Will	129-130

Contents

Preparation — 131
- Mortars & Pestles — 132-136
- Mincers & Grinders — 137-138
- Marrow Scoops & Scrapers — 140
- Scales — 141-142
- Apple Peeler — 143

Cooking in Cauldrons — 147
- Oxtail Stew — 149
- Beef Stew / Broth — 151
- Recipes & Quotes — 152

Roasting — 153
- Spit Roast Venison — 154-156
- Old English Pork Chop — 157-158
- Spit Roast Suckling Pig — 159
- Spit Roast Lamb — 160
- Roasting Beef — 161
- Game & Poultry — 163-166

Toasting — 167
- Forks — 167
- Downhearth Toasters — 168
- Bargrate Toasters — 171-174

Fish & Shellfish — 175
- Sea Fish — 175-184
- Fresh Water Fish — 185-187
- Shellfish — 188-192

Pies — 193
- Venison Pie, Game Pie — 193, 195-198
- Rolling Pins — 194
- Apple Pie — 199-200

Baking — 203
- Milling Flour — 204
- Quern — 204, 209
- Sieves — 205-206
- Bread & Baking — 207
- Bread Oven — 210
- Cloam Oven — 211
- Recipes — 214
- Baking Metalware — 215-216
- Waffles & Wafer Irons — 216

Dairy — 218
- Yokes & Milking Stools — 219
- Milk Buckets, Cans & Measures — 220
- Milk Settlers & Skimmers — 221
- Butter & Plunger Churns — 222
- Butter Workers — 224
- Butter Stamps — 225
- Butter Stamps, Curlers & Knife — 226
- Cheese Chissets, Corer & Scoops — 227
- Cheese Boards & Grater — 228
- Romance in the Dairy — 229

Moulds — 231
- Moulds — 231
- Terrines — 232
- Copper Jelly & Aspic Moulds — 233-224
- Gingerbread Moulds — 235-236
- Chocolate — 237
- Ice Cream & Biscuit Moulds — 238

Preserving & Spices — 239
- The Yeoman's Pig — 240
- Salting — 242-244
- Curing — 245
- Smoking — 246
- Jam & Preserving — 247-250
- Spices & Tea — 251-252
- Apples — 253-255

Contents

The Yeoman's Table	256
Treen Platers	257
Treen Bowls	258
Knives & Forks	261-263
Salt Pots & Spoons	264
China	265-266
Horn	267
Mugs	268
Tankards & Measures	269
Treen Goblets	270
Pewter	271-272
Jugs	273-275
Glassware	277-278
Corkscrews	279
Nut Crackers	280
Alms Dishes	281
The Aspiring Yeoman	282
Lighting	283
Making Rushlights	284
Rushlight Holders	285
Early Candlesticks	286
Brass Candlesticks	287
Hanging Candlesticks	288
Tinder Boxes & Pistols	289
Mechanical Candle Snuffers	290
Candles	291
Lanterns	293
Oil Lamps	294
Kitchen Garden	296
Herbs	298
Honey & Bee Keeping	299
Index	301-304
Bibliography	305

Carving and serving for the lord's table, taken from the early 14th century manuscript, the Lutterell Psalter.

Fire

Deer carcase waiting to be cooked on a spit by the river, note the smoke helping to keep the flies off the meat.

The Evolution of Cooking with Fire

Fire can be the most useful, destructive or comforting element in our lives.

At the dawn of time our primitive ancestors lived in caves or clearings in the primeval forest; they would have felt the effects of natural forest fires sweeping through the vegetation, having been started probably by a lightning strike in dry undergrowth or two sticks rubbing together. Fire has the ability to travel at awesome speed and with the wind behind it, can move faster than a man can run. Animals fleeing from the flames would panic and in the confusion run into the advancing fire. This would have given our primitive ancestor his first taste of burnt cooked food. Liking what he tasted, the smell of roasted meat would have awakened his taste buds – rather like that wonderful aroma wafting up the stairs on a Sunday morning, when bacon, eggs and mushrooms are cooking appetisingly in the kitchen below.

Man would have been living in a rudimentary shelter, and soon learned to strike two flints together or perhaps rub two sticks to produce a spark and start a fire in the mouth of the cave. This would have been a very useful defence against the legion of historical carnivorous predators that inhabited the land in those distant times. Wild bears were living in the British Isles until the 10th century and certain place names show that they were still around in early Saxon times.

Fire served not only as a defence, it was also a source of heat; the family would gather round it, a social tradition which continues worldwide today. When primitive man returned from hunting he would bring with him any edible animal he had been lucky enough to kill, and cook it on a stick anchored over the fire – the first spit. He also put food in the hot embers as we still do today when we roast chestnuts and bake potatoes in the ashes.

After early man had made a kill he realised that he would have to preserve it in some way: when hung outside, a dead carcase would attract flies and would not take long to putrefy and become infested with maggots which would make it totally inedible. What could be

---

"TO BURN ONE'S FINGERS"
To suffer loss by speculation or interference. The allusion is to taking chestnuts from the fire.

The Evolution of Cooking with Fire

A scene from the early 14th century Luttrell Psalter; a suckling pig and two geese or swans roasting on a spit.

done about this? He started to bring his meat into the cooler depths of the cave and this would enable him to feed his family for a week maybe. Perhaps one day someone left a piece of meat hanging over a particularly smoky fire and noticed that the result, the fore-runner of our smoked foods, kept longer and in fact had a better flavour when eaten. The same practices would have been adopted by the fish-eating fraternity and smoked fish also became part of man's diet. It was at about this time that salt, one of the most vital elements in the world, was discovered to be a preservative and put to use.

It soon became apparent that fire was the most important feature of early man's life. If he lived anywhere near moorland he learned to cut, dry and burn peat, while in forest areas an abundance of woods of all kinds was available for the fire.

Peat provided a slow burning and steady heat and is still used widely today as is animal dung in many parts of the world. Wood of course was the main source of fuel with many varieties having different qualities: for example pine and willow do not give out a great deal of heat and sparks fly everywhere, not so important in the mouth of a cave perhaps, but not ideal in a drawing room with carpet on the floors! Oak, ash and beech are some of the best woods for burning available in Britain and fruit wood and cedar burn well and produce a

A suckling pig roasting on a spit.

"POKE NOT FIRE WITH A SWORD"
Add not fuel to the fire.

The Evolution of Cooking with Fire

wonderful aroma. The hardwoods of the world make the best fires and give out the most heat. For a quick fire, stack the wood upright and to slow the fire down place the wood horizontally. This gives a good fire for cooking with a cauldron, spit or griddle etc.

As populations increased and became more static people began to build shelters or houses and so fires were moved to the centre of the main living area. The relocation of the fire from the mouth of a cave to the centre of a room enabled people to gather round it to cook, keep warm and benefit from the light of the flickering flames. The smoke would have wafted up and blackened the timbers of old houses as it filtered through the thatch. Later a hole covered with louvered boards was made to let the smoke out but stop rain coming in. Examples of central hearths still exist at Penshurst Place (Kent) and Stokesay Castle (Shropshire).

An important development in the history of the domestic fireplace was the use of an upright stone with a hollow in one side in which the fire was lit. A few still survive in early stone houses on outlying Scottish islands, in the Shetlands and Hebrides. The cauldron or pot was suspended over the fire by a chain or early crane.

Later, as house design progressed the fireplace was built against the outer wall and a chimney stack was added to conduct the smoke out of the living area. This development took place during the 16th century. Early fireplaces that have survived can be found in Rochester Castle and Glastonbury Abbey.

To begin with, fireplaces were purely simple and functional, but various improvements were added over the years and the hearth developed into an entire cooking area which included a bread oven and salt box, coppers for heating and boiling water and a smoking chamber. Some of these can still be seen in surviving inglenooks, with bread ovens especially in rural areas.

Since downhearth (cooking on a fire that was down on the floor) was the standard way of cooking on an

"THE FAT IS IN THE FIRE"
Something has been let out inadvertently which will cause a regular flare-up. The allusion is to frying: if the grease is spilt into the fire, the coals smoke and blaze thus spoiling the food.

The Evolution of Cooking with Fire

These pictures illustrate two main stages in the evolution of cooking with fire: (opposite left) downhearth, (above) bargrate.

open fire, many three legged implements rather than four legged ones, were used to maintain the balance on an uneven hearth: trivets, skillets, cooking pots and posnets were all used and are illustrated in the Downhearth chapter. Special downhearth pans with a leg on the handle were commonly used to heat small quantities of liquid or food, with the bowl of the pan resting in the embers and the handle supported by its leg.

To achieve a good result it was essential to have not only the right ingredients but also a skilled "operator", experienced in the art of cooking on a fire: the secret was in judging the strength of the fire as the heat it gave out depended on the wood burnt and the distance from it of the pot or cauldron. The aim was to control the fire so that nothing was burnt but was cooked at a steady temperature; flames would blaze up or ebb away, the pot's position needed constant adjustment and the fire had to be fed continually, unlike today when you can turn the oven on to gas mark 5 then walk away to do something else! In some large houses the fires were never allowed to go out and there are records of household fires burning continuously for over a hundred years!

Bargrates were first used in the 17th century. They began as simple bars resting on fire dogs and developed into a full basket. The culmination was the Georgian grate, familiar to all of us today.

A significant change in cooking with fire came with the discovery of coal. This marked the beginning of the age of the cast iron kitchen range and led to the extravaganza of the Victorian period before gas, electricity and oil took over and made so much redundant.

"THE POT CALLS THE KETTLE BLACK"

Said of a person who accuses another of faults similar to those committed by himself.
Pots were usually left rough cast on the outside, and were black from the fire. In former times the "kettle" was an open topped or sometimes lidded vessel which hung constantly over the fire; it contained boiling water for household use, and was thus usually black with soot on the outside.

Downhearth

Downhearth

This is the term used for cooking on the hearth stone. Everything to do with kitchens and cooking, even down to the tools we use, originated from when our ancestors were cooking on the hearth or "downhearth". The early toaster with hoops for holding the bread and the griddle for cooking meat in the embers, for example, have both developed into the modern electrical gadgets we use now in our 21st century kitchens.

Downhearth cooking would have started with a fire out in the open; with time this would have been moved inside to the middle of a room and from there to a wall with a chimney to take the smoke away. Eventually downhearth cooking was superseded in the 18th century by the bargrate and finally the iron kitchen range. In parts of the West Country downhearth cooking was practised into the 20th century, and is still the mainstay of life in some countries to this day.

The first thing that springs to mind in connection with downhearth cooking is the baked potato. Many of the older generation may remember baking potatoes and sweet chestnuts in the hot embers of the fire; I well recall waiting impatiently for them to be ready, then grabbing one with tongs or shovel and wiping it clean before cutting it open and eating it with a wedge of butter and grated cheese. It tasted wonderful, but I feel that was partly influenced by the excitement of having cooked it myself!

Potatoes were not brought to this country until Elizabethan times, and later became the staple diet of the Irish in the 19th century; when potato blight ruined the crops it caused one of the most notable disasters in history and necessitated the emigration of hundreds of thousands of people to all parts of the New World and the death from starvation of many who remained at home in Ireland.

"TO DINE ON POTATOES AND POINT"
To have potatoes without any relish or extras, a very meagre dinner indeed. When salt was expensive and the cellar was empty parents used to tell their children to point their potato to the salt-cellar, and eat it. This was potato and point, and the "joke" lies in the allusion to a "point-steak", which is the best portion.

Skillets & Posnets

Anglo – Roman cast and sheet copper alloy skillet.

English 13th / 14th century bronze posnet, photograph courtesy of Roderick Butler.

The earliest known dated English cast bronze skillet, dated 1591.

16th century bronze posnet made by Thomas Hatch of Broomfield, Kent.

17th century cast brass skillet.

Bronze hanging skillet dated 1710.

17th / 18th century leaded bronze skillet by John Fathers of Montacute, Somerset.

Late 17th century cast bronze Continental skillet.

17th century bronze skillet, south east region.

"TO SERVE THE SAME SAUCE"
To retaliate, to serve in the same manner.

Downhearth

The quantity of potatoes eaten in those days was quite prodigious!

Potatoes were also baked in the bread oven and the kitchen range. The potato rake was used to reach in and pull the hot potatoes from the oven and also would have been used to retrieve ones cooked in the ashes. Of course the fact that it is called a potato rake does not limit its use in the kitchen exclusively to potatoes!

A 17th century example made of iron and an 18th century one with a brass mounted handle are illustrated below.

Meat was cooked in various ways in early times: boiled in a cauldron, roasted either on a spit or bottle jack or grilled on a downhearth griddle. These were designed in many different ways, some of which incorporated a fat catching tray while other types revolved on a central spindle. Some of the later 19th century iron ones would have been enamel coated when the first enamelling became viable in cooking utensils around 1840. Regional variations are to be seen in the many different decorations and constructions of these kitchen implements (p.21, 22).

The grisset was another interesting receptacle in the hearth (p.9). It was used to hold fat or tallow and was put in the embers of the fire for the fat to melt so that it could be used for making rushlights, a vital part of life in times past. Most houses except those of the wealthy were lit by rushlights.

People living in rural areas, especially those in outlying districts, had very little opportunity or money to buy

19th century iron potato baker used for cooking potatoes in the ashes.

18th century brass mounted potato rake.

Large 17th century iron potato rake.

Mid 18th century brass & iron downhearth pan.

Late 17th century English brass skillet with maker's mark.

18th century adjustable iron trivet with 18th century brass long handled pan.

19th century Continental downhearth pottery cooking pot.

"MRS GLASSE"

This was the pen-name of Dr John Hill (1716 – 1765) who published "The Art of Cookery made Plain and Easy" in 1747, as "By a Lady". The pseudonym "Mrs Glasse" was added later.

Downhearth

16th century misericord from Bristol cathedral, depicting a domestic brawl.

the kind of diverse range of things we take for granted today. This is why most items had multiple uses and one cannot be categorical in assuming a specific use for them.

Another downhearth survivor, and a rare one, is the bacon cooker (p.9) which provided an effective method of cooking bacon. Certain foods such as hedgehogs and squirrels were baked in the hearth in clay shells which were broken open when the meat was cooked.

Most downhearth cooking was seasonal: game through the winter months, a good source of fresh meat when most people were surviving on salted meat or fish, with the addition of fruit and vegetables in the summer months.

My father maintained that English partridge cold for breakfast was the perfect start to any day. His other favourite was teal, a beautiful plump little duck with a wonderful delicate flavour. My long suffering mother, who was an excellent French cook, was constantly being presented with all manner of game and birds, including, on one occasion, Winston Churchill's black swan, shot accidentally one evening in mistake for a goose!!... Woodcock was a great delicacy, still much sought after today. Another country delicacy was the sparrow, and all finches, blackbirds, thrushes and fieldfares were very highly rated as well. In the Roasting chapter a lark spit is shown being used for quail, a small game bird still eaten frequently and readily available for anyone wishing to try and cook as their forefathers did.

"A LITTLE POT IS SOON HOT"
A small person is soon riled.

Downhearth

17th century wrought iron grisset.

18th/19th century cast iron grisset.

17th century wrought iron grisset for rushlight making.

18th century wrought iron bacon cooker

"HE LOOKS AS IF BUTTER WOULDN'T MELT IN HIS MOUTH."
He looks quite harmless, yet beware..

Cauldrons

Illustrated in the following pages are various cauldrons, including the early riveted and seamed variety and some later cast bronze and iron ones. The definitive book "English Bronze Cooking Vessels and Their Founders, 1350 – 1830" by Roderick Butler and Christopher Green, incorporates the wonderful collection put together by Roderick and Valentine Butler over many years; it is now in the possession of Taunton Museum.

16th century cast iron fire dog with wrought iron pot hook. 17th century bronze cauldron.

"DIED FOR WANT OF LOBSTER SAUCE"

Sometimes said of one who dies or suffers severely because of some trifling disappointment, pique or wounded vanity. At the grand feast given by the great Conde to Louis XIV at Chantilly, Vatel the chef was told that the lobster intended for the sauce had not arrived, whereupon he retired to his private room and leaning on his sword, ran it through his body, unable to survive such a dire disappointment.

Boiling, Seething and Simmering.

Cooking over, or in front of a downhearth fire only ceased relatively recently in this country although it is still practised today in some remote areas of the Continent.

Many different kinds of cooking could be carried out at the same time on the hearth: a cauldron would be hanging over the fire seething a stew while a spit rotated in front roasting a joint of meat, a posnet or skillet simmered in the embers and some bread toasted in a downhearth toaster.

Cooks in medieval times were usually men. They needed to learn a wealth of different skills that included not only the production of tasty meals (seasoning, basting etc) but also how to achieve the right kind of fire and maintain a steady temperature, more difficult than it sounds; old recipes frequently speak of a "soft fire" or a "quick fire". Added to this, were all the skills involved in using the different utensils and equipment for roasting, toasting, boiling, seething and simmering. This vital knowledge and experience would have been passed down through the generations; good cooks were highly prized and often handsomely rewarded by their masters.

The cauldron was the mainstay of downhearth cooking for many years. Early cauldrons were suspended on an iron chain hanging from the roof over the fire in the main living area. They were round bodied and were usually made of sheets of metal, often bronze, riveted together; they had no legs or lid.

Food could be cooked in several ways in a cauldron: a single dish such as a stew could be simmered for up to 7 hours, much longer than we would do today; alternatively, the cauldron could be filled with water (that was not consumed) and cloth bags would be immersed in the boiling liquid or covered pots floated on top, each

19th century copper cauldron with iron handle.

Rare surviving glazed terracotta cauldron.

containing different savoury foods or puddings. An example of this comes from a recipe of 1655 "To make Pyramidis Cream": the ingredients were all to be put into the (earthenware) "Bottle... stop it very close with a cork, and tye a cloth over it, put the Bottle into a Pot of Beef when it is boyling, and let it boyl three hours." The utensils most frequently documented for use with a cauldron are a flesh fork (p.12) for hooking out pieces of meat, a scummer (p.12, 104 - 106) for removing floating scum and a wooden paddle-shaped stick (p.15) for stirring the contents to stop food sticking or burning on the bottom. Many details of medieval life are illustrated in the Luttrell Psalter which was written in the 14th century for Sir Geoffrey Luttrell of Lincolnshire. It is a marvellous illuminated record of daily activities, and one of the illustrations shows a cook holding a flesh fork while skimming the contents of a cauldron with a scummer (p.12). Ladles were made of various metals such as iron, copper or brass (p.102, 103) and scrapers were important

English 17th century cast bronze cauldron. *18th century pot hook or hangol.*

"TO DINE WITH THOMAS GRESHAM"
To go dinnerless.

Cauldrons

17th century bronze Continental cauldron.

17th century English cast bronze cauldron.

Late 18th century French cast bronze cauldron.

Rare possibly 14th century flesh hook / fork and early copper scummer.

A cook using a scummer and flesh fork, taken from the early 14th century Luttrell Psalter.

"FIRST CATCH YOUR HARE"
This is a 13th century phrase.

Cauldrons

Possibly a cauldron stick, for stirring the contents of a cauldron.

Four 17th century English bronze cauldrons of distinctive bag shape. The legs of all these have been shortened by degradation in the fire.

"POT BOILER"
Anything done merely for the sake of the money it will bring in, because it will "keep the pot a-boiling".

Boiling, Seething and Simmering.

for cleaning out the inside of the cauldron after cooking. Of course there were some people who never bothered to clean theirs out properly so a hard crust of cooked food built up over the years, and can even be seen in some cauldrons today! Reading the Will of John Deeley (p.129, 130) you will see mention of many cooking utensils, an important part of any estate, and passed on in the family from one generation to the next. Their value can be appreciated by noting the repairs frequently made to vessels, prolonging their useful life (p.128).

As people gradually became more sophisticated their cooking methods changed as well: cauldrons became smaller so that they could be moved more easily, and the addition of legs or feet meant that they could be used in the hearth. They were hung from a pot hook (p.83) or hangol (p.11) which hooked into the lugs on each side of the cauldron. Adjustable cranes were developed so that the position of the cauldron could be altered up and down or in and out by means of a ratchet lever (p.81, 82, 84). Lids or covers were usually made of wood hence few have survived, but they were useful in keeping soot from falling into the pot and they speeded up the cooking time, so saving fuel.

(left) 18th century Continental cast bronze iron handled pot.
(below) 17th / 18th century apothecary or toy cauldron.

These types of pot were eventually superseded by cheaper mass produced iron ones with legs so they could stand on the floor when not in use; a Continental one is shown on page 15.

Posnets were developed in the 13th century (p.6). They were small cauldrons about 8 inches across or less with a side handle which often had a bracket to strengthen it (p.6). The name posnet is derived from the Old French and means "small pot". They often developed degraded legs as a result of being constantly dragged from the hot embers, and the front legs of posnets we see today are normally shorter than the back one.

Skillets seem to be the great survivors (p.6, 7) and many are still seen at auctions and in private collections. They became the every-day cooking vessel for many people in the 17th and 18th centuries, and were in use for a long time. They were approximately the same size as posnets but differed in that they were straight sided rather than pot bellied. They stood in the embers of the fire and were used for simmering small quantities of food. Incidentally, it should be noted that in North America the terms posnet and skillet were reversed for those vessels.

When coal became commonplace as a fuel the range was developed and things changed for ever: saucepans became flat bottomed instead of bag shaped (see for example the brass preserve pan at the bottom of page 250) and kettles and frying pans evolved until they became the familiar shaped items we use today.

All these developments took time of course, and the old ways lingered for many years in some rural parts of this country before dying out completely; but it is interesting to realise that so many of the kitchen utensils we use every day can trace back their origins hundreds of years to their original downhearth ancestors.

"CAULDRON OF OIL"
A cauldron of oil is the emblem of St John the Baptist.

Cauldrons

Early 19th century cast iron Continental cauldron.

19th century Continental cast iron cauldron.

Late Georgian steel flesh fork and contemporary French ladle.

19th century cast iron cauldron, by Carron of Falkirk.

"A BIG POT"
An important person, a personage.

Brandreths

19th century iron lark spit and downhearth cooking pot in the embers.

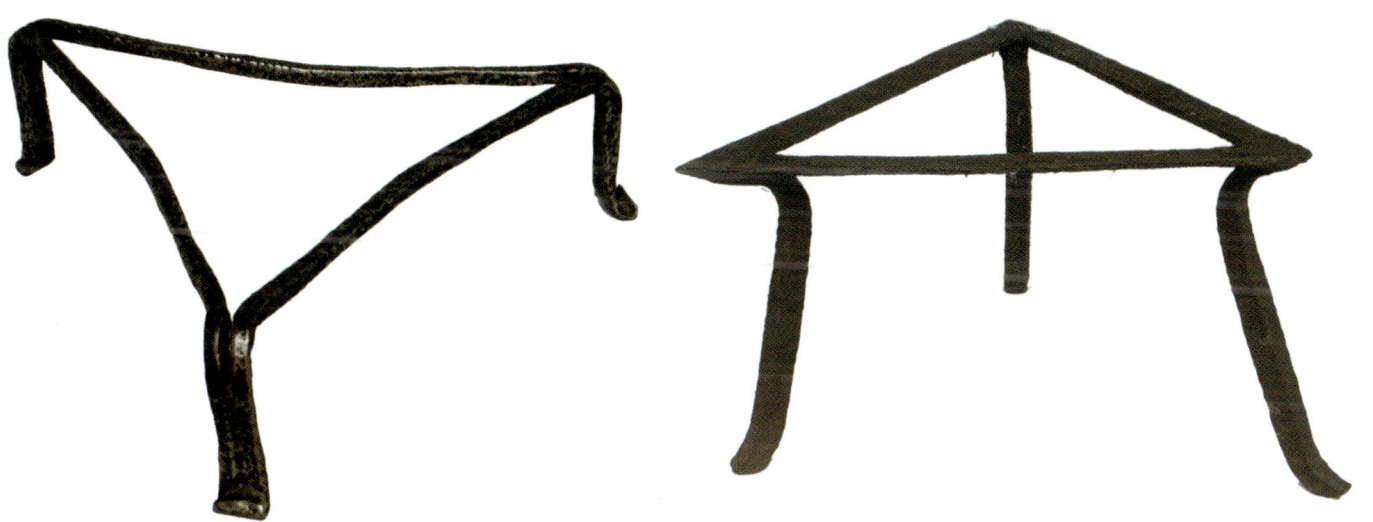

17th century wrought iron brandreth used for supporting a cauldron or a pot in the embers.

19th century wrought iron brandreth.

"KEEP YOUR BREATH TO COOL YOUR PORRIDGE"
Look after your own affairs.

Trivets

Early 19th century 'footman' trivet decorated with various re-used clock parts, dial, date-ring and spandrels in brass.

18th century steel trivet.

Late 19th century copper kettle trivet.

19th century cast brass and iron trivet.

"RIGHT AS A TRIVIT"
In the old days when floors were mostly stone paved and very uneven, a three legged trivit would keep the pot level.

Frying Pans & Long Handled Skillet

18th / 19th century tinned copper frying pan with wooden handle.

18th / 19th century French copper & iron long handled frying pan.

19th century French long handled iron frying pan.

18th century wrought iron hanging brandreth with mid 18th century brass and iron downhearth pan.

"A FLASH IN THE PAN"
A failure after a showy begining, a nine days' wonder.

Pans

Illustrated are various frying, saute, fish and fruit pans, in use from the 17th to 19th century.

Late 16th/ early 17th century cast bronze downhearth frying pan.

18th century seamed copper fat catcher with iron handle.

18th century French copper downhearth fruit pan.

Late 18th century English tinned copper frying pan with iron handle.

"OUT OF THE FRYING PAN, INTO THE FIRE"
In trying to extricate yourself from one evil you fall into a greater one. The Greeks used to say "Out of the smoke, into the flame."

Pans

19th century French tinned copper saute pan.

19th century fish frying pan and lid with inner griddle for lifting the fish out whole.

Rare early 19th century cast brass frying pan with iron handle.

Late 19th century iron frying pan.

"A SCOTCH BREAKFAST"
A substantial breakfast of sundry sorts of good things to eat and drink.

Pieces of beef cooking on an English early 19th century wrought iron revolving griddle.

Unusual late 18th century downhearth revolving gridiron cooking a beef steak.

19th century enamel griddle and fat catcher for basting, with an enamel grisset in the hearth. Enamel was first used for cooking equipment circa 1845.

"AFTER MEAT, MUSTARD"
A phrase meaning doing something, or offering a service when it is too late, or when there is no longer need thereof.

Griddles or Gridirons

Steel gridiron dated 1697.

18th century iron revolving gridiron.

18th century wrought iron revolving gridiron.

19th century wrought iron revolving gridiron.

19th century wrought iron revolving downhearth gridiron.

"CARBONADO"
Grilled meat or fish. Strictly speaking a carbonado is a piece of meat cut crosswise for the gridiron.
(Shakespeare "…let him make a carbonado of me…"
1 Henry 1V, V, 3.)

Early cooking hearth showing brass 17th century spit engine and rare curved low stool; a similar example of this stool is in the collection of the Weald and Downland Museum.

Fire Dogs

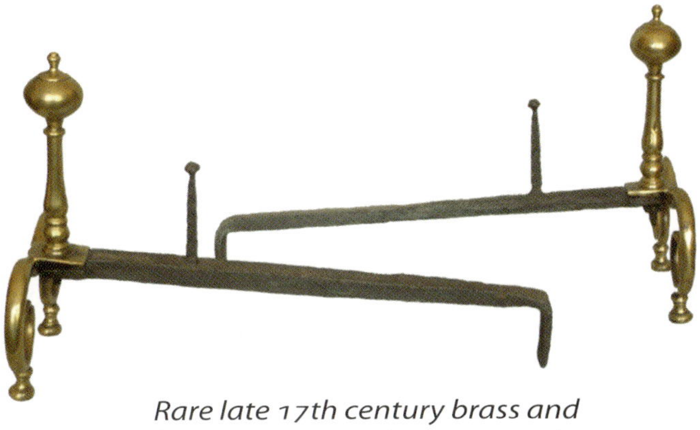

Rare late 17th century brass and iron creepers used to support the logs in the fireplace.

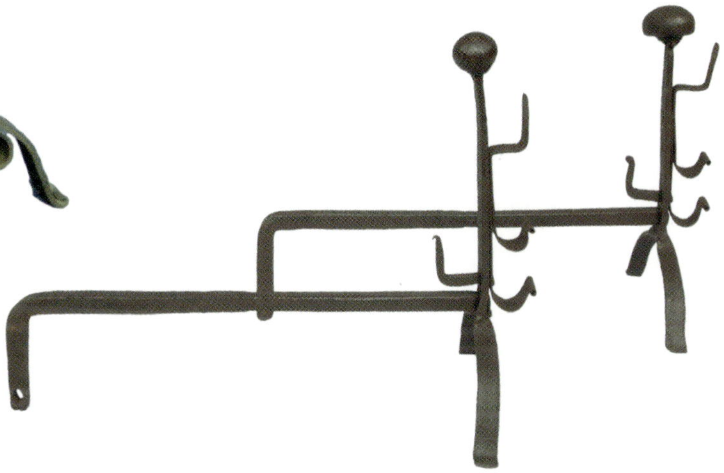

17th century English brass knobbed wrought iron spit dogs.

Late 17th century / early 18th century wrought iron spit dogs.

18th century wrought iron adjustable height spit dogs.

19th century wrought iron spit dogs.

"ANDIRONS"
A pair of firedogs for supporting logs in an open fireplace. The word is from the Old French "andier" of unknown origin, and has nothing to do with iron.

Porte de Chimenee

These cressets may have been used for supporting small vessels to keep the contents hot.

17th century free standing porte de chimenee of Continental origin for use with a spit jack.

"WITH A GRAIN OF SALT"
There is some truth in the statement but we must use great caution in accepting it.

Cob Irons & Curfew

Continental fire keep (or curfew) hanging above the fire. The basket spit is turned on the cob irons driven by the spit engine, with a bread oven in the background.

"CAKES AND ALE"
A jolly good time.

Flesh Forks

A selection of 17th-19th century flesh forks and a toasting fork with heat shield.

"TO FORK OUT"
Fork is old thieves' slang for a finger, so to "fork out" is to produce and hand over or to pay up.

Toasting & Cooking Forks

A selection of 18th -19th century forks for birds, with a brass inlaid flesh fork.

"TO PLUCK A PIGEON"
To cheat a gullible person of his money.

Toasting & Cooking Forks

Toasting fork cooking a gobbet of venison.

"THERE IS REASON IN ROASTING EGGS"

Even the most trivial thing has a reason for being done in one way rather than another. When wood fires were usual, it was more common to roast eggs than to boil them, and some care was taken to prevent their being "ill-roasted, all on one side."

"One likes the pheasant's wing, and one the leg;
The vulgar boil, the learned roast the egg." (Pope, Epistles ii)

Toasting & Cooking Forks

Enlargements showing details of 18th century bird fork.

Enlargement showing a bird detail on a bird cooking fork.

Enlargement showing fish decoration on fish cooking fork.

"A SALT EEL"
A rope's end used for scourging; at one time eelskins were used for whips.
"With my salt eele, went down in the parlour, and there got my boy and did beat him."
(Pepys' Diary, April 24th).

Toasting & Cooking Forks

A selection of 19th century toasting forks.

"A GREEN CHEESE"
An unripe cheese, also a cheese that is eaten fresh (like a cream cheese) and is not kept to mature. Bread and Cheese – food of a frugal nature.

Toasting & Cooking Forks

Toasting & Cooking Forks

(left to right) Rare 18th C. combined bread & flesh fork - Welsh copper fork circa 1840 - 19th C. wirework fork - 18th C. silver tipped fork - two 19th C. copper forks.

"SILVER FORK"
A school of early 19th century novelists. A writer of this accomplished stamp informs you that the quality eat fish with silver forks.

Toasting & Cooking Forks

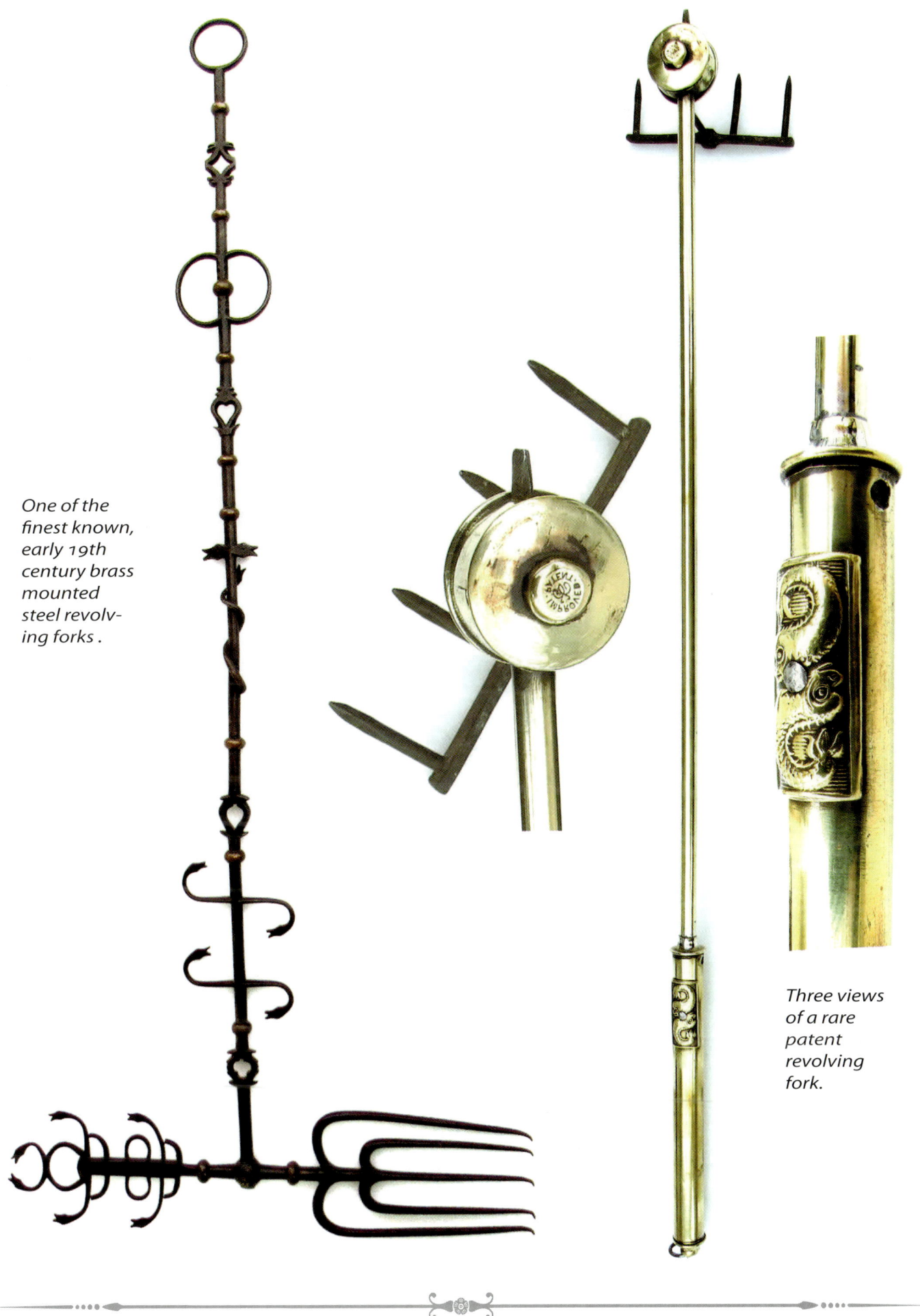

One of the finest known, early 19th century brass mounted steel revolving forks.

Three views of a rare patent revolving fork.

"BLOOD WITHOUT GROATE IS NOTHING"
Family without fortune is worthless. The allusion is perhaps to black pudding, which consists chiefly of blood and groats (coarse meal) formed into a sausage.

Curfews

Early 17th century German fire-keep.

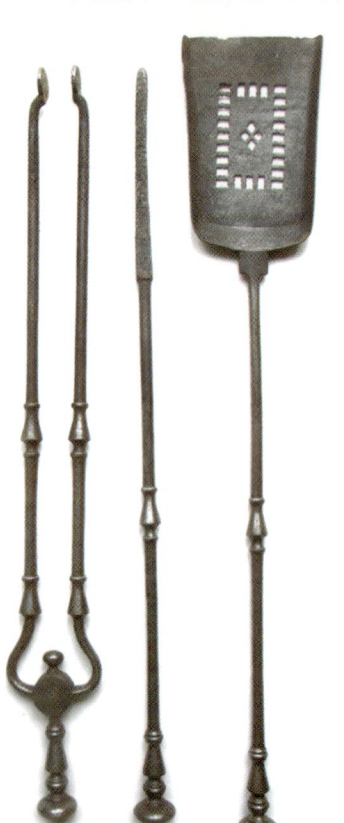

Mid 19th century steel fire-iron set.

Late 17th century Dutch brass curfew.

"A SOFT FIRE MAKES SWEET MALT"
Too much hurry or precipitation spoils work, as too fierce a fire would burn the malt and destroy its sweetness.

Fire Tools

Ember tongs

These were made in many different shapes and metals, and were used for various reasons, removing glowing embers from the fire to transfer them to another fire, or to light a candle for example. The articulated iron lazy tongs are a wonderfully ingenious piece of engineering as shown in the photograph. You could use them to pick up something as small as a stamp from the floor without bending down.

Mid 19th century Welsh copper fireguard.

19th century steel lazy tongs.

18th century ember tongs.

Late 18th century miniature ember tools for use with a chafing dish.

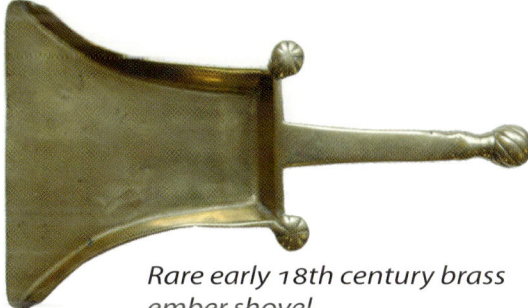

19th century leather and wood bellows.

Rare early 18th century brass ember shovel.

Fine example of a Georgian log fork about 50 inches long.

18th / 19th century blow pipe made from a re-used gun barrel.

"CULROSS GIRDLES"
The thin plate of iron used in Scotland for the manufacture of oaten cakes is called a girdle, for which Culross was long celebrated.

Fire Baskets

17th century iron fire basket with decorative brass knobs.

18th century iron fire basket with cresset holders.

Late 18th century wrought iron fire basket.

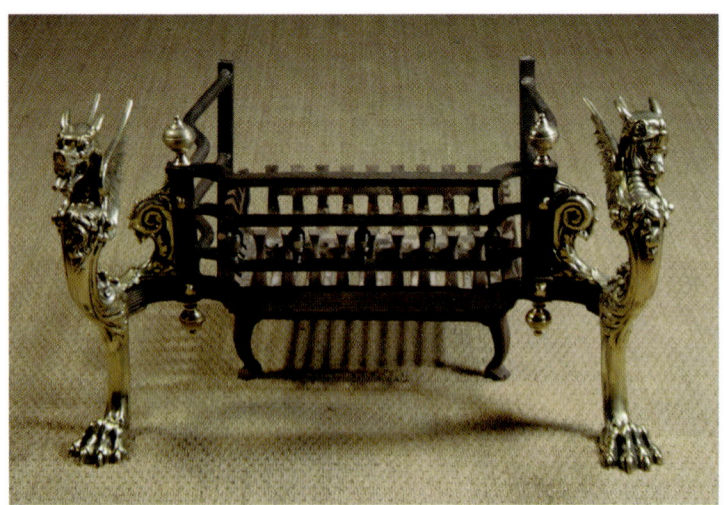

Fine Victorian fire grate shown without its fire back, the culmination of the evolution of the fire basket into the grate.

"SIGHING FOR THE FLESH-POTS OF EGYPT"
Hankering for the good things no longer at your command.

Rare surviving terracotta cauldron with a bronze 17th century cauldron over the fire in the background.

"TO ADD FUEL TO THE FIRE"
To say or do something that increases the emotion of a person.

Bargrate

Bargrate

Bargrates were first used in the 17th century and the early ones were exactly as the name implies, bars resting above each other on two fire dogs (brandirons) with no basket; the fire was kept behind the bars and cooking utensils could be hung from them. Later the full basket became common and the culmination of this development was the Victorian grate (p.37) which we are familiar with today. In the 18th century an adjustable grate (p.42) was devised which allowed one to alter the width of the fire by means of a winding mechanism, therefore concentrating the heat in a small direct area. Dutch ovens (p.85), which were used in conjunction with the bottle jack (p.62, 90) to reflect the heat, were particularly useful for cooking in front of a bargrate.

19th century brass bargrate trivet.

"FEAST OF REASON"
Conversation about, and discussion of learned and congenial subjects.
The phrase comes from Pope's "Satires of Horace", 1733.

Bargrate

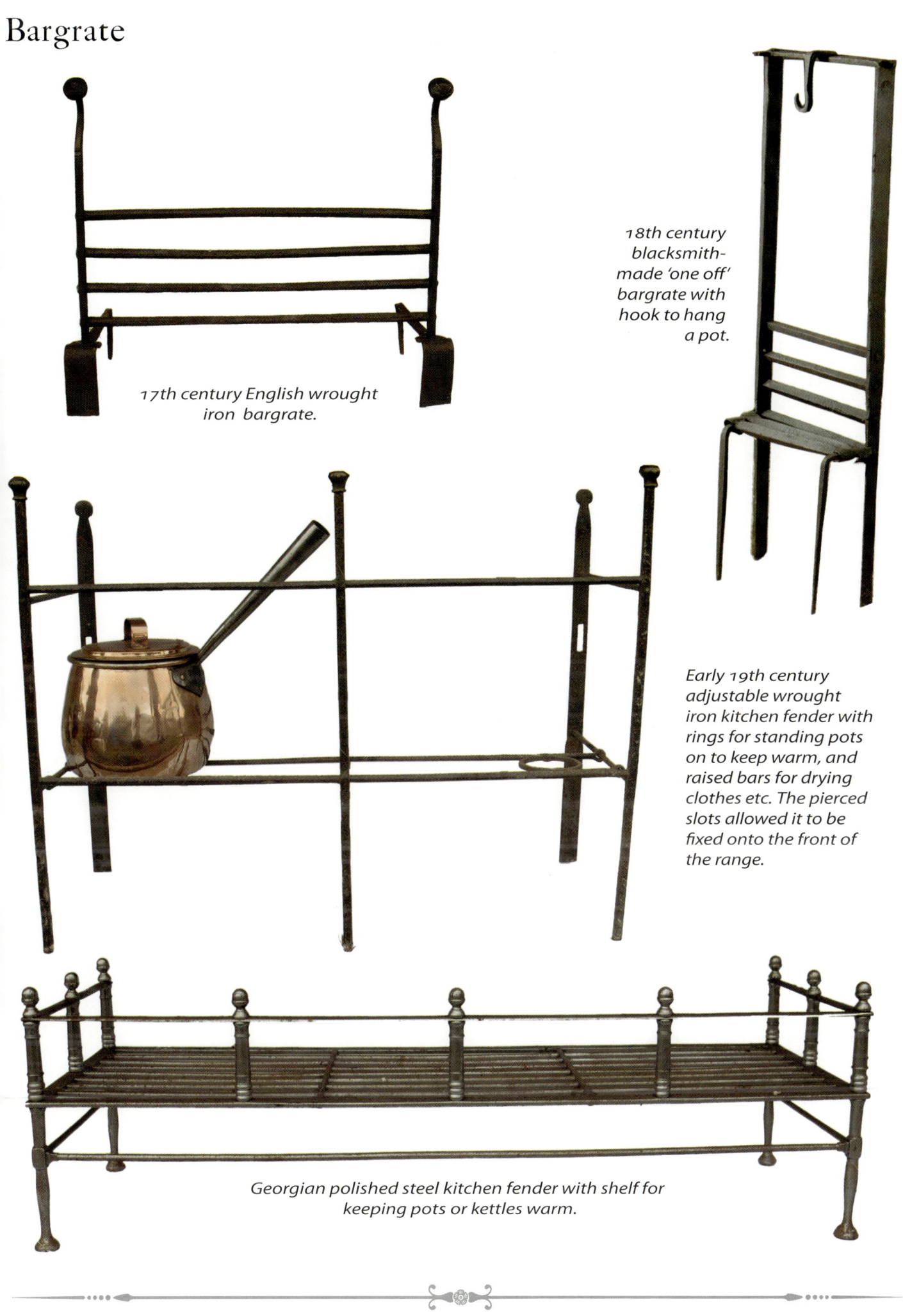

17th century English wrought iron bargrate.

18th century blacksmith-made 'one off' bargrate with hook to hang a pot.

Early 19th century adjustable wrought iron kitchen fender with rings for standing pots on to keep warm, and raised bars for drying clothes etc. The pierced slots allowed it to be fixed onto the front of the range.

Georgian polished steel kitchen fender with shelf for keeping pots or kettles warm.

"NEITHER HAWK NOR BUZZARD"
Of doubtful social position, too good for the kitchen, and not good enough for the family.

Cauldron suspended by a hangol from a crane over a bargrate fire, with a bargrate toaster cooking a beef steak.

Bargrate

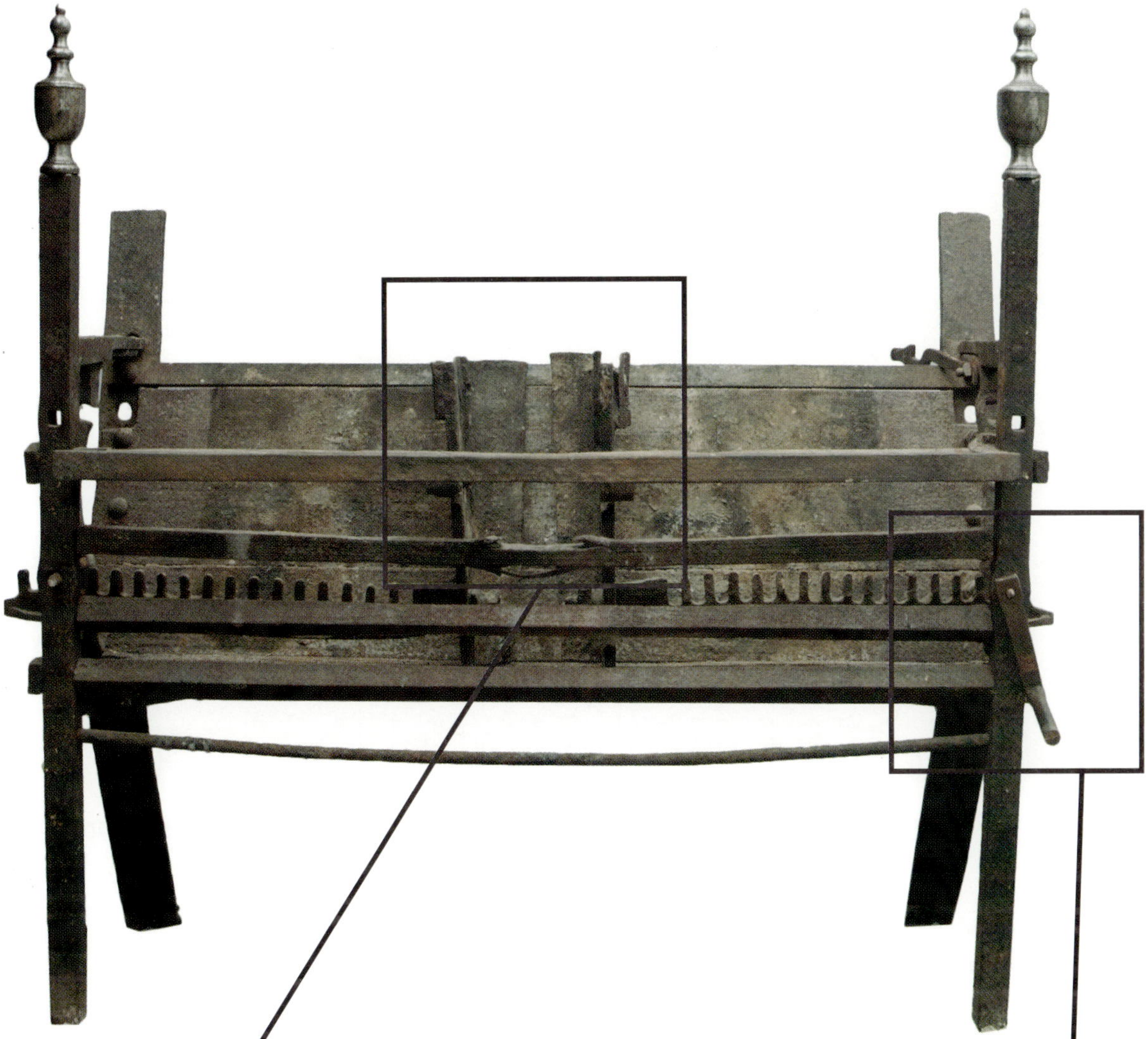

Detail of moveable 'cheeks'.

Detail of winding apparatus.

18th century wrought iron bargrate with adjustable 'cheeks'.

"AWAY WITH THE JOINT STOOLE, REMOVE THE COURT-CUPBOARD, LOOK TO THE PLATE, GOOD THOU, SAVE ME A PIECE OF MARCHPANE"

Shakespeare, Romeo and Juliet. Marchpane was the old name for the confection of almonds, sugar etc. that we call marzipan.

Fire Backs

Cast iron fire back for an early bargrate, dated 1641, with 3 masks and initials in the decorations.

Cast iron fire back, dated 1608.

"MACFARLAN'S GEESE LIKE THEIR PLAY BETTER THAN THEIR MEAT"
One day James VI visited the chieftain of Loch Lomond and was highly amused by the gambols of the wild geese, but the one served at the table was so tough that the King exclaimed "Macfarlan's geese etc"

Fire Backs

Early 17th century cast iron fire back illustrating dog, lion, cauldron and skillet.

18th century cast iron fire back.

"RUMP AND DOZEN"
A rump of beef and a dozen of claret, or a rump steak and a dozen oysters. A not uncommon wager among sportsmen of the late 18th and early 19th century.

Bargrate Attachments

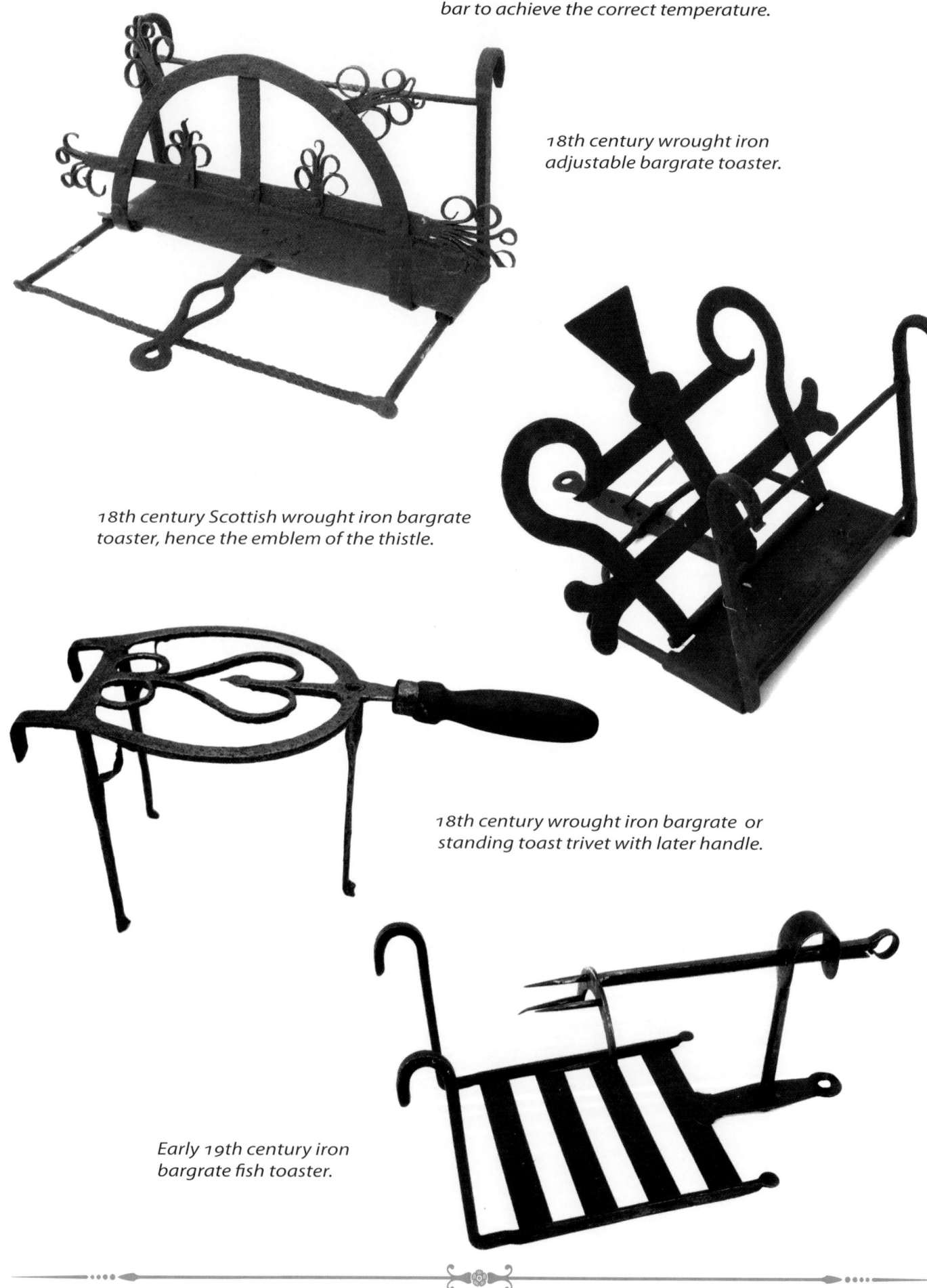

The pair of hooks on these attachments allowed them to be raised or lowered to the appropriate bar to achieve the correct temperature.

18th century wrought iron adjustable bargrate toaster.

18th century Scottish wrought iron bargrate toaster, hence the emblem of the thistle.

18th century wrought iron bargrate or standing toast trivet with later handle.

Early 19th century iron bargrate fish toaster.

"IRON RATIONS"
Bully beef, tinned meat. Emergency rations.

Trivets

1840 bronze and iron fish toaster which fits beneath a bargrate toast trivet.

Brass Georgian bargrate trivet.

C.1860 combination bargrate toast trivet. When combined with an iron heating block it could be used as a plate warmer.

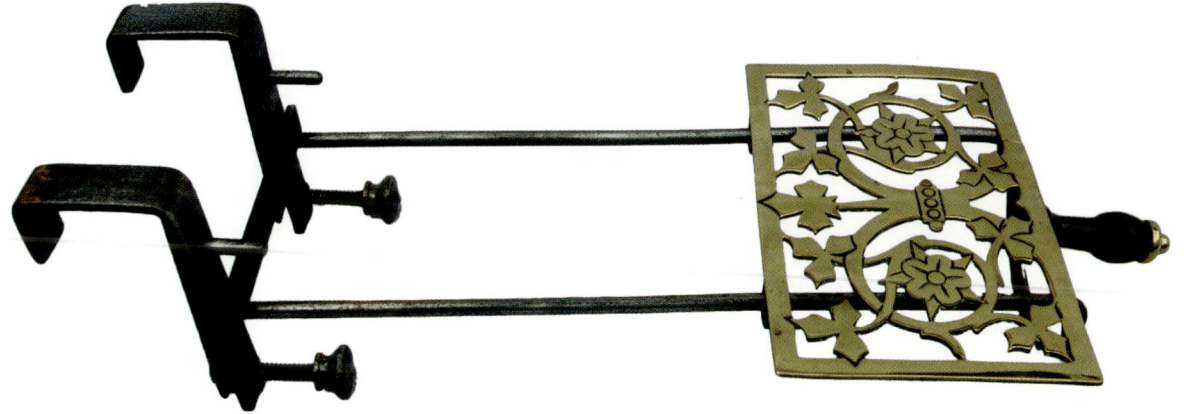

Late 19th century iron & brass adjustable bargrate toast trivet.

"TO HAVE MANY IRONS IN THE FIRE"
To be involved in many projects.

Cauldron cooking over a very early bargrate which is dated 1641 and was found in Ludlow, Shropshire; an 18th century plate warmer stands in the foreground with pewter plates.

"TO DINE WITH DUKE HUMPHREY"
To go dinnerless.

Keeping Food & Plates Warm

When downhearth cooking was in vogue, one of the main problems, as you can imagine, was keeping food and plates warm without an oven. Our ancestors overcame this problem in a variety of ways. The photograph (p.50) shows a late 17th century brass brazier still complete with the original pan below to hold charcoal, and lugs on top to rest a dish on. It could also be used for cooking or keeping food warm. Sauces were often cooked at the table in dishes heated by a brazier.

Another way to keep food hot was to use a piece of equipment called a hastener which was placed in the hearth facing the fire; the shelves inside were made of thin sheet iron and plates of food were put on the shelves to keep warm until needed.

Some people had special hollow "water jacket" plates made of pewter, copper or porcelain which could be filled with hot water and used at the table, and there were also three-legged brass or iron stands called "cats" where dishes could be placed to keep warm in the hearth. Cats derived their name from the fact that however they fell they landed on their feet; they were used as toasting stands§ and to catch the fat from roasting meat.

There were also various other ways of keeping plates hot. The photograph on the right shows a revolving iron frame on a tripod base, a rare survivor; (most implements that could not conveniently be used or adapted were quickly disposed of – you only have to think of gadgets in our kitchens 40 years ago that are now collectors' items and rarely seen). A copper Georgian plate warmer is also shown on the next page; it looks similar to an enlarged coal scuttle, and was used rather like a hastener, with the plates stacked inside facing the fire.

Back view of a 19th century plate warmer / hastener, the open side with the plates faced the fire, access was gained via a door at the rear.

16th/17th century bronze chafing dish.

18th century brass chafing dish with turned wooden ebonised handle.

18th century brass chafing dish with iron 'slug' for heating in the fire.

Mid 18th century steel revolving plate warmer.

Circa 1780 English brass three legged cat, used as a toasting stand.

19th century iron & brass chafing or warming dish.

"TO KILL THE FATTED CALF"
To welcome with the best of everything, from the parable of the prodigal son
(Luke XV, 30)

Rare late 18th century copper plate warmer.

"TO EAT ONE OUT OF HOUSE AND HOME"
To eat so much that one will have to part with house and home in order to pay for it.

17th century Dutch brass standing brazier / chafing dish for light cooking with charcoal.

"THE ANSWER'S A LEMON"
A senseless and ridiculous repartee used as a form of reply to some particularly silly or unanswerable conundrum.

Late bargrate. Victorian cast iron grate (about 1860), mass produced for small houses or cottages, to provide heat and fire for cooking.

Spits

Pheasant roasting on a spit supported by cob irons and driven by a spit jack over a fat catcher.

From the earliest days when people began to cook their food, the spit, supported on forked sticks over the fire, was an essential tool in the preparation of cooked meat. Meat cooked on a spit needed to be quickly sealed on the outside to keep the juices in. Once the meat was sealed, the spit was moved further away from the heat, allowing the joint to cook slowly, sometimes for 4 or 5 hours; it had to be kept turning to prevent it from burning. Wooden spits were still being used in 13th century England and were easily replaceable for every roast.

The first iron spits were manually turned and rested on two iron supports, or spit dogs as they were called. In most early descriptions of the workings of a medieval kitchen, the boy who turned the iron spit was called the turnspit; he was the lowest member of the kitchen staff and his was a menial and uncomfortable job, crouched in front of the fire, endlessly turning the spit.

As the workload increased in the kitchen, people began to look for a more efficient method of turning the spit; the dog wheel was developed and used mainly in the West of England and parts of Wales. This was similar to a modern day "hamster wheel" only larger; the dog was put inside and ran continuously on the spot, turning the wheel which turned the spit and because it was such strenuous work, dogs were often used in pairs, one taking over from the other at the end of its shift. Dr Caius, founder of Caius College, Cambridge, in the middle of the 17th century, wrote about the "curs of the coarsest kind, a certain dog in kitchen service". These poor dogs were described in the eighteenth century as "long bodied, crooked legged and ugly dogs with a suspicious unhappy look about them". In some areas geese were used instead of dogs (p. 72).

Various examples of dog wheels still exist, and can be found at Lacock in Wiltshire, Fagins Castle in Cardiff, Newcastle Emlyn in Wales and No.1, the Royal Crescent, Bath.

The dangle spit was developed in the late 18th century and used until the 19th century. Dangle spits (p. 61) were made in a variety of styles with many variations; some

"TURNSPIT"

One who has all the work but none of the profit; he turns the spit but eats none of the roast. The allusion is to the turnspit, a small dog which was used to turn the roasting spit by means of a kind of tread wheel.

Spits

18th century hand-turned iron spit.

18th century fire dogs with 19th century spit jack powered basket spit.

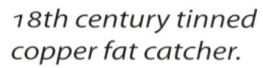

18th century tinned copper fat catcher.

18th century spit jack powered iron spit.

18th century iron spit jack powered basket spit.

Early 19th century iron spit jack powered basket spit.

"IT IS MEAT AND DRINK TO ME"
It is something that is almost essential to my well-being or happiness;
something very much to be desired.

Spits

Wild trout cooking on a spit by the river.

were made of iron, brass or copper (the latter usually associated with Wales). There were hooks for holding the meat incorporated into the design, with weighted arms giving an added momentum when the dangle spit holding the meat was spun round by hand. It would gradually unwind and needed constant rewinding.

An alternative to the dangle spit was a clockwork version called the bottle jack, a good reliable instrument which would work for 20 to 45 minutes. One of the first patents taken out was by Joseph Merlin (patent no. 1032) in 1773. Illustrated are some of the many varieties of bottle jack (p 62, 90); they survive in considerable numbers, as they were mass produced by various makers such as Salter or Linwood and were sometimes used in conjunction with Dutch ovens. This combination worked very well and was an extremely efficient way of cooking the roast. The tin surround of the Dutch oven reflected the heat and cooked the meat from both sides, so a smaller fire was needed, saving fuel. Once the meat had been suspended from it and the jack had been wound up with its key, it would rotate first one way, then with a loud click start to rotate the other way and this would continue as long as someone remembered to wind it up at regular intervals. This provided a very satisfactory form of cooking, so much easier to operate than the hand turned spit.

Three other spit turning devices were developed during the 15th and 16th centuries, designed for cooking larger joints of meat, whole animals, or several animals or birds at the same time. These were the weight driven jack, the smoke jack and the spring driven horizontal jack.

The weight driven jack consisted of a rectangular iron frame containing a barrel with a rope wrapped round it. The rope passed over a pulley high up near the ceiling and came down again to the iron or stone weight. Once the weight reached the floor the rope was rewound by turning the barrel using the small handle on the end. A system of gears and a flywheel stopped the weight from immediately dropping back, and drove the large iron wheel just behind it within the frame. This mainwheel drove a smaller wheel or pinion which in turn drove two smaller wheels. These were each attached to a spit which was supported at the other end in a "v" shaped

"I'LL PLUCK HIS GOOSE FOR HIM"
Comparing the person to a goose, the threat is to pluck off his feathers in which he prides himself.

Spits

Roast chicken on a spit with several iron skewers holding it in place.

bracket on the side of an andiron. Another set of gear wheels incorporated a governor and enabled the speed of the spits to be adjusted.

The smoke jack would have been made entirely of iron and steel by a blacksmith. It had "windmill" like vanes which fitted closely inside the chimney to catch as much as possible of the hot air rising up from the fire. These vanes turned a shaft which in turn was linked to the spit via a chain. Smoke jacks needed a great deal of maintenance and also required a very substantial fire to enable them to function properly.

In the 15th century the spring driven jack was invented on the Continent. A spring mechanism was used instead of a weight to drive the jack and a tapered device called a fusee (also used in clocks) was incorporated to regulate the power of the spring from the time it was fully wound up until it needed rewinding; thus the spit was able to turn at the same speed all the time without gradually slowing down.

"CAPON"

Properly a castrated cock but the name given to various fish by friars who wished to evade the Friday fast, and so eased their consciences by changing the name of the fish.

Chicken – a fish out of the coop
A crail's capon – a dried haddock
A Glasgow capon – a salt herring
A Severn capon – a sole
A Yarmouth capon – a red herring

Spit Racks

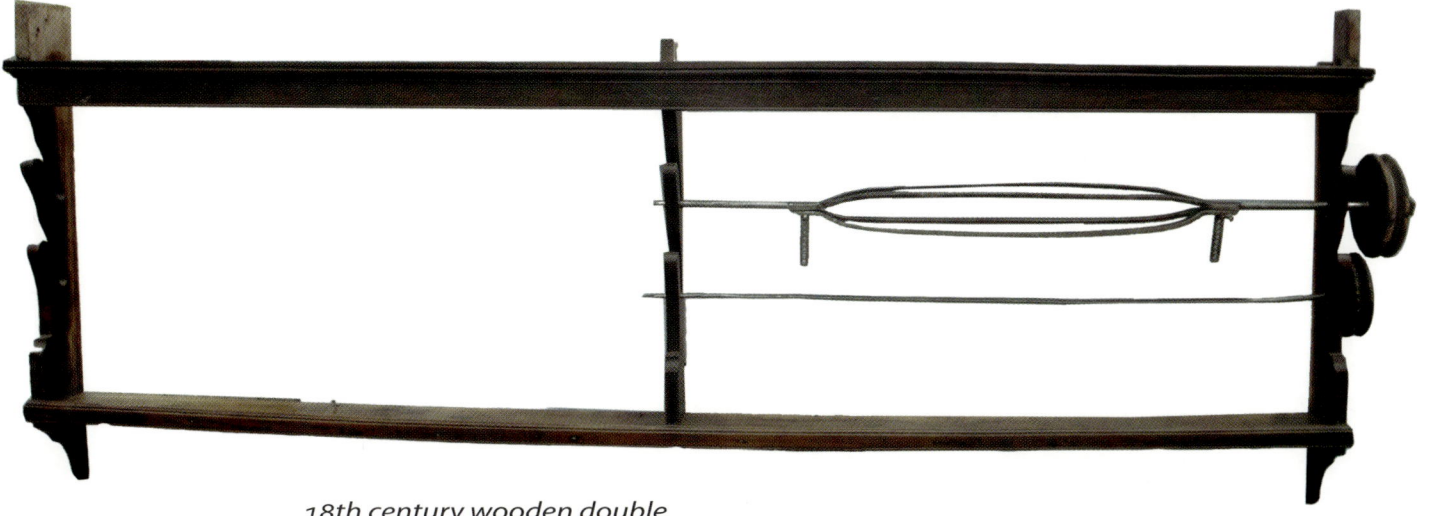

18th century wooden double spit rack (above & below left), which would have been mounted above the fireplace.

18th/19th century chestnut single Continental spit rack.

"HE WON'T EARN SALT FOR HIS PORRIDGE"
He will never earn a penny.

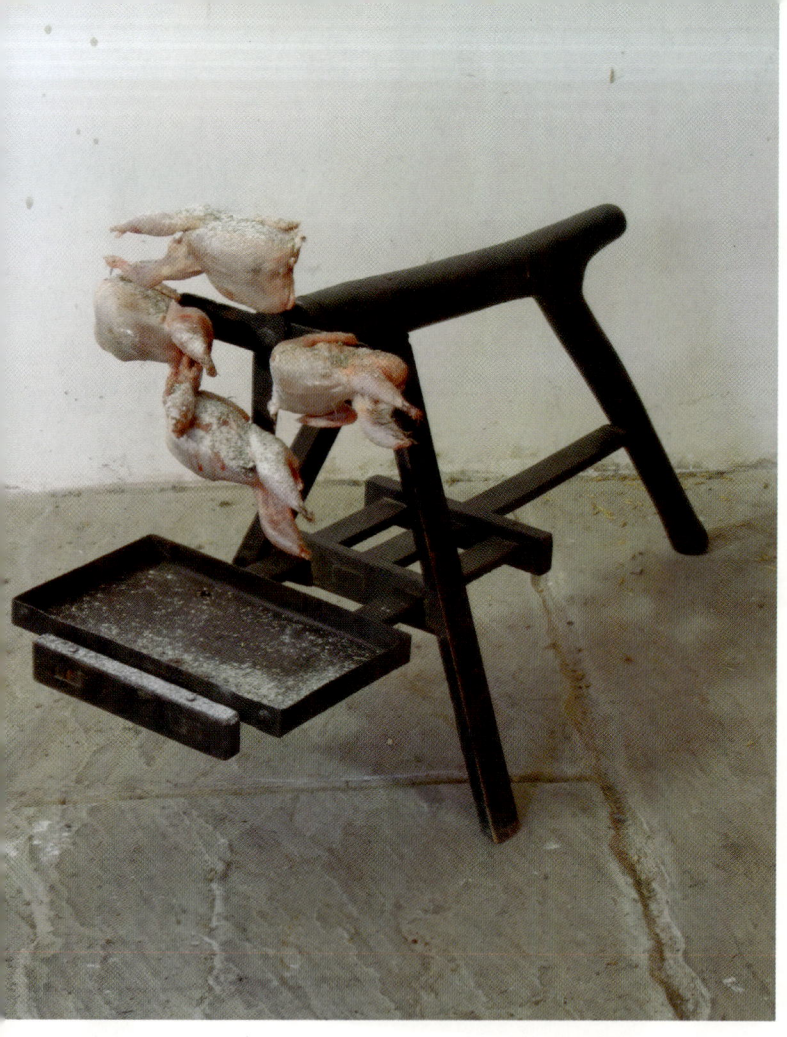

A good example of a "toasting dog" with birds attached, in this case quail. It would have been used to cook all manner of small birds, blackbirds, finches, sparrows, larks etc. We must remember that in years gone by all garden and wild birds were fair game. It is only recently that social conscience has dictated which species can be eaten and which protected.

A larkspit with six pairs of prongs to impale the birds. This example can be adjusted up and down, and it revolves to cook the back as well as the breast of the birds. It also incorporates a tray or fat catcher so the birds can be basted while they are cooking. It can be used with a bargrate.

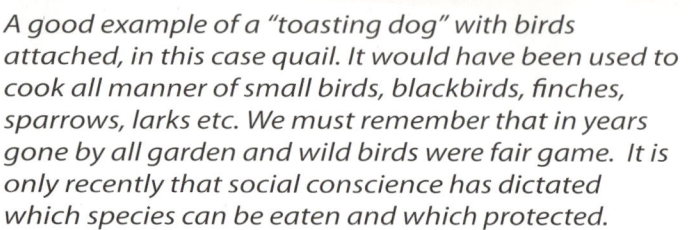

A well made tinned 18th century copper fat catcher of Welsh or English origin incorporating a lip at one end to pour off excess fat; nothing was wasted in those days.

18th century iron fat catcher.
A rare survivor which has been much used, this is a primitive fat catcher with wooden socket handles.

"BIRDS OF A FEATHER FLOCK TOGETHER"

Those of similar taste congregate in groups. This proverb has been in use since at least the mid 16th century. In 1545, William Turner used a version of it in his papist satire The Rescuing of Romish Fox:
"Byrdes of on kynde and color flok and flye allwayes together."

Fire Screens

A woven fire screen providing protection from the heat of the fire.

The only respite from the heat was gained from a woven screen, and not surprisingly, very few of these have survived; they were regularly doused with water to stop them from catching fire, which also hastened their demise! A non-adjustable one is illustrated above. It was apparent that the adjustable one shown right had been used in a kitchen because when it was discovered it still retained some of its original woven screen. It was taken to the Willow and Wetlands Trust in Somerset and they wove a beautiful exact copy of the original screen. Wooden framed screens decorated with embroidery and protected with glass were called Pole Screens, and were used in 18th century drawing rooms to shield the ladies from the heat of the fire.

A very rare surviving example of an early 19th century adjustable wickerwork fire screen.

"IF YOU CAN'T STAND THE HEAT GET OUT OF THE KITCHEN"
If you can't cope when things get too much, walk away.

Skewers

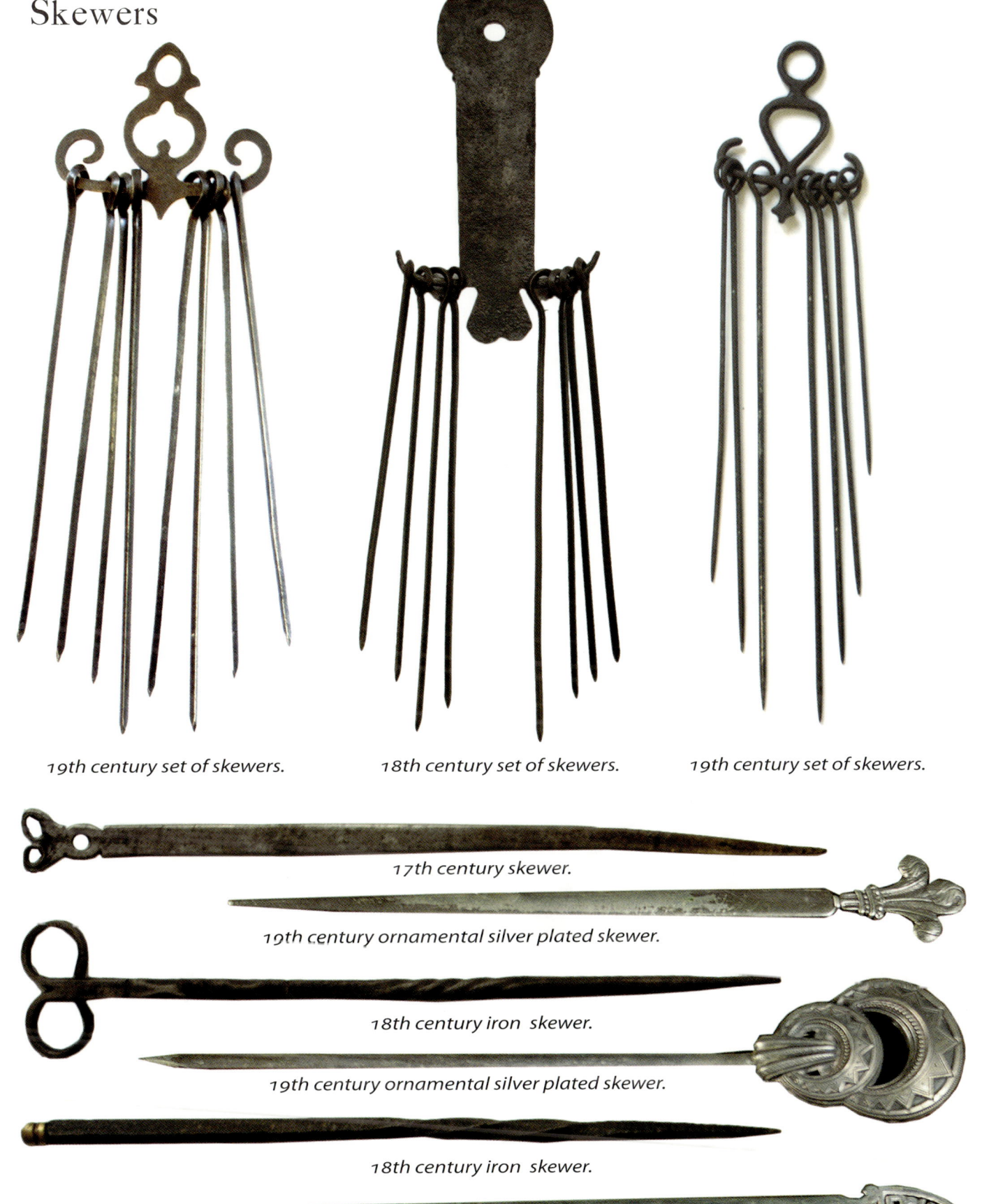

19th century set of skewers. 18th century set of skewers. 19th century set of skewers.

17th century skewer.

19th century ornamental silver plated skewer.

18th century iron skewer.

19th century ornamental silver plated skewer.

18th century iron skewer.

19th century ornamental silver plated skewer.

19th century iron skewer.

"PAY ON THE NAIL"
In the Middle Ages "nails" were flat topped columns in market places. When a buyer and a seller agreed a deal, money was placed on the nail for all to see.

Dangle Spits

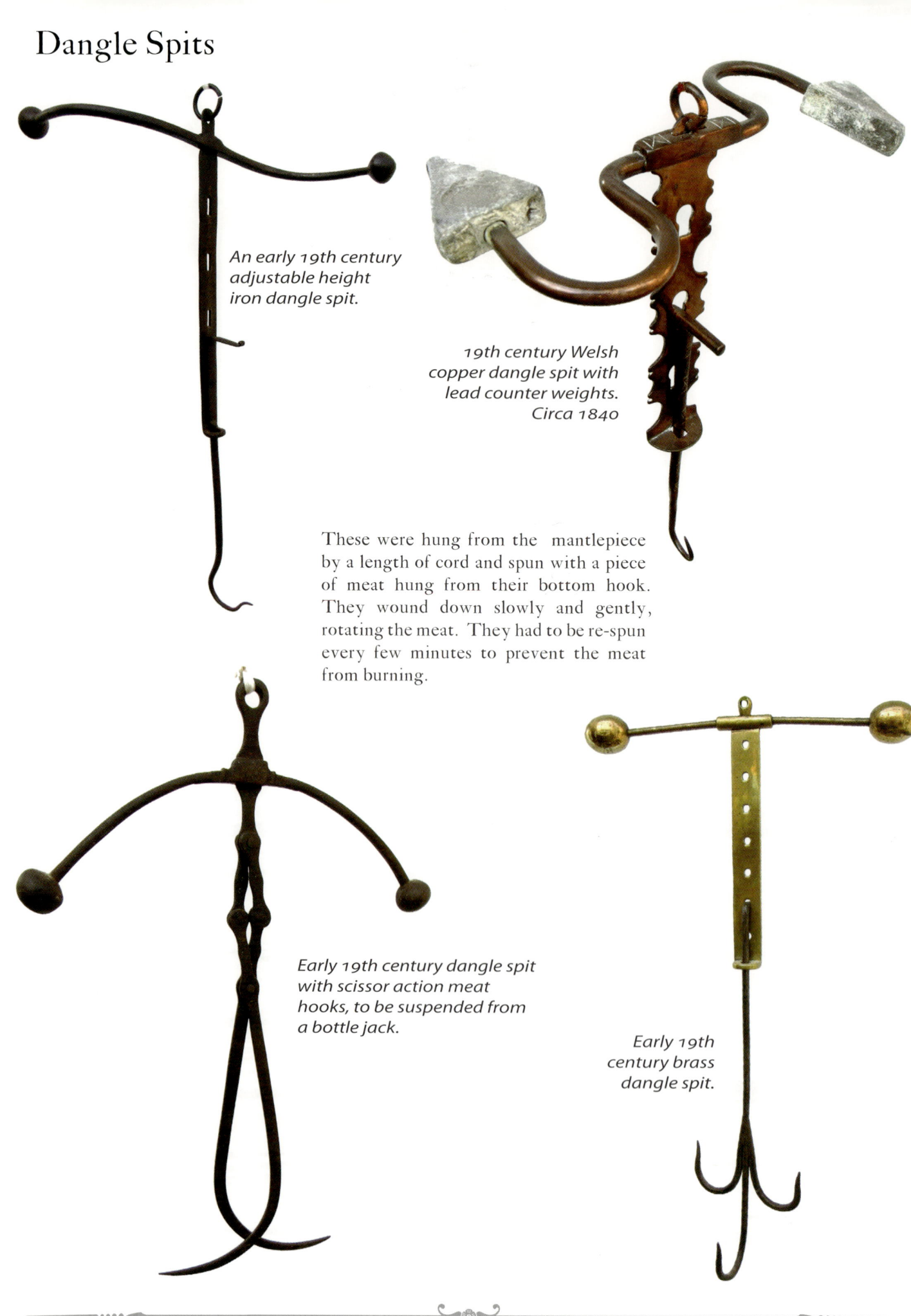

An early 19th century adjustable height iron dangle spit.

19th century Welsh copper dangle spit with lead counter weights. Circa 1840

These were hung from the mantlepiece by a length of cord and spun with a piece of meat hung from their bottom hook. They wound down slowly and gently, rotating the meat. They had to be re-spun every few minutes to prevent the meat from burning.

Early 19th century dangle spit with scissor action meat hooks, to be suspended from a bottle jack.

Early 19th century brass dangle spit.

"TO THINK SMALL POTATOES OF IT"
To think very little of it.

61

Bottle Jacks

A 19th century brass jack-rack used for hanging bottle jacks on, and a selection of 18th/19th century clockwork bottle jacks; some would have had a 'wheel' fitting as shown on page 90.

"JACK OF ALL TRADES AND MASTER OF NONE"
A term of contempt for someone who tries everything but is not an expert in any one field.

Spit Jacks

Rare late 17th century side mounted, brass and iron jack of 'Moxon' type.

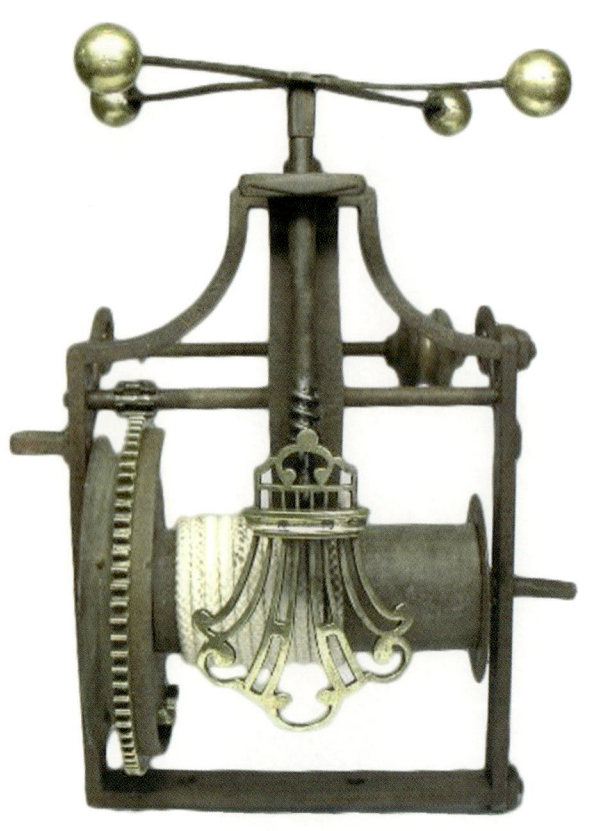

Late 18th century French brass & iron weight driven spit jack.

French 18th/19th century spit jack which would have been contained in a wooden case. The bell sounds when the jack needs rewinding.

Mid 18th century wrought iron London style jack.

"CAROUSE"
To drink deeply, to make merry with drinking.

Spit Jacks

Two views of a mid 18th century wrought iron London style spit jack with clutch mechanism.

Late French bronze and iron spit jack, a real miniature with an interesting system of pulley wheels to grip the rope.

"DOGS MEAT"
Food unfit for consumption.

Late 18th century spit jack probably made by the Cornish clockmaker, Broad of Bodmin.

Spit Jacks

17th century brass spit jack having many features of English lantern clock technology. Note the wonderful castellated brass nuts.

"I'LL BASTE YOUR JACKET FOR YOU" i.e. cane you.
"I'll give you a thorough basting" i.e. beating.

Spit Jacks

Stone weights used to drive spit jacks as shown in the main photograph.

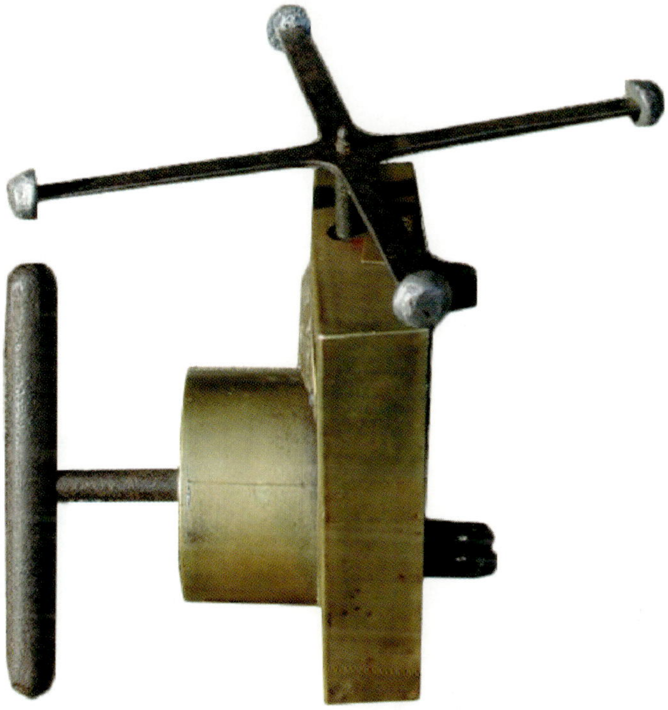

Spit Jacks

These photographs show four views of the same clockwork spit jack, including an enlargement of its patent embossed stamp. This type of spit jack was attached to a special fire dog by brackets on the back, and the gear on the underside engaged with a gear on the spit itself, giving it a direct drive. The mechanism was wound up by the handle to activate the spit, and the fly weights at the top spun round to help regulate the momentum.

"EISELL"
Old name for vinegar.

Spit Jacks

19th century French floor standing clockwork spit jack in operation.

Two 19th century French floor standing clockwork spit jacks with an iron and brass adjustable spit holder.

"TO DINE WITH DEMOCRITAS"
To be cheated out of one's dinner. Democritus was the derider, or philosopher who laughed at men's folly.

Smoke Jacks

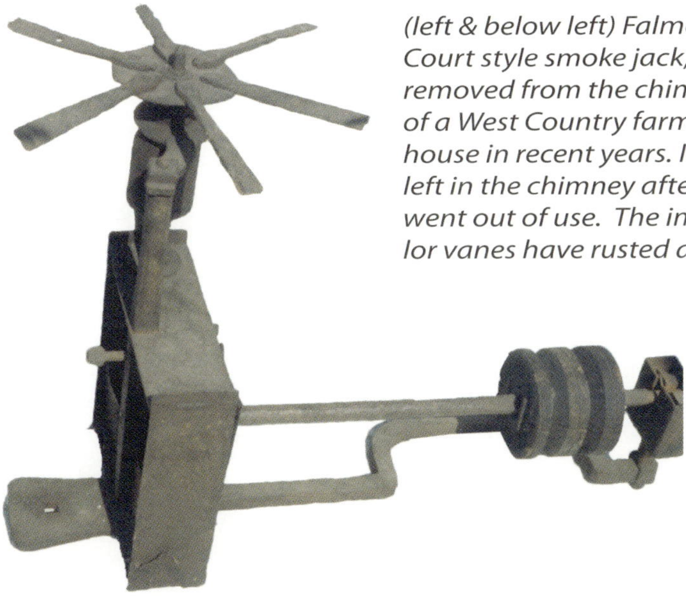

(left & below left) Falmer Court style smoke jack, removed from the chimney of a West Country farm house in recent years. It was left in the chimney after it went out of use. The impellor vanes have rusted away.

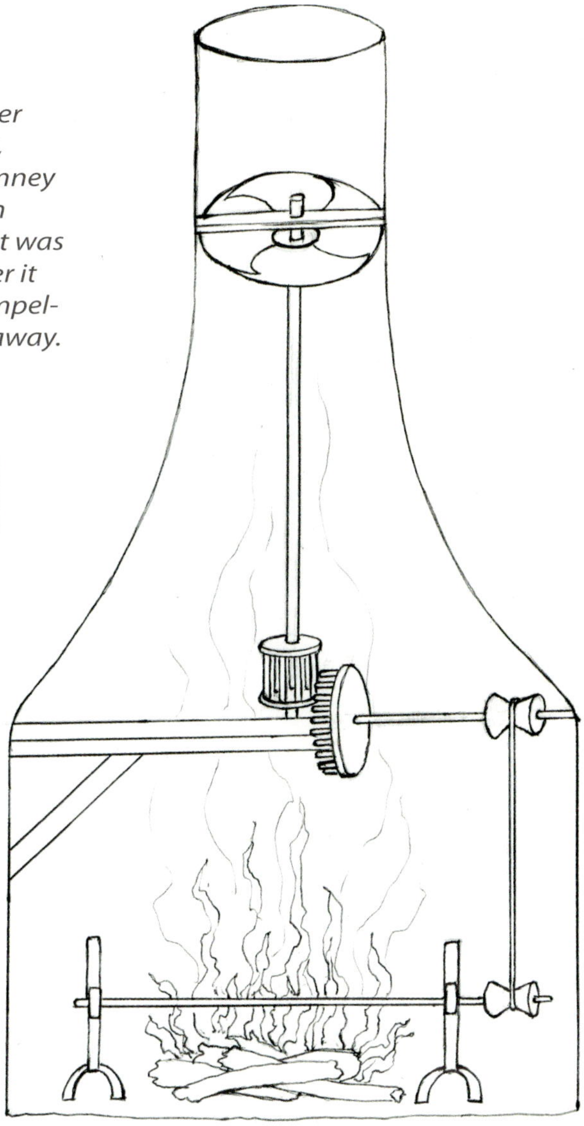

The bearings and gears ran in oil baths to help to keep them working in the hot smoky chimney.

An illustration of an early smoke jack.

An illustration of a smoke jack from Falmer Court, Sussex.

Water Jacks

Water driven jacks gained their power from a small water wheel worked by a stream outside. It was connected to a spit by means of a rod which came through the wall bearing a pulley. To our knowledge no examples survive.

"DOGS' NOSE"
Gin and beer.

THE LITTLE DOG THAT TURNED THE SPIT

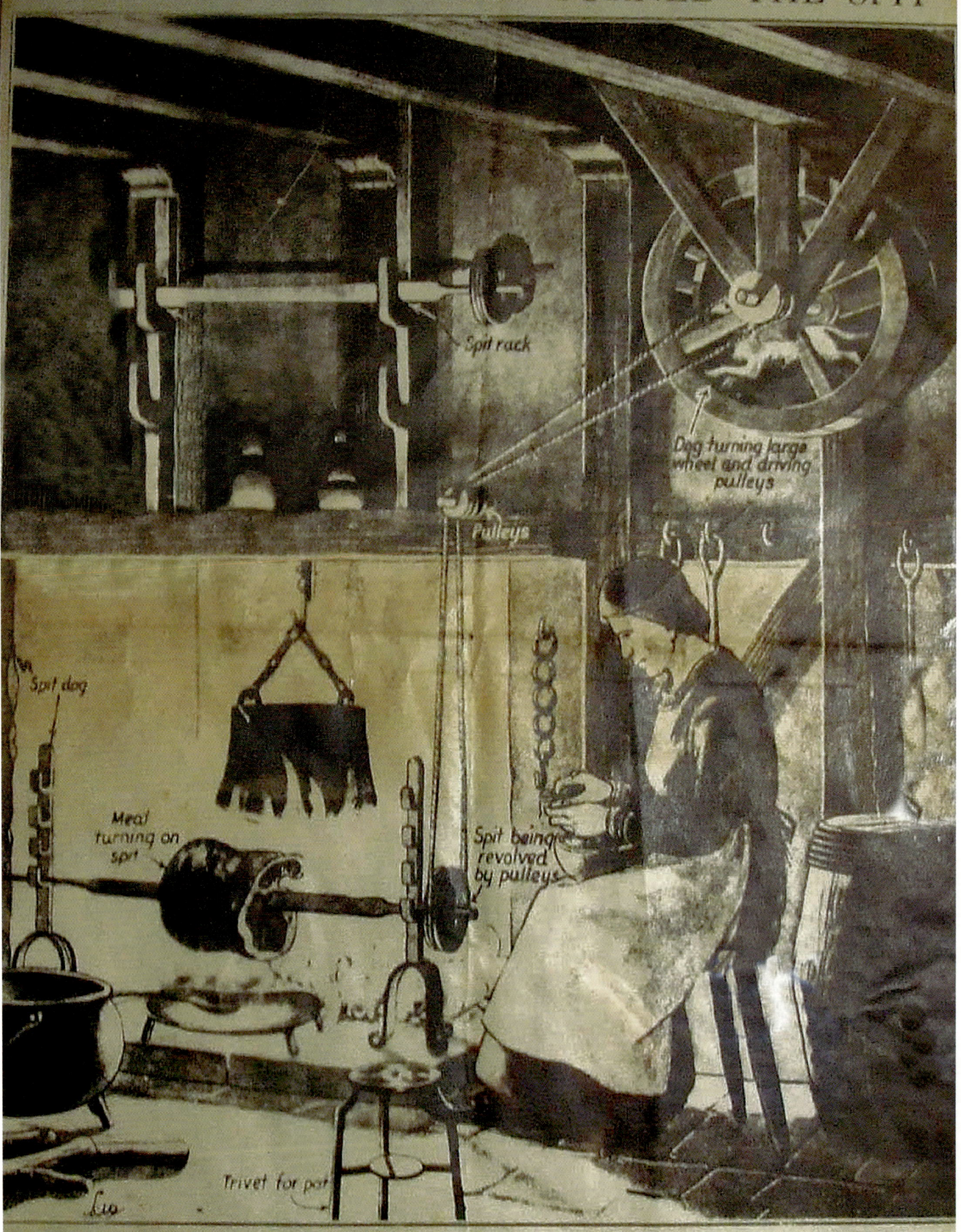

the Middle Ages the joints of meat and birds were cooked by roasting them in front of the fire. They were impaled upon a spit. was turned so that all parts of the joint or bird might receive the heat and be properly cooked. Sometimes the spit was turned boy, but towards the end of the fifteenth century little dogs came to be used for this purpose. Somewhere near the fireplace anged a wheel, not unlike that which is found in a squirrel's cage. The dog was trained to go through the motions of reby turning the wheel, and by means of a rope attached to a pulley the wheel turned the spit. The unfortunate dog was his work by means of a live coal put in the wheel behind him. If he stopped running the cinder burned his hind paws. kept on a rack above, and as we can see, both here and on page 416, cooking was rather more complicated than it is

Turnspit Dogs - (Canis familiaris)
A labour saving device.

Dog wheels were once common in certain areas of the country. They were normally made of wood or iron, and there were several designs and lay-outs with different diameter wheels. Some drawings showing the dog wheel above the fire obviously employed a lot of artistic licence, as clearly the animal inside would have died of heat exhaustion in that position, and the cook would have needed a ladder or tall chair to place the dog in the wheel.

From our studies of the lay-out, we have found that the dog wheel was sometimes in a separate room adjacent to the cooking fire, and was usually positioned at waist or shoulder height in a recess in the wall. The shaft from the dog wheel would have gone through the wall into the side of the fireplace where it was attached to a pulley; this in turn was attached with a rope, chain or leather belt to the pulley on the end of the iron spit on which the meat was cooked. The wooden pulleys would have varied in size, with the largest being on the spit. It was important that the spit was turned gently and slowly, so that the fat was not thrown out into the room or onto the fire which would have caused the flames

A medieval oak bench-end made in the early 15th century, in All Saints Church, East Budleigh in Devon. It shows a lady clasping a spit dog by the tail. There is a dressed bird (perhaps chicken) ready for roasting, in the top left hand corner.

to flare up and burn the meat. It would have taken perhaps three or four hours to roast a suckling pig for example, so two dogs would have been used in relays. Turnspits were a recognised breed of dog which varied regionally to some extent in size and shape, similar to a small Jack Russell type of terrier. The recess in the wall of one private house (where there used to be a dog wheel) measured about 40 inches in diameter and about 8 inches deep, clearly made for a small dog. It is likely that many people have found a round recess in an old house and have not realised the significance of it, taking it for a blocked up window or serving hatch perhaps.

Dog wheels were popular in coaching inns where parties of ravenous travellers would arrive throughout the day; they were also found in town and country houses and large farm houses.

Although some people used geese or ponies to turn spits, dogs continued to be used in the West Country and Wales long after the rest of the country had turned to mechanised spit engines or jacks.

17th century dog wheel that would have driven the spit.

"DOG DAYS".
The hottest period of the year. From the old days, the heliacal rising of Sirius, the Dog Star.

Turnspits & Spit Dogs

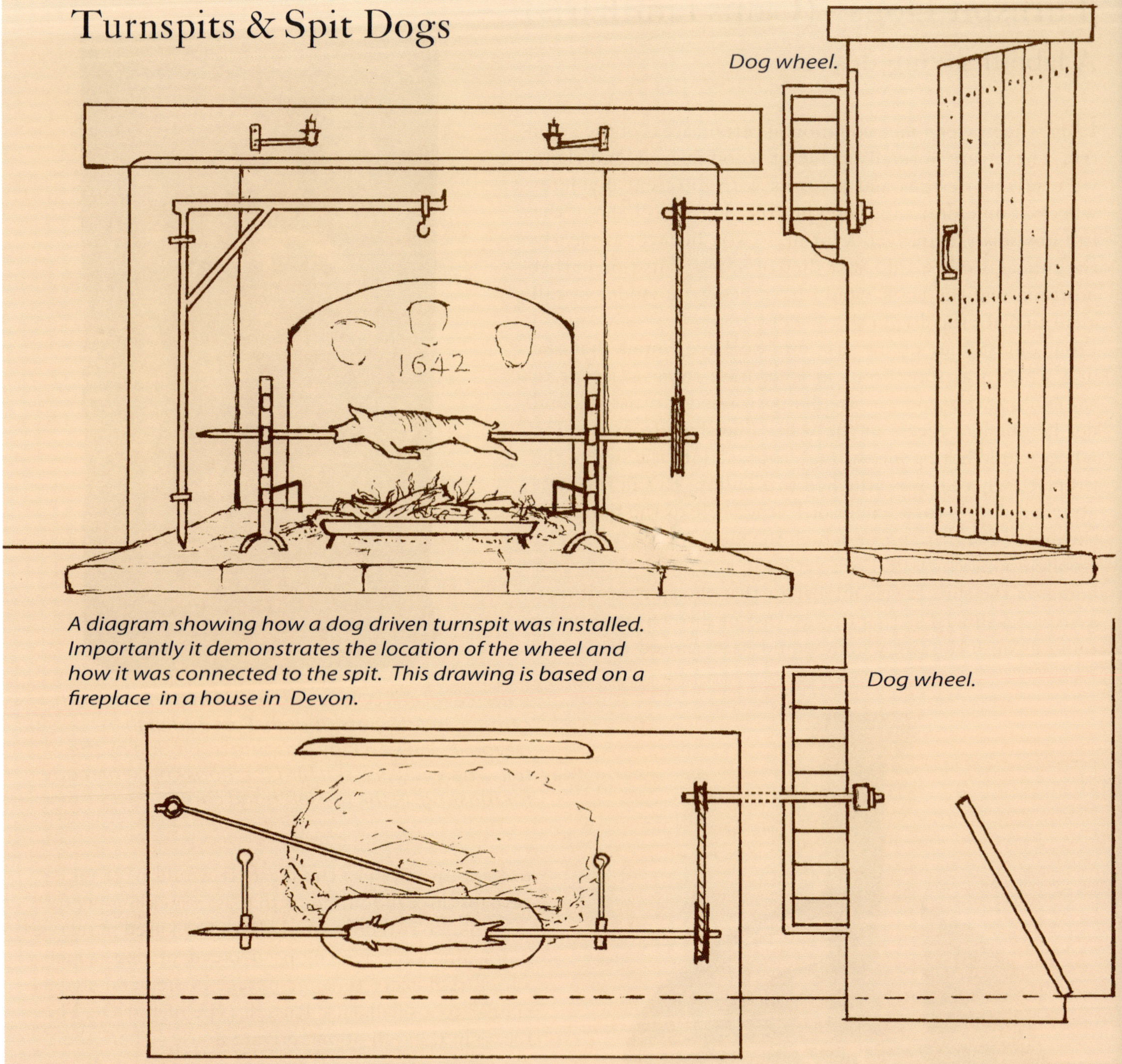

Dog wheel.

A diagram showing how a dog driven turnspit was installed. Importantly it demonstrates the location of the wheel and how it was connected to the spit. This drawing is based on a fireplace in a house in Devon.

Dog wheel.

Whiskey, the last known spit dog, stuffed and now residing in Abergavenny Museum, Wales.

THE TURNSPIT

"THE BITER BEING BIT"

This old saying has nothing to do with animals. In the 17th century a biter was a con man. "Talk about a biter being bitten" was originally a phrase about a conman being beaten at his own game.

Does your grill provide such delicate control?

Cranes, Pot Hooks & Kettles

A bargrate in use with a hanging cauldron and fat catcher in the embers, beneath a cooking chop.

Kettles & Kettle Tilts

Early kettles were round bottomed vessels made of beaten or sheet copper or brass; they had no fixed handle or spout. They hung in the hearth and were used mainly for heating water. Later kettles were also made of iron and in the 18th/19th centuries, all households would have had one hanging in the hearth. The kettle as we know it went through many evolutionary changes, from the original hanging pot through to the copper or iron cistern which was equipped with a tap for drawing off hot water, avoiding the risk of being scalded.

The kettle tilt came into use in the 18th century, making it easier and safer to deal with boiling water; many examples can still be seen and some are illustrated opposite, from the highly decorative to the plain utilitarian.

"TEA KETTLE BROTH"
Poor man's soup consisting of hot water, bread and a small lump of butter with pepper and salt.

Kettle Tilts

Late 18th century wood handled wrought iron Scottish kettle tilt with 18th century Dutch swing handled copper kettle.

18th century iron kettle tilt, adjustable for use with kettles having different sized handles.

19th century iron kettle tilt.

Late 18th / early 19th century wrought iron kettle tilt.

18th century brass knobbed iron kettle tilt.

"A STORM IN A TEACUP"
A mighty to-do about a trifle; making a great fuss about nothing.

76

Early Kettles

Possibly late 16th century riveted sheet brass oval kettle.

18th century French seamed thin sheet copper pot with iron fittings. Made for downhearth use, probably for boiling water.

"BUB"
Particularly strong beer.

Kettles

Early/mid 18th century copper kettle.

Mid 18th century brass kettle.

Late 18th century English kettle.

Mid 19th century Continental brass kettle.

Late 19th century one gallon kettle.

Late 19th century one gallon kettle.

"KETTLE"
Old thieves' slang for a watch. A tin kettle is a silver watch, a red kettle is a gold one.

Kettles

18th century English seamed brass kettle.

19th century copper 'half' range kettle.

19th century English Britannia metal kettle.

19th century cast iron and brass kettle.

"CLARET CUP"
A drink made of claret, brandy, lemon, borage, sugar, ice and carbonated water.

Cranes

An 18th century chimney crane holding a 17th century bronze cauldron.

19th century iron adjustable chimney crane for use over a fire.

Late 18th century iron bar. This was mounted above the fireplace and the adjustable pot hook could be moved left or right to control the cooking temperature.

"CHIRPING CUP"
A merry-making glass or cup of liquor.

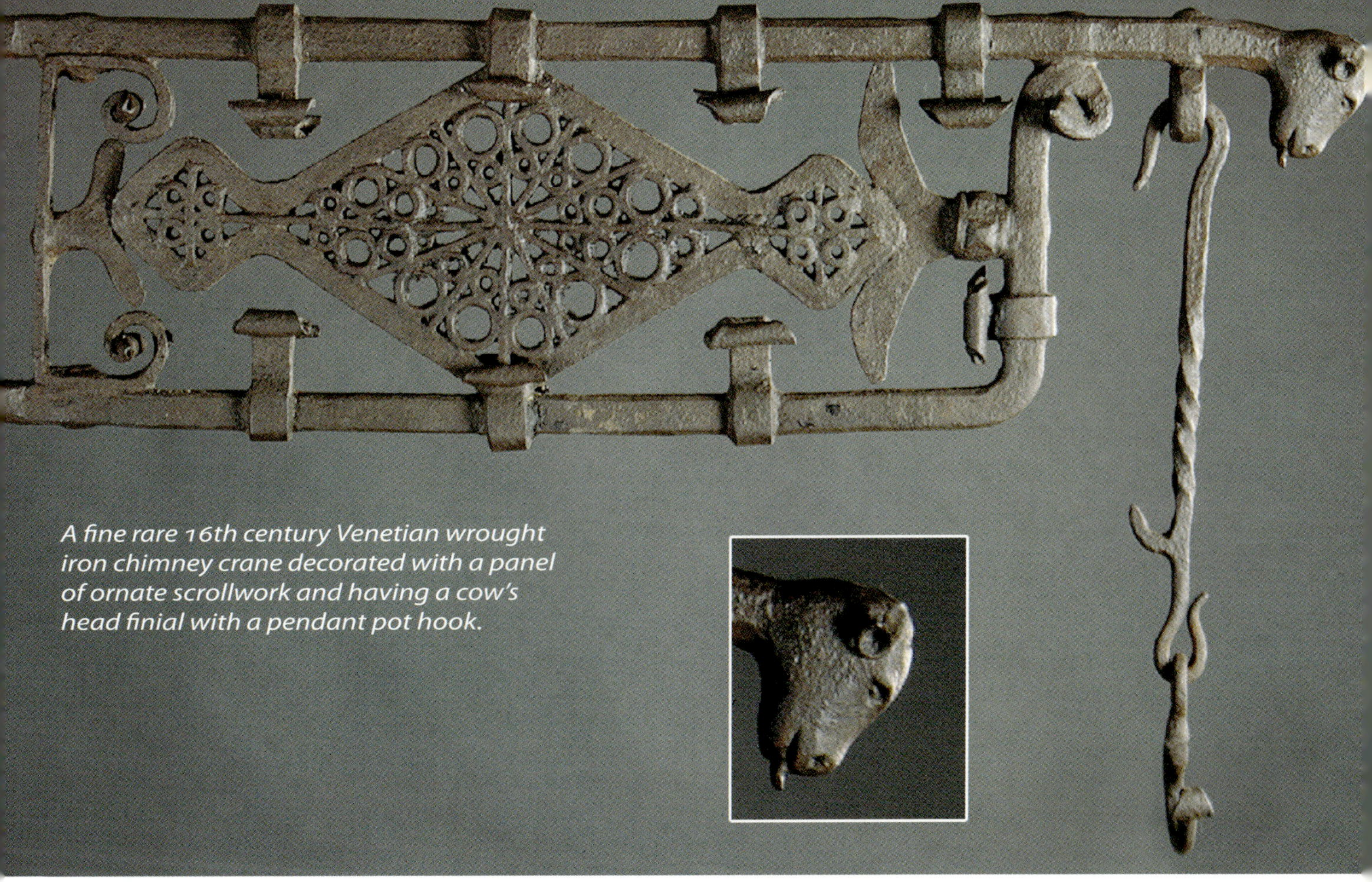

A fine rare 16th century Venetian wrought iron chimney crane decorated with a panel of ornate scrollwork and having a cow's head finial with a pendant pot hook.

18th century English three way chimney crane in situ, with a ratchet lever for adjusting the height of the pot or cauldron.

Pot Hooks

Four 18th century wrought iron adjustable pot hooks, a rare example on the right with brass mounts.

"TO GIVE HIM HIS GRUEL"
To give him severe punishment; properly to kill him. The allusion is to the practice, in 19th century France, of giving poisoned possets – an art perfected by Catherine de Medici and her Italian advisers.

Dutch Ovens

Large 19th century floor standing tin hastener showing boned and rolled shoulder of lamb cooking on a bottle jack. The rear door shown open for basting.

Dutch Ovens

The designs of English made Dutch ovens (or hasteners as they were also called), were many and varied, with both downhearth and bargrate versions.

They were made in great quantities in the late 18th and early 19th centuries, mainly from sheet tin. This was a good material until it rusted, which is why not many survived once they became redundant, unlike the decorative brass bottle jacks which were used in conjunction with them.

Many an old cook in the past has told how the clicking of the bottle jack in the Dutch oven was one of the most familiar sounds in the late 18th and early 19th century kitchen.

Dutch ovens were designed to reflect the heat of the fire and catch the fat that dripped from the joint. Most of them had a door at the back which allowed one to baste the meat cooking inside and keep an eye on its progress. Smaller horizontal ones had a spit passing through that could revolve on 5 or 6 different settings so the meat would not get burnt; these also incorporated a fat catcher so the joint could be basted while cooking; other fat catchers had a spout on one end so that when the meat was done the juices and fat could be poured out into a bowl to be used again later for cooking, lard and dripping, or turned into rush lights. The dripping was often eaten on bread or toast, a practice long since frowned upon by the medical profession!

"RULE THE ROAST"
To be in charge, have full authority; from the mid 16th century. The now more common "Rule the Roost" is recorded from the mid 18th century.

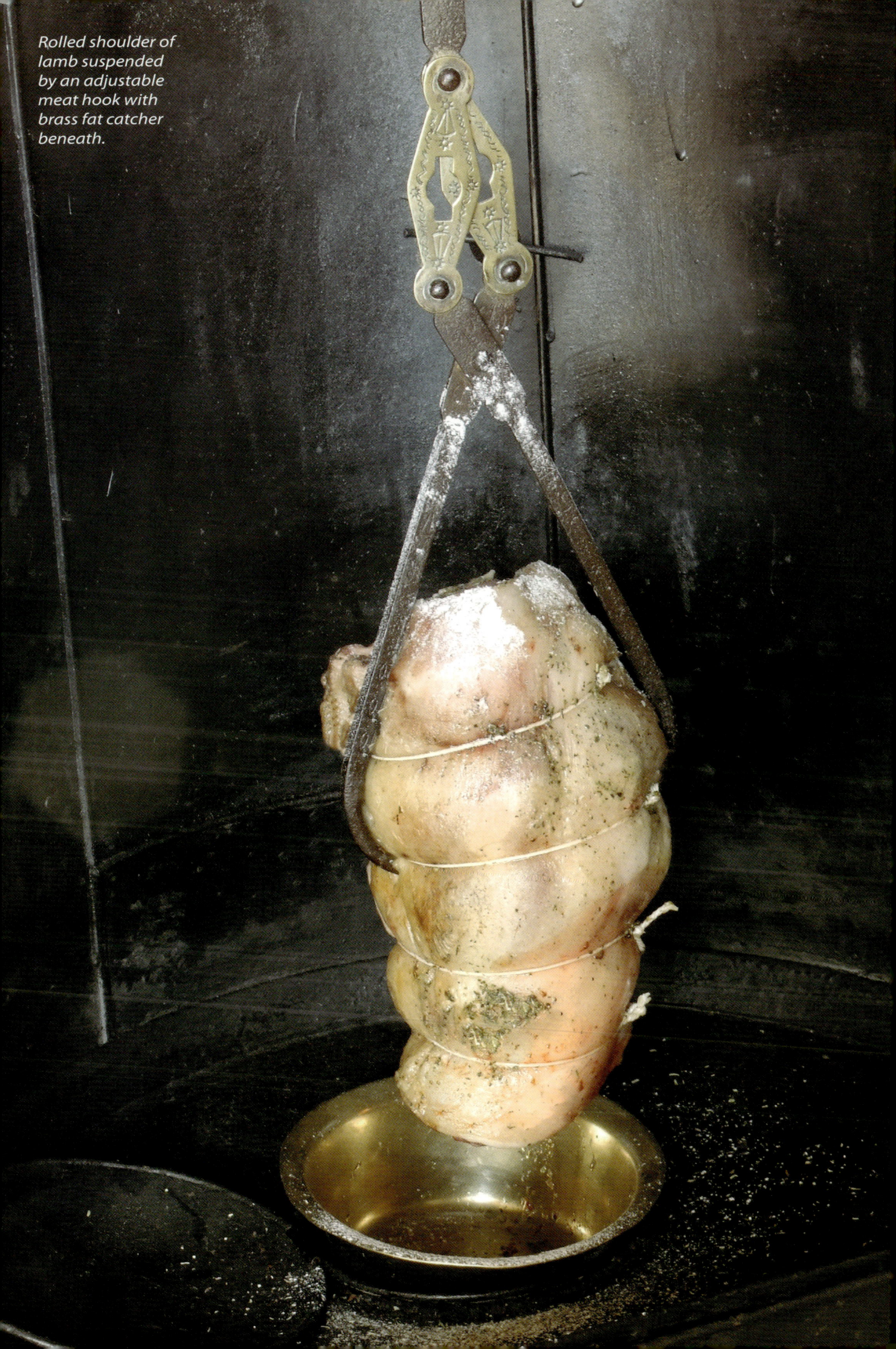

Rolled shoulder of lamb suspended by an adjustable meat hook with brass fat catcher beneath.

Dutch Ovens

One of the smallest types of Dutch oven was used by sliding it onto the bars of a bargrate, giving the cook some control over the amount of heat she needed.

Various Dutch ovens are illustrated in this chapter, including a small copper game oven which incorporates a bar and hooks to hang the bird on (p.91). At the begining of this chapter, a large free-standing one is shown (p.85) cooking a boned and rolled shoulder of lamb. The lamb was well basted with a mixture of butter, olive oil, rosemary and thyme, salt and pepper; the photograph shows the door open at the back while the basting was being done. The cooking time varied according to the strength and proximity of the fire.

A fine skewer would be inserted into the joint to test whether it was cooked; if the juices that ran out were still bloody it needed more time, if the juices ran clear it was ready, so could be taken out of the Dutch oven and allowed to rest before being carried to the table for carving.

If someone decided to try using a Dutch oven or hastener today, it would be possible to restore its reflecting ability by lining the inside with aluminium baking foil to reflect the heat and speed up the cooking.

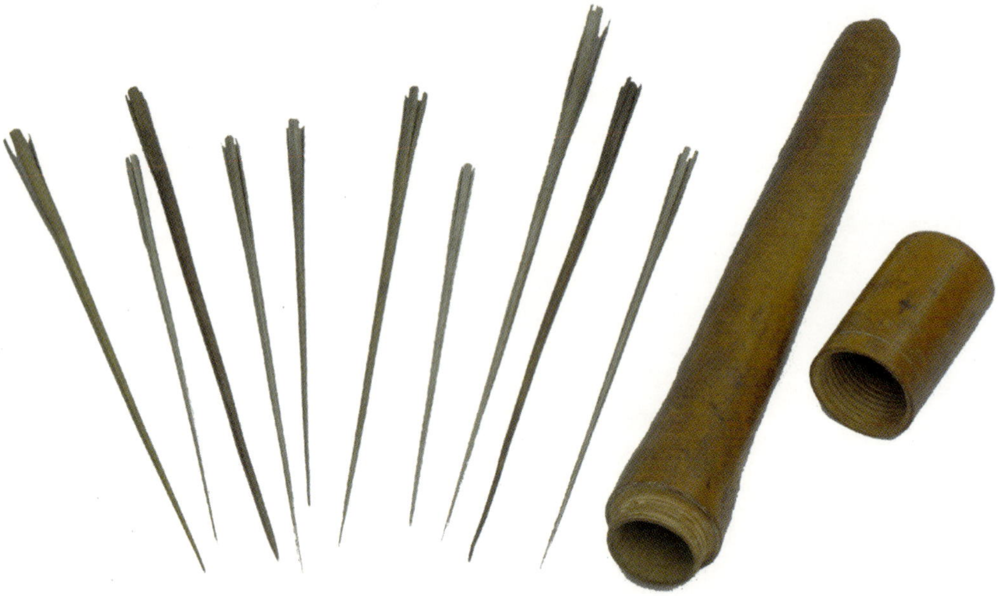

Rare set of 18th century steel larding needles with a treen case.

Larding needles

These were used for threading fat (often pork fat or lamb "caul") through meat. Some meats, venison for example, had very little fat, so the needles were used to thread the fat through, thus keeping the joint moist when cooking. The photograph shows a treen (wooden) case with a graduated set of needles.

19th century iron and brass adjustable height, meat scissor hooks, to be suspended from a bottle jack.

"TO SHOW OR GIVE ONE THE COLD SHOULDER"
To assume a distant manner towards a person. The reference is to a cold shoulder of mutton served to a stranger at dinner; there is not much of it and even what is left is but moderate fare.

Early 19th century bottle jack hanging in a 19th century hastener.

Marriott (Dutch) Oven

Clockwork mechanism inside housing.

Reverse view of the clockwork housing.

A very rare Marriott (Dutch) oven, possibly a unique survivor. It is made of tin so has been very susceptible to rust. This 'improved version' relates to the fact that the device was designed to turn a horizontal spit in addition to the vertical one.
Henry Marriott worked in Fleet Street, London from 1812 to 1822, and died a wealthy man in 1848 at the age of 70.

A selection of bottle jacks.

Dutch Ovens

Small 19th century floor standing reversible hastener.

A rare copper Dutch game oven, note the hanging bar inside.

Small 19th century tin hasteners and an iron spit (below) which was inserted through the hole on each side of the hastener. Note the small prong on the spit used for adjusting the postion of the meat by locking into the little holes on the side of the hastener.

"WHAT'S SAUCE FOR THE GOOSE IS SAUCE FOR THE GANDER"
Both must be treated exactly alike. Apple sauce is just as good for one as the other.

Roast lamb which has just been removed from the bottle jack.
Note the two rare 18th century skewers.

"ONE MAN'S MEAT IS ANOTHER MAN'S POISON"
What suits one man may be anathema to another.

The Yeoman's Kitchen

Life in the yeoman's house changed slowly, and gradually improved. Times were difficult and people had to work hard to keep a roof over their heads, with enough to eat and a bed to sleep in; the cattle housed at one end of the building would have helped to keep the house warm in winter.

The yeoman's kitchen must have been one of the most important and busy rooms in the house. Many tasks as well as cooking were carried out there: cleaning, maintenance and mending clothes by the light of the fire, to name but a few.

The room would have been simply furnished with tables, benches or chairs, hanging food cupboards and a settle by the fire perhaps. Everything, including tools and utensils, would have been handed down through the generations, including, most importantly, the vast wealth of knowledge that the cook had acquired during a lifetime of hard work.

The arrival of the Industrial Revolution put an end to this way of life; nothing was ever the same again after mass production took business away from rural craftsmen such as blacksmiths, coopers and wheelwrights.

"DOG LATIN"

A law report (Daniel v Dishclout). Stephens' definition of a kitchen as the Law classically expresses it: a kitchen is "camera necessaris pro usus cookare, cum saucepannis, stew-pannis, scullero, dressero, coacholo stovis, smoak-jacko, pro roastandum, boilandum, fryandum, et plum-pudding-mixandum".

Chopping Boards & Peel

18th century Continental chopping board.

18th/19th century chopping board and selection of knives.

19th century elm peel with tapered working edge.

18th century carved chopping board and horn handled chopper.

19th century bread board and bread knives.

"BREAD AND CHEESE"
The barest necessities of life.

Kitchen Treen

Many items used in the kitchen were made from wood. Turned items such as bowls, cups, condiments, mortars etc were made from woods appropriate to their purpose. Mortars were often made from heavy, dense lignum vitae, bowls were made from sycamore and ash and drinking cups from many different woods.
Staved pieces of wood, held together by iron or wicker bands were used to make some of the earliest vessels. They were easily constructed and could be kept watertight by adjusting the bands.

18th/19th century treen masher and platter.

Treen cooking spoons made from various woods.

"HE HAS SUPPED ALL HIS PORRIDGE"
He has eaten his last meal, he is dead.

Treen Spoons & Spurtle

Treen cooking spoon.

19th century treen spurtle / stirrer.

A selection of bone spoons.

"TO HAVE A BONE TO PICK WITH ONE"
To have an unpleasant matter to discuss and settle. Two dogs and one bone invariably form an excellent basis for a fight.

Kitchen Utensils

Various 17th to 19th century copper, brass and iron kitchen implements on an early 19th century painted wooden rack.

18th & 19th century iron slices and peels.

"EVERYTHING BUT THE KITCHEN SINK"
Everything you could think of, usually excessive luggage or belongings when travelling.

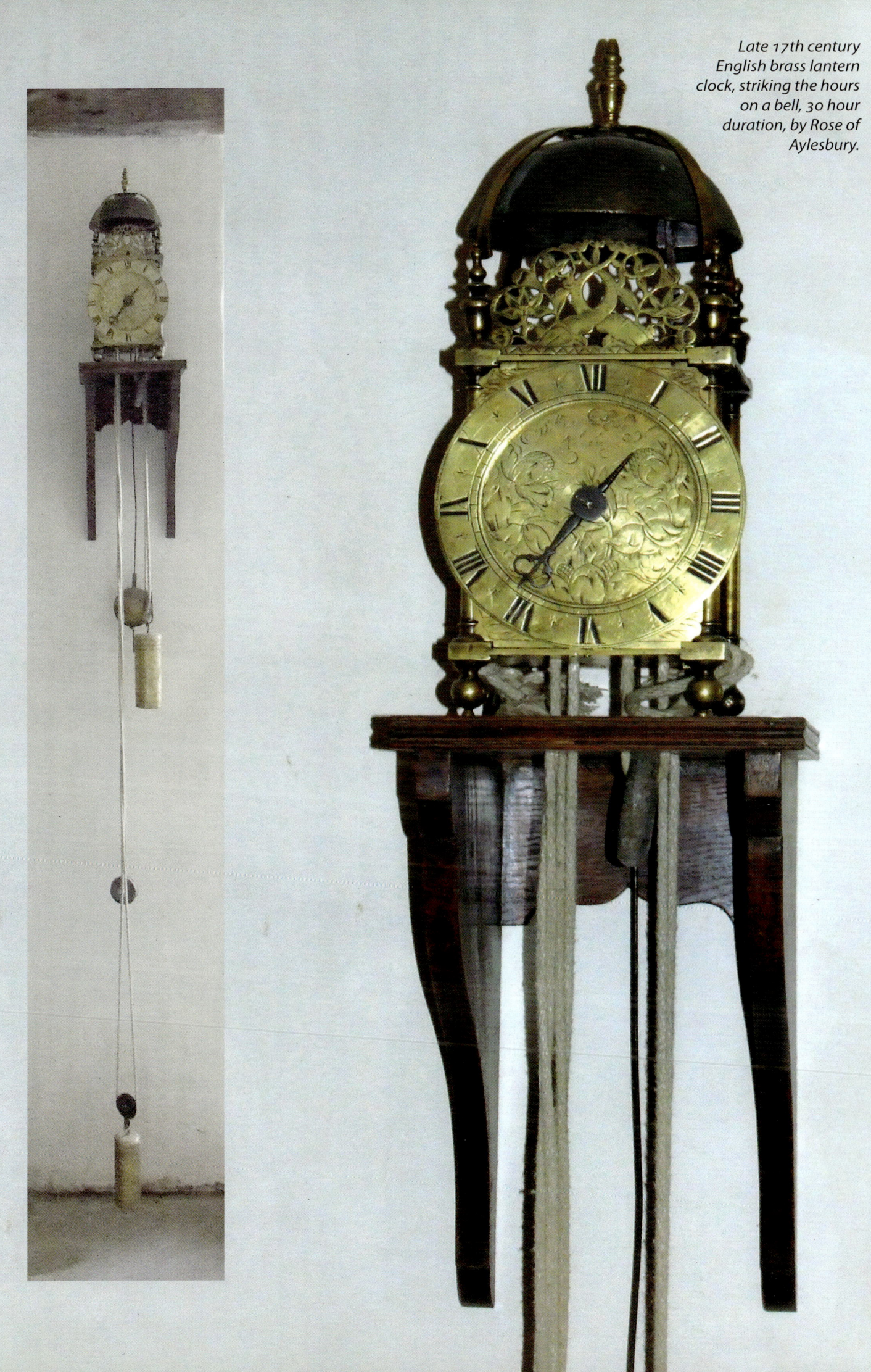

Late 17th century English brass lantern clock, striking the hours on a bell, 30 hour duration, by Rose of Aylesbury.

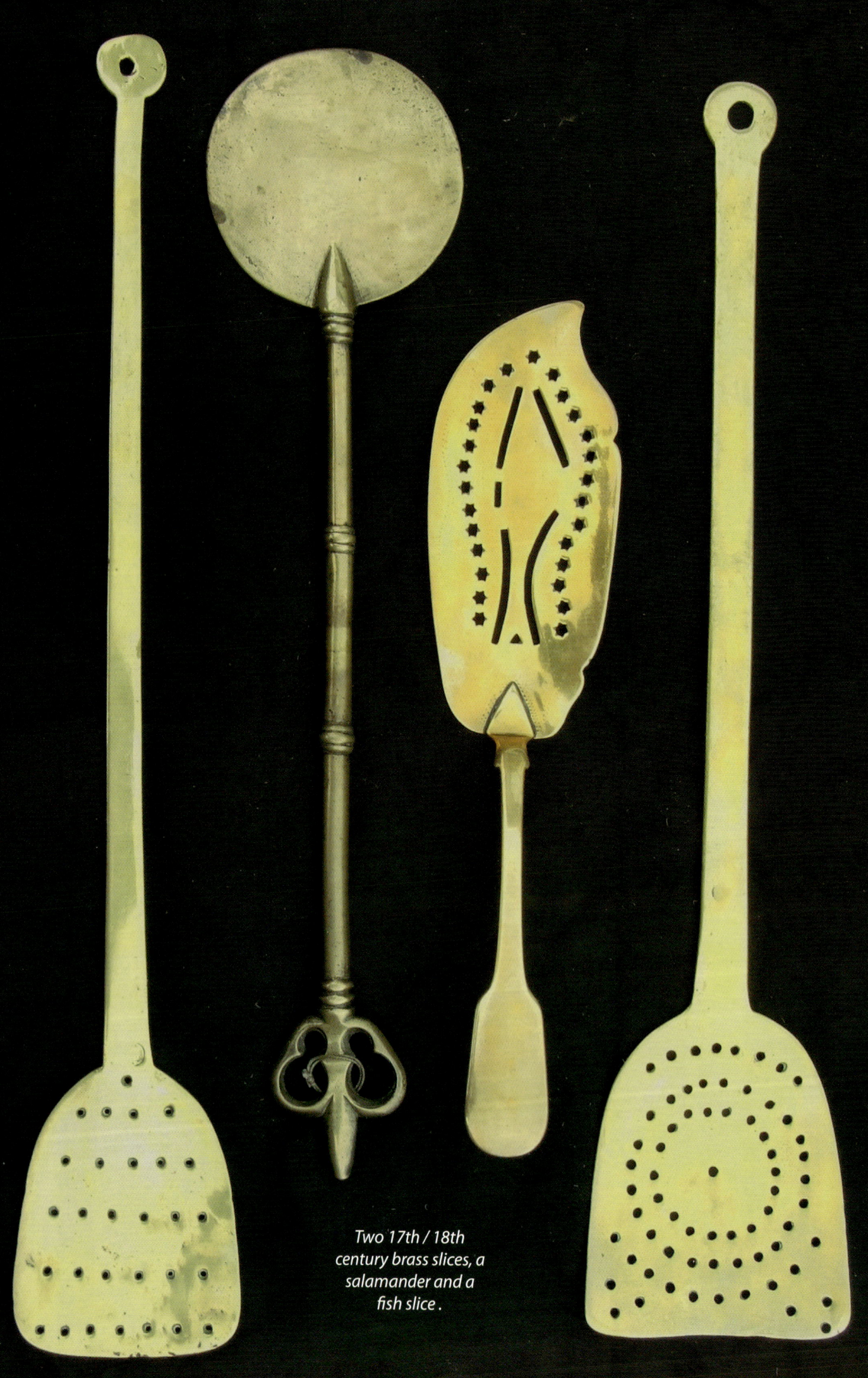

Two 17th / 18th century brass slices, a salamander and a fish slice.

Ladles

Ladles have always been important implements in the kitchen, and can be traced back to the very earliest days of cooking. Serving any liquid such as soup, stew, broth or potage from a cauldron, saucepan or skillet required the use of a ladle; joints were basted with the meat juices, butter and herbs from the fat catcher, so straining ladles with perforated or partially perforated bowls, were essential. A drawing from a late 18th century print by Rowlinson shows a cook sitting by a dog spit in front of the fire holding a basting ladle (p.74). They were made of wood, brass, copper or iron as illustrated below.

A ladle is described in Johnson's Dictionary circa 1812, as "a large spoon, a vessel with a handle". Ladles came in a variety of shapes and sizes with many regional characteristics; for example, there is a form which has extended sides and a pierced bowl for straining liquids. Much early cooking was done in a cauldron or iron pot, hence the need to scum the contents; perforated ladles must have done the same job as certain scummers. There are still many examples of perforated ladles and spoons to be seen, as illustrated below.

Early ladles were most likely carved from wood, a tradition that continued until the time when machines were developed to make the wooden kitchen spoons that are used today. There has always been a strong tradition of wood carving in Wales where wooden love spoons or tokens are still made. Carved wooden ladles continued to be used alongside iron, copper and brass ones, the latter being made from either cast or sheet brass.

Basting ladles usually have a flat profile meaning that the bowl is in line with the handle. They were used in conjunction with the drip pans illustrated in many early paintings, to collect the juices and fat for basting the joint. They worked well because of the low profile of early fat catchers.

The ladle used for serving soup or gravy at the table was a different shape from the basting ladle as it had a very bent profile (see below) which was necessary for getting into a steep sided tureen. Many examples of these followed the designs of the silversmiths of the times, but were made of copper, brass or iron instead. In most homes from the 16th to the 20th century, life revolved around the kitchen fire with people cooking, eating, and often sleeping in cupboard beds in the same room. When the potage was cooked it would be served out to the family and workers, one large ladleful in a bowl for each person.

19th century copper straining spoon.

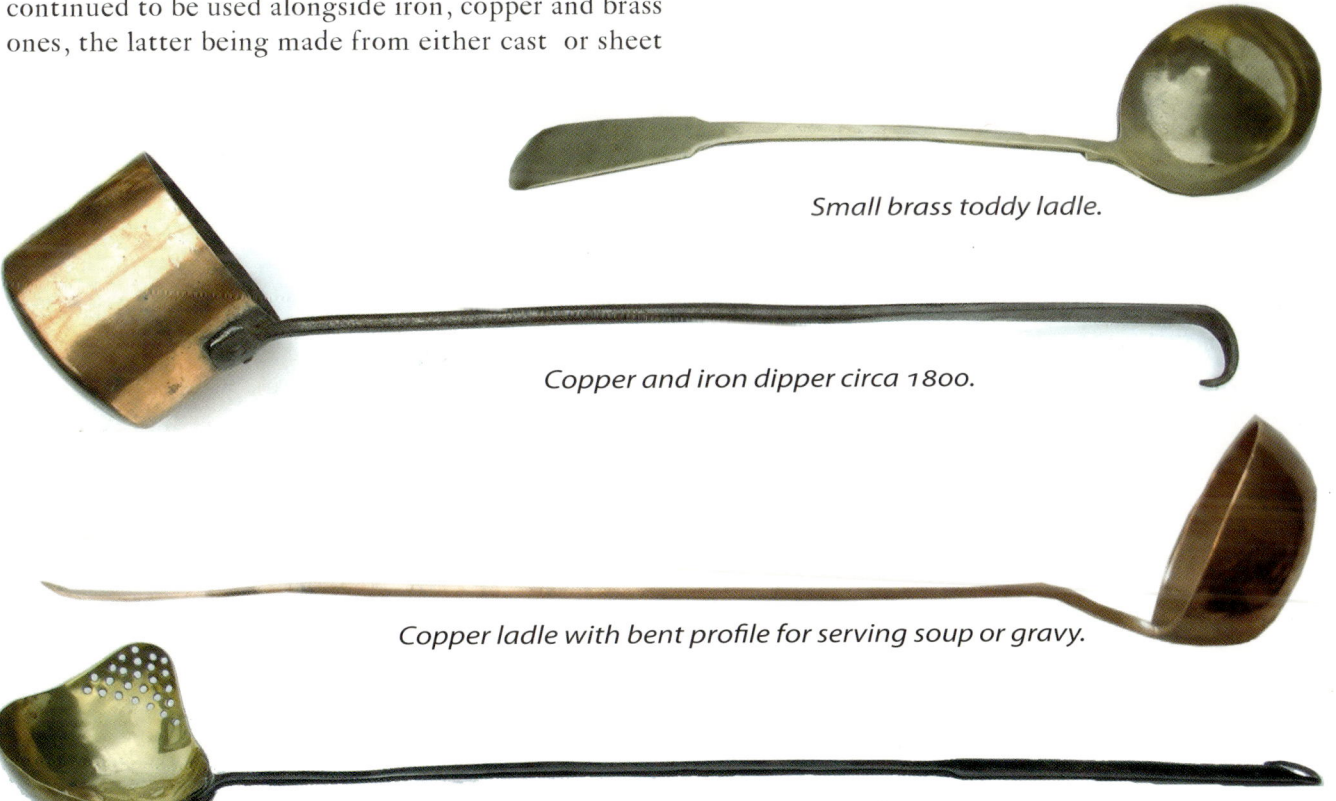

Small brass toddy ladle.

Copper and iron dipper circa 1800.

Copper ladle with bent profile for serving soup or gravy.

Iron and brass half strainer ladle.

"ST MARTHA'S LADLE"
Sister of Lazarus and Mary and friend of Jesus. She is portrayed as the type of woman constantly busy with household affairs; her emblem is a ladle, a broom or a bunch of keys.

18th/19th century brass ladles.

Skimmers & Scummers

These two groups of implements were frequently put in the same category in the 20th century but there is one fundamental difference between them: a skimmer is used to remove the cream from the top of the milk, leaving a useful end-product, a scummer removes a by-product which has no value and is discarded. (Nowadays "scum" is a term of abuse to denigrate people or substances.)

A 14th century inventory mentions: "A brandreth, flesh fork, a scummer, a ladle, a pot stick" which would indicate that scummers were being used in domestic households at that time. Another quote from 'The Academy of Armoury' circa 1668 states: "cooks take away all the filth and scum from the boiling pot, the liquor remaining". This does not sound very appetising! There is mention in a medieval recipe of scum being removed from a cauldron of boiling fish. Another recipe, "To Boil a Chine of Mutton" says: "boil in a glazed pipkin (earthernware pot) being well scummed then a faggot (bundle) of sweet herbs being finely boiled down, serve it on snippets, pieces of toasted or dry bread".

The large holed implement made of cast brass with a riveted socket to take the wooden handle (right) is similar to one found on the Mary Rose, Henry VIII's flagship which sank just off the south coast near Portsmouth. When she was lifted from the sea, a remarkable collection of artefacts was discovered inside her which has greatly added to our knowledge of life in those days. She is a great national treasure! Since the holed implement was found on a ship at sea, it seems clear that it would not have been used for milk but to remove the scum from a cauldron cooking meat or fish, or the froth from beer for example. The smaller holed varieties were probably used for skimming cream from milk.

Marked brass skimmers were made by the Worshipful Company of Founders of London who passed an ordnance in 1614 stating that "every person or persons using the art or Mastery of making brass and copper works shall from time to time mark the same work with their own proper and several marks where by the wares and workmanship which they make, may be known when they shall be viewed and searched and found defective." According to Rivington's New York Gazette, dated July 29th 1773, William Bayley in his store and warehouse in Beaker Street and in his store (or shop) in the Fly Market, New York, specified that they had for sale "reasonable, both wholesale and retail, imported in the latest vessels from England, brass scummer ladles and slices".

A selection of skimmers and scummers is illustrated to demonstrate the diversity of these important and much used pieces of domestic kitchen equipment. They are made from a wide range of metals: copper, iron and

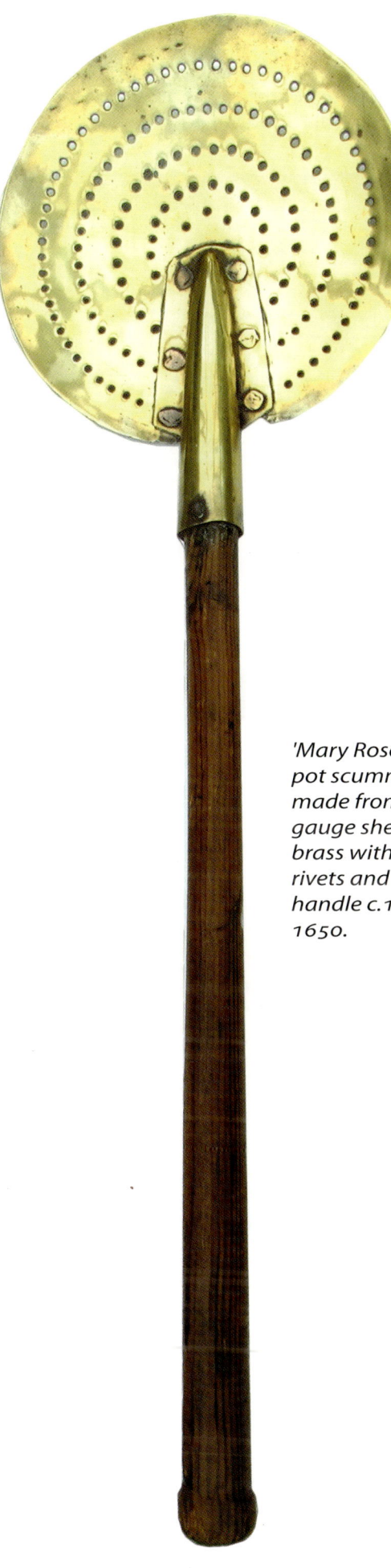

'Mary Rose' type pot scummer made from thick gauge sheet brass with rolled rivets and wood handle c.1550-1650.

"SKIMMER OR SCUMMER"
'Tis only a fool that knoweth not his skimmer from his scummer.

Skimmers & Scummers

17th century English cast brass pot scummer or milk skimmer showing early repair.

19th century iron handled sheet brass milk skimmer.

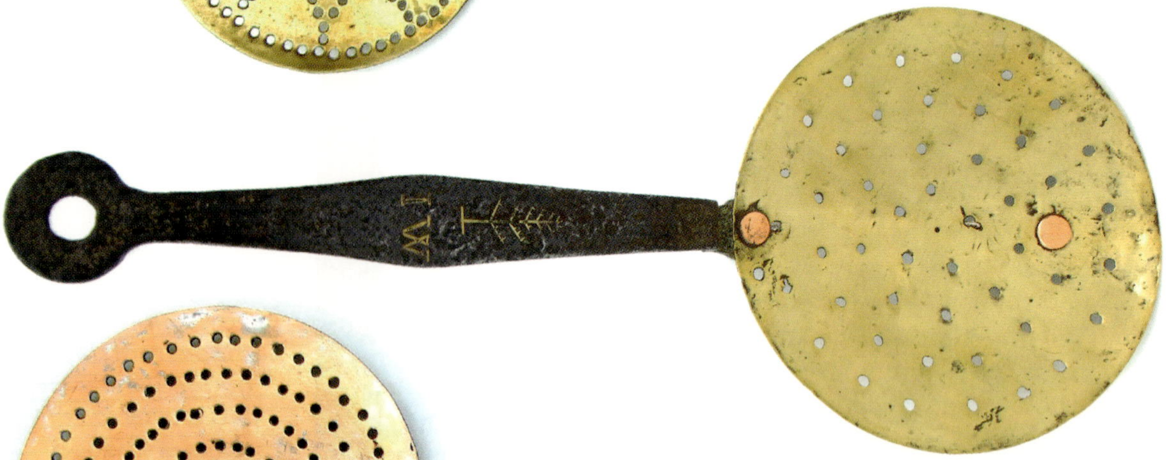

19th century iron handled sheet brass milk skimmer with brazed 'inlay' I.W and a primitive tree (presumably a pun on his name 'Wood').

19th century tinned copper pot scummer.

more usually brass. Later brass ones were produced in their thousands for purely decorative purposes; they were made of a very soft yellow brass unlike the early hard brass ones of former times.

Many skimmers were produced with the iron handle extending across most of the back. One example incorporates the unusual feature of a step in the handle which is inlaid with the brass letters I.W. and a primitive tree (see above). Enamel milk skimmers (see opposite), which were usually white, came in about 1840 when enamelling became commercially viable.

Skimmers and scummers usually have a hole or an oblong slot pierced in their handles; on the Continent they are frequently fitted with a hook instead. 19th century English implements sometimes had a French style hook handle.

Here is a recipe for Milk Punch by Eric Quale: "To twenty quarts of the best rum or brandy, put in the peel of thirty Sevill oranges and thirty lemons, as soon as it boils up and when a cup of scum rises to the top, take off the pot and skim it perfectly clear, then put on again with some more of the beaten eggs and skim again as before. Do the same with the remainder of the egg until it is quite free from "dirt". This punch will keep for many years." (Today it would seem obvious that the use of the word "dirt" implies it should certainly not be kept too long!)

105   "TO STEW IN ONE'S OWN JUICE"
To suffer the natural consequences of one's actions.

Skimmers & Scummers

19th century iron handled sheet brass milk skimmer.

19th century copper pot scummer with 'French' pattern hook.

19th century tinned iron pot scummer.

19th century iron handled sheet brass milk skimmer.

19th century iron handled sheet brass milk skimmer.

19th century enamelled skimmer.

"SKIMMINGTON".
A procession made through a village to ridicule or make an example of a nagging wife or an errant husband. This saying may come from a skimming ladle used during the procession.

Kitchen Utensils

Pewter measure.

19th century copper bread proving bowl.

19th century terracotta glazed colander.

19th century French copper porringer.

19th century brass serving spoon.

Large 19th century whisk.

Salts, peppers and a flour dredger, all brass.

"TO PEPPER ONE WELL"
To give one a good basting, thrashing.

Miscellaneous Kitchen Items

19th century oak salt box; it would have hung by the fire to keep the salt dry.

Early 19th century hour glass used to keep time when cooking.

18th century brass hinged, wooden kettle lifter, used to protect the cook's hand from being burned on the metal handle.

Small 18th/19th century English lignum vitae pestle & mortar and a string box. This wood was imported from the West Indies and is one of the few which is so dense that it sinks in water! The name means "wood from the tree of life", derived from its supposed life-giving properties. The heart wood is light coloured and the outer, dark. Lignum is also "self lubricating" and maintains a shiny finish.

"TO DINE WITH THE CROSS LEGGED KNIGHTS"
To have no dinner at all.
The knights referred to are the stone effigies of the Temple Church, where at one time lawyers met their clients. A host of vagabonds used to hang about the church all day in the hope of being hired as witnesses.

Ale Mullers

Three 19th century copper 'ass's ear' ale mullers.

19th century copper 'slipper' ale muller.

"COOPER"
Half stout and half porter. The term arose from the old practice at breweries of allowing the coopers a daily portion of stout and porter. As they did not like to drink porter after stout, they mixed the two together.

Costrels

An early 17th century leather costrel.

18th century leather saddle bottle for taking beer outdoors.

An 18th century wooden bottle. Probably common in most kitchens but a rare survivor today.

18th century iron bound costrel, prepared in the kitchen for use in the fields.

Three 19th century wooden costrels for farm workers to take beer / cider into the fields.

"THOSE WHO DRINK BEER WILL THINK BEER"
Attributed to Warburton, Bishop of Gloucester. (1698-1779)

Basting / Glazing Pot & Bain Marie

An early 19th century tinned copper basting / glazing pot and brush, separate parts shown on the left with the assembled pot shown on the right.

Late 19th century tin, copper and porcelain bain-marie.

"TO BASTE YOUR BACON"
To strike or scourge someone. Bacon is the outside portion of a side of pork, and may be considered generally as the part which would receive a blow. Formerly swine's flesh formed the staple food of English rustics.

Bed Warming Pans

18th/19th century bed warming pans, often stored on the kitchen wall and filled with hot embers from the kitchen fire to warm the bed last thing at night.

"WARMING PANS".

A nickname for Jacobites. It is said that James ll's child was surreptitiously introduced into the queen's bed in a warming pan as a substitute for a stillborn baby.

Chestnut & Coffee Bean Roasters

19th century roaster.

19th century chestnut roaster.

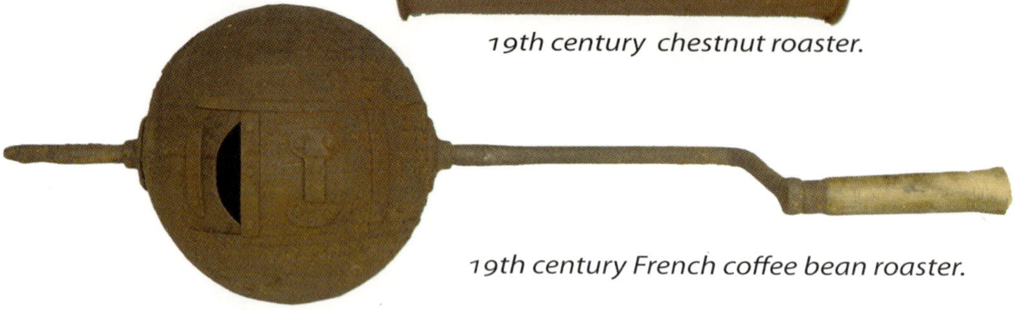

19th century French coffee bean roaster.

Sweet chestnuts had many uses when in season. They were fed to poultry, and pigs foraged for them in the woods. They could be roasted and ground into flour or made into porridge. There was even a special kind of beer brewed from them. Chestnuts were also used in the production of charcoal.

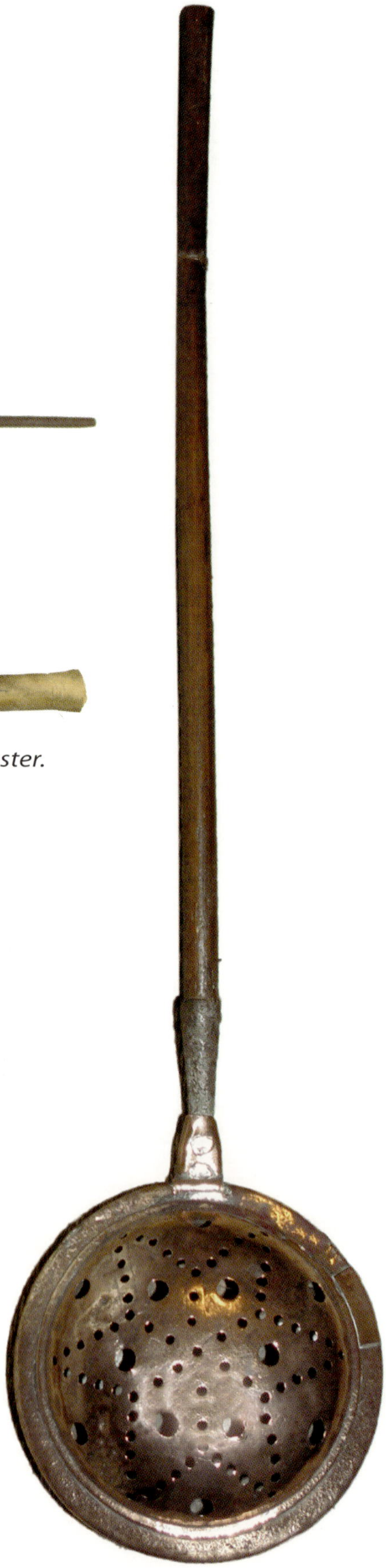

18th century Continental chestnut roaster.

"CHESTNUT"
A stale joke.

Eggs

Broody Box

The broody box would have been hung on the wall in the kitchen, out of the reach of dogs, cats or children. The hens would have lived outside in barns or outbuildings; poultry houses were not common until Victorian times.

Once a hen became broody she would have been put into the box to sit on some fertile eggs. She was taken out once a day to be given a drink of water and scraps of bread and grain on the kitchen floor. When she had emptied herself she was put back inside the box to continue incubating her eggs.

Dated 1815 kitchen broody coop.

19th century Staffordshire sitting duck egg container.

19th century Staffordshire sitting hen.

18th/19th century rustic copper egg cup.

Rare 18th century tinned copper small bird egg poacher.

A set of 19th century treen egg cups and stand.

"I GOT EGGS FOR MY MONEY"
I gave valuable money and received such worthless things as eggs.

Sugar

Sugar was first found and used in Polynesia from where it spread to India, then Persia, North Africa and Spain via the Arabs. This "new spice" was brought to Western Europe by the Crusaders in the 11th century, and in 1493 Columbus took some sugar cane plants to the Caribbean where they flourished. So began the colonisation of the West Indies where more and more plantations were developed and more and more slaves were imported to work them.

Due to politics and taxation, it was only the raw dark sugar that was allowed to be exported to England and Europe where it was refined in a series of boiling and filtering processes. When it was considered ready for granulation it was poured into inverted conical moulds and allowed to cool, then the cones of sugar (right) were tapped out of their moulds, trimmed and wrapped in blue paper to enhance their whiteness.

These sugar cones / loaves were very hard and a small sugar axe (opposite) was used to break them up, sugar snips (below) then broke the chunks into usable pieces.

Loaves varied greatly in size: the larger the loaf the lower the grade of sugar. Some were as big as 3ft high and some as small as 5 inches. Sugar was sold in this form well into the 20th century until bagged granulated sugar became available.

A pair of Georgian sugar nips.

"STOLEN SWEETS ARE ALWAYS SWEETER"
Things procured by stealth, and game illicitly taken, have the charm of illegality to make them the more palatable.

Sugar

A pair of 18th century hand held sugar nips.

Fine 18th century steel sugar axe.

Rare 18th century treen sugar bowl and lid.

"TO THE HUNGRY SOUL EVERY LITTLE THING IS SWEET"
To a hungry man every morsel is good.

Kitchen Storage

Rare pitched roof early 18th century oak hanging food cupboard. It hung from the ceiling to prevent larger vermin from eating the food.

18th century Continental wrought iron 'Dutch crown'.

18th century English 'Dutch crown'.

17th century pierced mural food cupboard.

17th century oak grain ark which would have stood in the kitchen to keep the grain dry.

"CAGMAG"
Offal, bad meat, also a tough old goose; food which none can relish.

HOUSEHOLD WANTS INDICATOR

ALMONDS.	CREAM OF TARTAR.	MARGARINE.	SARDINES.
APPLES.	CURRANTS.	MARMALADE.	SAUCES.
ARROWROOT.	CURRY P^DR.	MATCHES.	SAUSAGES.
AMMONIA.	CUSTARD P^DR.	METH. SPIRITS.	SEMOLINA.
APRICOTS.	DISINFECT^ANT.	MILK.	SOAP.
BACON.	DOG BISCUITS.	MIN. WATERS.	SODA.
BAK^G POWDER.	EGGS.	MUSTARD.	SOUPS.
BAKED BEANS.	EMERY PAPER	NIGHT LIGHTS.	SPICES.
BARLEY.	ENAMELINE.	NUTS.	STARCH.
BATHBRICK.	ESSENCES, FL.	NUTMEGS.	SUET.
BEER, STOUT.	FIGS.	OATMEAL.	SUGAR.
BEEF, PRES^D.	FIRELIGHTS.	OIL. OLIVES.	SYRUP.
BEESWAX.	FLOUR.	ONIONS.	TAPERS.
BISCUITS.	GELATINE.	ORANGES.	TAPIOCA.
BIRDSEED.	GINGER.	PAPERS, DISH.	TEA.
BLACKING.	GRAVY COLOR.	PEAS.	TOMATOES.
BLACKLEAD.	HADDOCKS.	PEACHES.	TONGUE.
BLUE.	HAM.	PEARS.	TOOTH PAST^E
BORAX.	HARICOTS.	PEEL.	TREACLE.
BOVRIL, OXO.	HEARTH ST^ONE.	PEPPER.	TURPENTINE
BRANDY.	HERBS.	PICKLES.	VEGETABLES
BRUSHES.	HOUSE FLAN.	PINEAPPLE.	VERMICELLI.
BUTTER.	HONEY.	PIPECLAY	VINEGAR.
CANDLES.	HOMINY.	PLATE P^DR.	WASH LEAT^HR
CAPERS.	INFANT FOOD.	POLISH, BOOT.	WASHING P^DR
CARB. SODA.	ISINGLASS.	POLISH, BRASS	WHITENING.
CAKE.	JAM.		
CHEESE.	JELLY.		
CHOCOLATE.	KIPPERS.		
CHUTNEY.	LAMB.		
CHICORY.	LARD.		
COAL, ETC.	LEMONS.		
COCOA.	LEMON CURD.		
COCOANUT, D^ES.	LENTILS.		
COFFEE.	LOBSTER.		
CORNFLOUR.	MACARONI.	SALAD CREAM.	

CHARLES LETTS &

A Victorian Grocer's Ledger

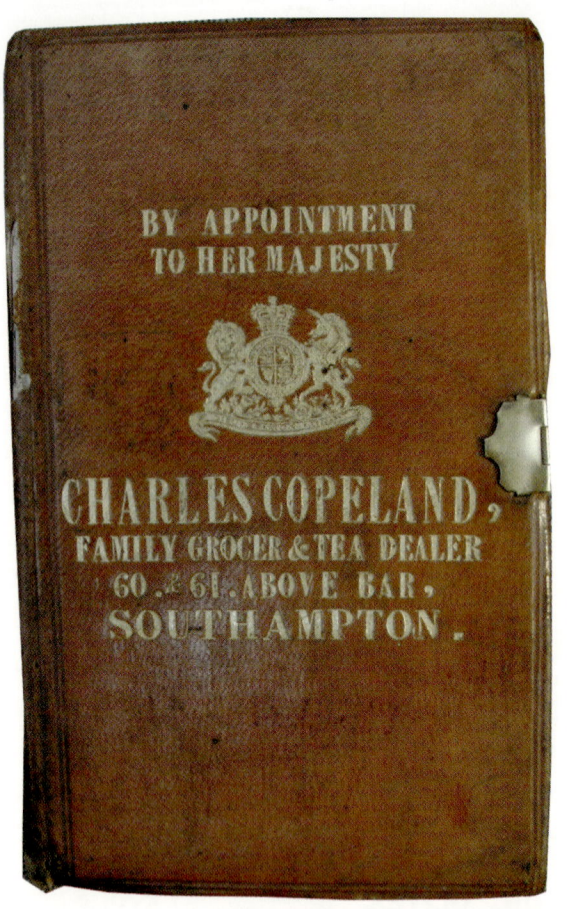

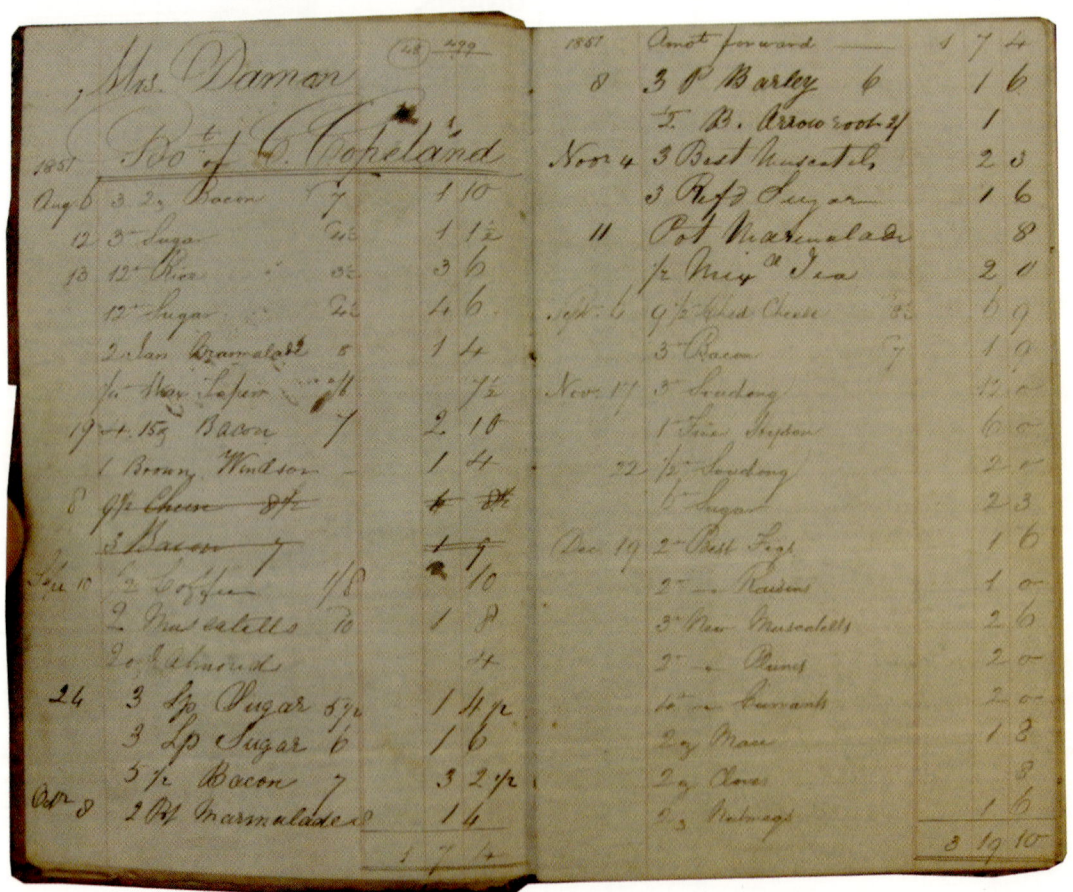

A ledger of the grocer Charles Copeland, of Southhampton, dated 1857.

The lady of the house would settle the debts built up over a period of time by the cook who bought supplies for kitchen and household use.

"TO COOK THE BOOKS"
To falsify a financial account or reckoning to make it more acceptable or palatable as if by cooking.

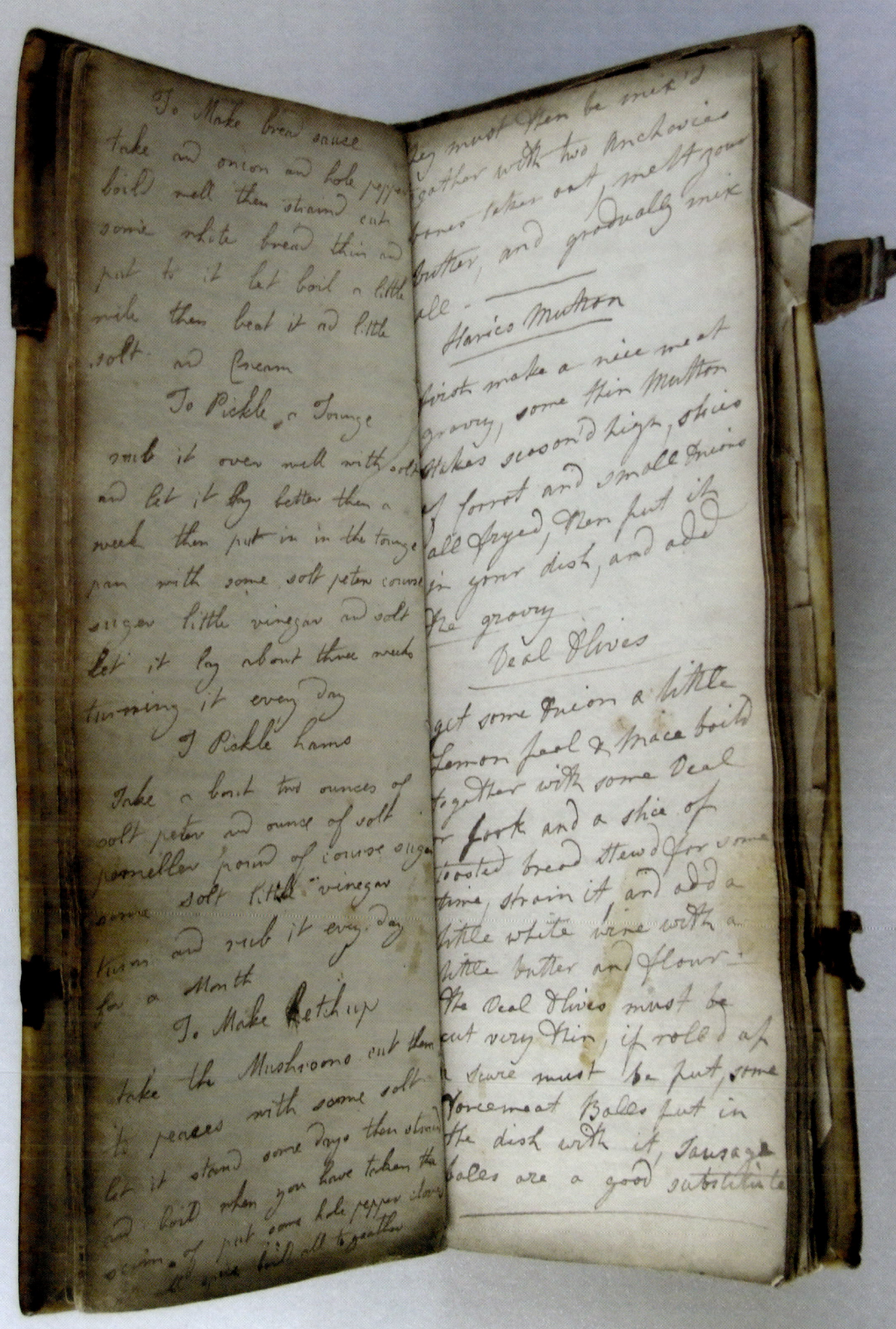

Early 19th century hand written recipe book. Recipe books in the past often contained recipes for medicines as well as food. Common remedies were usually prepared in the kitchen.

Settles

Large open fires needed a substantial draught in order to draw well. Free standing settles were placed in front of the hearth to provide some protection from the cold air drawn in by the fire. Many household tasks were carried out while people sat in the warmth and light of the flames on cold winter evenings.

An early 18th century West Country oak bacon settle. The panelled section opens to reveal the hooks where bacon was hung for storage.

An early 18th century downhearth settle that would have been next to the hearth.

"THE DUNMOW FLITCH"
A side of bacon awarded at Great Dunmow in Essex on Whit Monday to any couple who could swear that they had not quarrelled or repented of their marriage vows for at least a year and a day. The custom is said to have been started by Lady Juga Baynard in 1104 and restored by Robert Fitzwalter in 1244.

A well earned rest.

Traps & Vermin Control

Glass gudgeon trap.

Glass Gudgeon Trap
The gudgeon is a small freshwater fish. The trap would be baited with maggots, small red worms or bread paste, then would be placed on the river floor where the gudgeon feed. They were normally eaten fried like whitebait.

17th century flintlock gun. These were often kept above the fire in the kitchen; shown with four shot or powder flasks.

19th century glass wasp trap.

Vermin were always a problem in the home, especially during the winter months when rats and mice were drawn into the house because it offered warmth, food and shelter from the weather. Their numbers were kept in check by dogs and cats, and mice were caught in traps such as the ones illustrated opposite; in households where cats were not permitted mice were prevented by the use of chloride of lime.

Insects were also a problem, but were largely kept at bay by the smoky atmosphere in the house, and bunches of tansy were often hung by joints of meat to keep flies away. The ingenious English trap (below right) was used to catch cockroaches, and wasps and flies were caught in special glass traps (right) which were designed to hold cider or watered-down jam as bait.

Large chests or arks (p.117) were used for storing grain, spices, herbs and valuable dried medicinal plants; these arks were hung from hooks in the ceiling, along with game and poultry, to keep them out of reach of dogs and cats. Later, wire mesh or gauzed cabinets made of wood or steel were introduced to protect food from flies. Most food was stored in wooden bins or barrels, earthenware pots and glass or stone jars, as there was always a problem with weevils, silver fish, beetles and ants etc.

19th century cockroach trap.

"A FLY IN THE OINTMENT"
The trifling cause that spoils everything. A phrase of Biblical origin.

Vermin Control in the Kitchen

Wire mouse trap.

The 'opposition', our resident mouse.

19th century wood mouse trap. The unfortunate mouse was squashed by the wooden block.

Our rodent control officer.

"'TIS AN OLD RAT THAT WON'T EAT CHEESE"
Only a very cunning rat knows that cheese is a mere bait.

Buckets

Rare West Country 18th century dug-out bucket.

Two 19th century brass bound wooden coopered buckets.

18th century brass water bucket.

19th century English brass and copper malt bucket.

19th century English iron bound copper water bucket.

"TO BUCKET ALONG".
Originally, to ride a horse at full pelt, thus pushing him or taking it out of him "by the bucket".

Cleaning & Hygiene

When the realisation started to dawn on people that cleanliness was next to Godliness, they began to wash themselves and their clothes.

Soap had in fact been around for a very long time; it was first mentioned by the Romans, and Pliny maintained that it originated in northern Europe. To begin with it was made from tallow or animal fat, vegetable or olive oil and wood ash; ash is alkaline and when mixed with animal fat it produces a grease which dissolves dirt. Certain plants, nature's natural alternatives, were also used: soap wort for example, was gathered from streams and river banks and the leaves were boiled in a cauldron. The mixture was then distilled to leave a thick residue which was used for washing clothes in a nearby stream or the village washing trough; washing is still done like this in rural parts of Europe as well as in the developing world. Soap was not recommended for cleaning spits in the kitchen as it would taint any meat subsequently put on to cook. Tight bundles of tough twigs were used as scourers, below, and it was possible to get cooking utensils quite clean using these along with some sand and plenty of elbow grease.

Pomanders and later pot-pourri were made to counteract the many pungent smells that often occurred in the kitchen.

To make a pomander these days, you will need: an orange, some cloves, ground cinnamon, orris root powder (made from the roots of Mediterranean irises), masking tape and some ribbon.

First divide the orange into four quarters by sticking the masking tape round it. Insert the cloves into the peel, leaving room round each one as the orange will dry out and shrink. Mix together the cinnamon and orris root powder and put the mixture into a paper bag. Add the orange and roll it round in the bag to coat it well with the spices. Put the bag and its contents somewhere warm, and leave it for at least three weeks for the orange to dry out. If there are any signs of mould developing, throw it away and begin again. When the orange has dried out completely, replace the masking tape with ribbon and hang up your pomander to scent the room.

Twig kitchen scourers.

Kitchen tidy.

"Making a Pomander
To make Pomanders, take two penny-worth of Labdanum, two penny-worth of Storax liquid, one penny-worth of Calamus Aromaticus, as much Balm, half a quarter of a pound of fine wax, of Cloves and Mace two penny-worth ... and of Musk four grains: beat all these exceedingly together, till they come to a perfect substance, then mould it in any fashion you please, and dry it."
Gervase Markham, "The English House-Wife (1675)

"Mixing Pot-Pourri
A quicker sort of pot-pourri - Take three handfuls of orange flowers, three of clove-gillyflowers, three of damask roses, one of knotted marjoram, one of lemon-thyme, six bay leaves, a handful of rosemary, one of myrtle, half of mint, one of lavender, the rind of a lemon, and a quarter of an ounce of cloves. Chop all, and put them in layers, with pounded bay-salt between, up to the tip of the jar. If all the ingredients cannot be obtained at once, put them in as you get them; always throwing in salt with every new article."
Sarah Hale, "The New Household Receipt-Book" (1854)

19th century Masons' ironstone potpourri vase with pierced lid.

"TO MAKE A NAPKIN OUT OF ONE'S DISH-CLOUT"
To marry one's cook, or contract some such misalliance.

19th century copper for boiling water and washing clothes. Only the lid is visable.

Repairs

An interesting working repair on an 18th century French copper fruit pan.

Two views of an 18th century cast bronze skillet with a tinker's repair of sheet brass held in place by copper rivets.

Multiple intricate repairs to a large pan.

Stapled repair of 18th century Delft plate.

"HE HAS NOT A DOG TO LICK A DISH"
He has quite cleared out, he has taken away everything.

A Typical Will and Inventory of an 18th century Yeoman

This is the Will and Inventory of John Deeley of the village of Launton, near Bicester, Oxfordshire, who died in 1716. He was a yeoman farmer, and would have known of the Washington family, who lived at Sulgrave Manor about 14 miles away. John Deeley is an ancestor of Robert Deeley, the author of this book.

Personal estate to his son William Deeley, daughters Joanna, Mary and Sarah Deeley & their survivors for their maintenance until 21 years or married then the principal money to be divided amongst them. Sarah to have £20 more than the others of my younger children. And if any dye to pay the sum to my son John Deeley............. Executors Jo. Box of Marsh Gibbon, Thos. Tossill Blake, Northants. Signed and sealed this 25 day of March 1716
John Deeley
Witnesses Martha Theed Jo Jones J Egerton

A true and perfect inventory of the goods & Chattells, rights & credits of John Deeley, late of Launton in the county of Oxon taken & approved on April 24th 1716

	£	s	d
Weaking apparel & money in his purss	20	00	00
Item Plate & six gold rings	8	00	00
Item Linen, being twenty nine pair of sheets, a doz of pillow drawers, one doz & three table clothes five doz & 4 napkins & 4 towels	10	02	00
In the Parlor chamber one joint bedstead, curtains & Vallens, feather bed, bolster & pillows, blankets & quilt, a chest of drawers, a table, a looking glass, seven chairs, one stool, window curtains, brass andirons, fire shovel & tongs	12	10	00
In the clossetts, some books, glasses & other things	10	00	
In the buttory chamber, one joint bedstead, 1 feather bed, curtains & vallons, bolster & pillows, blanckets a quilt, chest of drawer, 1 table, a trunk, six chairs & window curtains	6	10	
In the Hall chamber 1 feather bed 2 flock beds blankets	2	01	06
In the kitchen " " " " & other lumber	3	06	08
In the Garrotts a malt garenor with malt in it, bedsteads, bedding etc.	4	12	06
Bacon & Cheese	3	03	04
In Parlor 14 cain chairs, 2 tables, looking glass, bellows, fire doggs etc. & picture	1	16	00
In kitchen a furnace, brass pan, skillets, skimmer, ladles, frying pan, gridirons, pott hangers, pair			

doggs 1 doz & 2 pewtor dishes, 2 doz & 11 plates, 4 porringers, 2 salts, a bason, spoons & other small items	2	05	00
In Dairy leadon milk pan, churn, kivors, trough, Pans, tables, shelves, potts etc.	2	3	00
In Buttory kivors, buttory, barrolls, stands, spinning wheel etc.	1	10	00
Pump in back yard etc.		10	00
Cow cribbs & dung in back yards	1	5	00
Firewood & poles " " "	3	10	00
2 waggons, 3 carts & an old malt mill	16	00	00
Ploughs, harrows, timber, ladders etc. & all other implements	5	00	00
A load of slats & 8 doz hurdles	2	15	00
2 wheat stadles & 2 bean hovels	3	00	00
The wheat & rye in the rick in the barn	24	00	00
The beans in the hovel & in the barn	16	00	00
The hay & straw at home & in the ground	17	10	00
Eight horses, mares & colts & harness	28	00	00
26 cows & heifer, 3 young bulls, 2 yearling bullocks & 4 calves	65	00	00
128 sheep & 32 lambs in field	48	00	00
126 " " 50 lambs in the ground at Hungerill	1	10	00
14 sheep in the home close	10	17	00
5 store hogs & a sow & pigs	7	15	00
The poultry in the back yard		10	00
Wheat growing in the field, barley & beans & all other grains	61	1	00
	56	1	00
The debts owing to the testator at the time of his death	4	13	00
Total	£620	13	10

William Rawlins
Edward Hitchcock   Appraisors
William Marriott   July 11th 1715

"WHERE THERE IS A WILL, THERE IS A RELATIVE."
An old Warwickshire saying.

Preparation

A selection of kitchen tools used for preparing food.

Preparation

So much of our food today is already pre-cooked, canned or bottled that it is easy to forget what is involved in preparing food properly from scratch.

Choppers were produced in a bewildering array of regional designs, with double- and even triple-bladed herb choppers. The more ornate ones would have come from wealthier households, the simpler, plain ones belonging to the poorer homes. In the West Country they were used mainly to chop potatoes and as general kitchen choppers. A variety of different ones is illustrated; the large one (far right) is a 19th century cleaving chopper for splitting a pig. The author used one 40 years ago to split a carcase right down the centre of the spine, a job that required some skill as one had to avoid splintering the bones.

(right) 18th century brass inlaid iron meat cleaver. (far right) 19th century cleaver with turned wooden handle and brass ferrule.

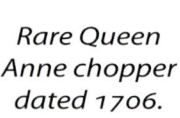

Rare Queen Anne chopper dated 1706.

131

"BATCHELOR'S FARE"
Bread and cheese and kisses.

Mortars

Large 17th century Continental mortar made from a hollowed out single piece of wood.

A large English, lignum vitae, mortar circa 1700.

(top & middle) Floor standing mortar, (bottom) a mess of pounded chicken on a pewter plate.

"TO GRIND ONE DOWN"
To reduce the price asked. A knife is gradually reduced by grinding.

Mortars and Pestles

The mortar is the "vessel" and the pestle is the "club" shaped implement.

Mortars in one form or another, have been around since man walked on our planet; indeed, bonoboes (relatives of the chimpanzee) have been observed using stones to crack nuts open on a hard surface, surely the start of mortars and pestles!

It would not have taken man very long to work out that if the hard surface had a depression in it to contain the object to be crushed, it would be more efficient and less wasteful than pounding on a flat surface.

Although mortars and pestles are often associated with apothecaries, undoubtedly the earliest and most common use would have been in food preparation, as virtually nothing up until the 19th century was available in powdered form. Mortars and pestles would have been essential in the manufacture of products as diverse as paint and gunpowder as well as in the preparation of food and medicines.

It was important that both mortars and pestles were harder than the substance being pulverised so that no contamination occurred. It was also important that the materials used did not absorb flavours or vice versa and whereas the internal surface of the mortar had to be smooth, the pestle, although also normally smooth,

Probably 16th century stone mortar with walnut cover and pestle. It's rare to retain the cover, which was used to keep the contents in whilst pounding.

Two examples of 17th/18th century lignum vitae mortars and pestles.

"ENOUGH IS AS GOOD AS A FEAST"
A proverbial saying from the late 14th century.

Mortars and Pestles

Mid 17th century cast leaded bronze two-handled mortar, dated 1640, probably by George Oldfield of Nottinghamshire.

Leaded bronze mortar by Edward Neale of Burford dated 1688 and made for John and Mary Whipp.

17th century leaded bronze mortar with portrait of Charles II, probably from the London 'unknown' foundry. Many were produced after the restoration of Charles II.

Large leaded bronze West Country mortar cast for John Galton of Taunton, dated 1705.

was sometimes roughened to facilitate grinding. Mortars were made of many different materials including wood, brass, bronze, hard ceramic, iron, marble and granite; they also came in many different sizes from very small to extremely large, so big, in fact, that some required mechanical help to operate the pestle. After the introduction of sugar, some people in the past would not have had the perfect, shiny white teeth that you see in period films today; many would have lost teeth at an early age and therefore their food needed to be mashed to aid digestion.

The majority of kitchens would have had some form of mortars and pestles, poorer homes perhaps one or two, but large affluent households would have had a range of sizes and materials that could be used for a variety of different types of food preparation, from the breaking up of sugar and salt to the grinding of herbs, spices, peppercorns etc.

"TO MAKE MINCEMEAT OF"
To utterly demolish, to shatter to pieces; mincemeat is meat cut up very fine.

Pestles of various dates and materials.

Mincers and Grinders

Mincers and grinders became more common in the 18th century. Until then many foods, that is herbs, spices and meats, were crushed in a mortar, and the term a "mess" of food, meat etc, was coined. From this came the Officers' Mess where the food was prepared and eaten; the term "Mess bill" comes from the same derivation.

The first mincers were made of iron, sometimes with brass bushes or bearings which would have been made by relatively skilled craftsmen. The earliest mincers would have been fixed in position permanently while later ones were clamped to the table and could be removed when not in use. They are now hard to find as most of them would have been thrown away as soon as they were superseded by a better model.

A collection of treen, iron and brass grinders is shown. Grinders made from treen are very much sought after by collectors.

Two views of an 18th century lignum vitae wood mortar / grinder, fitted with metal grinding plates.

Late 18th century lignum vitae grinder.

A mid 18th century lignum vitae coffee grinder with lid, and folding handle usually kept inside.

Late 18th century lignum vitae coffee grinder with screw-on lid, and folding handle usually kept inside.

"TO TAKE A GRINDER"
To insult another by applying the left thumb to the nose and revolving the right hand round it, as if working a coffee mill.

Grinders

Two views of a mid 19th century Kenrick gothic style cast iron coffee grinder.

Rare 17th/18th century wall mounted Scottish iron grinder (possibly for oats) on orginal mounting block.

Three 18th century Continental grinders.

"GLIM"
A cup of coffee with brandy in it instead of milk.

Marrow Scoops & Scrapers

Marrow scoops can sometimes be confused with cheese scoops. In days gone by all large bones had the marrow extracted, something which is no longer practised. The photographs show two marrow scoops: the silver one (second down) is unusual as it has a point for prizing out the marrow, unlike the more standard design illustrated.

Medieval people liked marrow and used it for a variety of dishes. Here is an old recipe: simmer 2 cupfuls of pearl barley in milk until the grains are soft and swollen, then put 2 tablespoons of finely chopped marrow in the bottom of a dish and pour the barley on top. Cover with honey, treacle or a sprinkling of sugar, then put the rest of the chopped marrow on top and Currants, raisins or sultanas can be added if desired.

In the 18th century marrow bones were served baked with the ends of the bones stuffed with bread to stop the marrow drying out during cooking. The marrow was dug out of the bones at the table with marrow scoops, and eaten on toast. It was said that Queen Victoria ate marrow toast most days! This was not actually a very healthy dish for those on a diet as it had a very high fat content.

One of the last hotels known to serve marrow bones at the table was the Mitre in Oxford; the marrow was also served like butter, having been melted out of the bones and coloured with saffron.

18th century bone marrow scoop.

18th century silver marrow scoop; the pointed end was used for loosening the marrow in the bone.

19th century bone marrow scoop.

Rare 17th/18th century iron cauldron scraper inlaid with brass and copper.

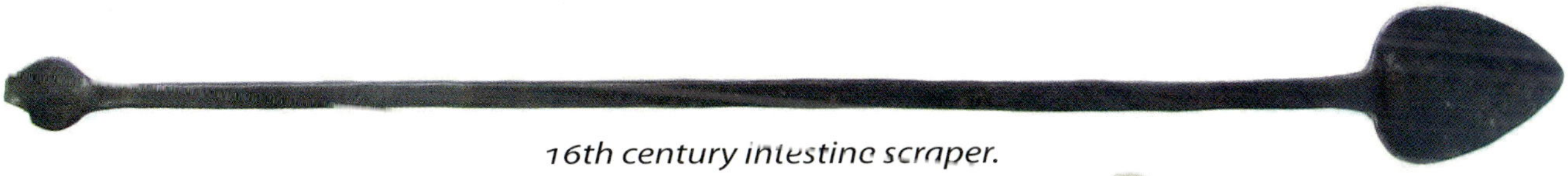

16th century intestine scraper.

Intestine scrapers were used for cleaning offal and intestines which were then used as the casings for sausages.

"To make the Sausages"

"To make the best Sausages that ever was eat. Take a leg of young Pork, and cut of all the lean, and shred it very small, but leave none of the strings or skins amongst it, then take two pound of Beef Suet, and shred it small, then take two handfuls of red Sage, a little Pepper and Salt, and Nutmeg, and a small piece of an Onion, chop them altogether with the flesh and Suet; if it is small enough, put the yolk of two or three Eggs and mix altogether, and make it up in a Past if you will use it, roul out as many pieces as you please in the form of an ordinary Sausage, and so fry them, this Past will keep a fortnight upon occasion."

Bones showing the nutritious marrow inside which was easily extracted with a marrow scoop.

"DOWN ON YOUR MARROW BONES!"
"Down on your knees!" A humorous way of telling a person he had better beg pardon.

Scales

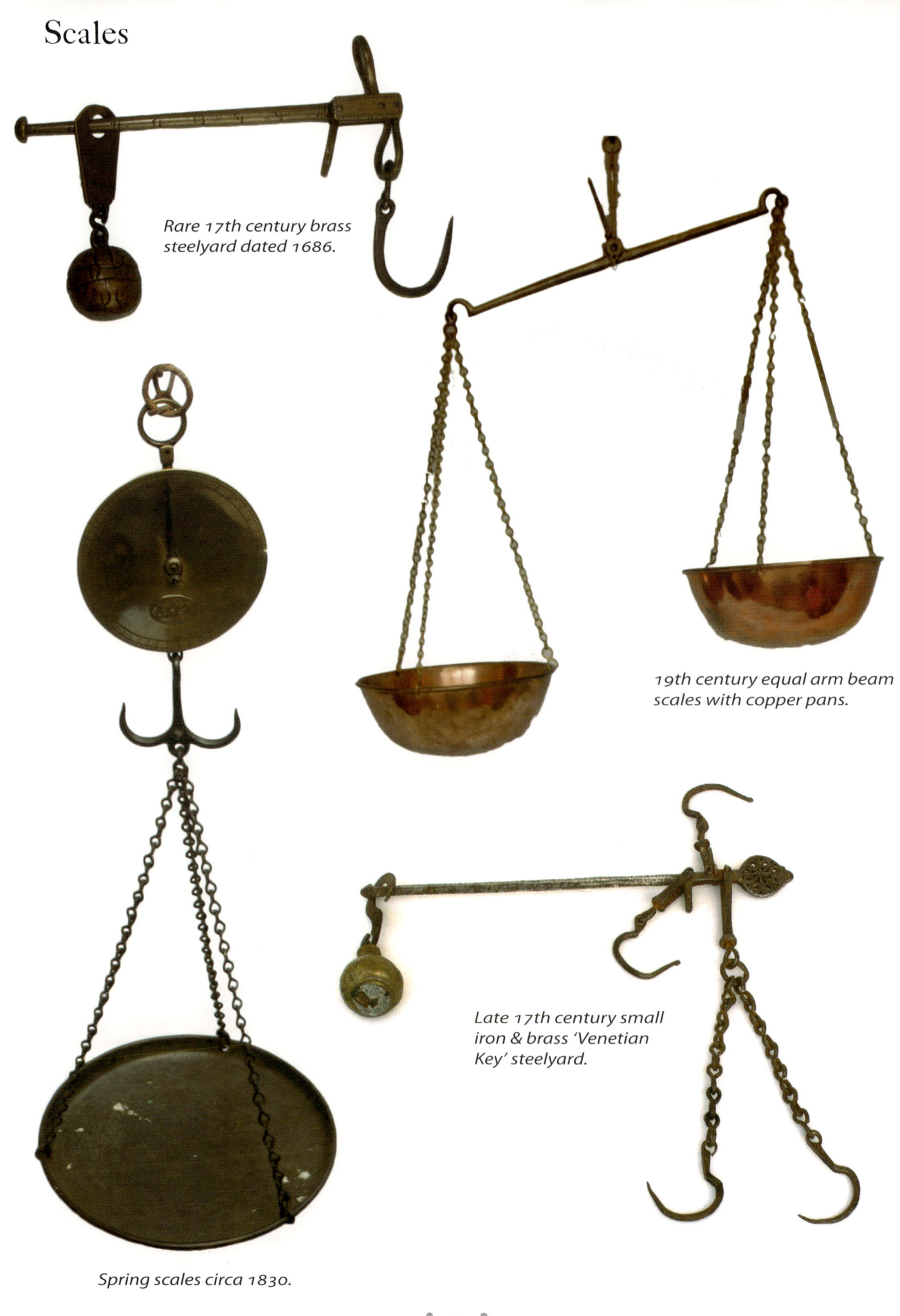

Rare 17th century brass steelyard dated 1686.

19th century equal arm beam scales with copper pans.

Spring scales circa 1830.

Late 17th century small iron & brass 'Venetian Key' steelyard.

"IT'S HANGING IN THE BALANCE"
The outcome could go either way.

Scales

Mid 19th century wrought iron balance with copper pans.

19th century Roberval cast iron kitchen scales with brass pans.

Late 19th century Salter butter scales.

"TO BE WEIGHED IN THE BALANCE & FOUND WANTING"
To be thoroughly examined & still found lacking.

A Victorian apple peeler.

19th century pantry.

Cooking

The variety of food available to us today would have been unheard of in the past, and no one except the king and members of the aristocracy would have been able to enjoy such luxury. One must remember that in those days food was locally and seasonally sourced; venison, pheasant and pigeon would have been common in the forests, and fish and shellfish plentiful by rivers and on the coast. Country folk and town dwellers alike often kept a pig as well. The local manor usually had a dovecot which was able to provide a constant supply of meat, the squabs (young pigeons) being very useful additions to the menu.

Cooking in Cauldrons

Cauldron of vegetables and bouquet-garni of fresh herbs.

Cooking in Cauldrons

It was not long before early man discovered that a piece of meat dropped into a pot of boiling water made a good nourishing meal. As cooking in cauldrons or pots evolved, herbs were added to flavour and tenderise the meat; herbs in those early days were all wild plants gathered from nearby forests or meadows.

Early cauldrons were made of pottery, then bronze or brass, and were different from the Continental types having a sag-bottom and no legs. Because of this, iron stands called brandreths (p.16) were made. They could be square, round or triangular and enabled the brandreth away from, or closer to the fire; in this way it was easier to maintain a regular temperature for simmering or boiling liquids.

As with roasting, one of the secrets of good cauldron cooking was control of the fire: it was vital not to boil away the liquid but to keep it simmering gently, hence the importance of the adjustable crane and chain. This is all covered in depth in "Boiling, Seething & Simmering" which can be found in the Downhearth chapter.

"TO EAT THE LEEK"
To be compelled to eat your own words, or retract what you have said.

The cauldron before cooking, with vegetables, herbs and oxtail. There is more liquid than would have generally been used, to show the contents of the pot for the photograph.

"A WATCHED POT NEVER BOILS"
Said as mild reproof to one who is showing impatience.

Ingredients to be prepared for the cauldron.

Oxtail Stew

"The tails should be sent from the butcher ready jointed. Soak and wash them well, cut them into joints, or lengths of two or three joints, and cover them with cold broth or water. As soon as they boil, remove the scum, and add a half-teaspoonful of salt, or as much more as may be needed, and a little common pepper or cayenne, an onion stuck with half a dozen cloves, two or three small carrots, and a bunch or two of parsley. When these have simmered for two hours and a quarter, try the meat with a fork, and should it not be perfectly tender, let it remain over the fire until it is so. Ox-tails sometimes require nearly or quite three hours stewing: they may be served with the vegetables, or with the gravy strained from them, and thickened."

"TOO MANY COOKS SPOIL THE BROTH"
By the hands of many a great work is spoilt.

The cauldron starting to cook over the fire.

"POT LUCK"

In medieval times it was the custom to have a pot on the fire with various meats and vegetables cooking in it continuously and extra ingredients added as they became available. As a result some of the contents would become very unpalatable while some would still be good, and you never knew what you would get.

Methods of Cauldron Cooking

Stew simmering in the cauldron. It tasted A LOT better than it looks!

Peiouns ystewed - (Stewed Pigeons)

"Take peiouns (pigeons) and stop hem with garlic ypylld (peeled) and with gode erbis ihewe (chopped herbs), and do hem in an erthen pot; cast therto gode broth and whyte grece (lard), powdour fort (a mixture of hot spices such as pepper and ginger), saffron, verjuice (juice of unripe fruit) and salt."

Beef Broth

"Wash a Leg or a Shin of Beef very clean, crack the bone in two or three places, (this you should desire the Butcher to do for you,) add thereto any trimmings you have of Meat, Game or Poultry, (i.e. heads, necks, gizzards, feet, &c) and cover them with cold water, - watch and stir it up well from the bottom, and the moment it begins to simmer, skim it carefully – your broth must be perfectly clear and limpid; - on this depends the goodness of the Soups, Sauces and Gravies, of which it is the basis: - then add some cold water, to make the remaining scum rise, and skim it again; - when the scum has done rising, and the surface of the broth is quite clear, put in one moderate-sized Carrot, a head of Celery, two turnips, and two onions, - it should not have any taste of sweet herbs, spice or garlic, &c. – either of these flavours can easily be added immediately after, if desired, - cover it close, - set it by the side of the fire, - and let it simmer very gently (so as not to waste the Broth) for four or five hours, or more, according to the weight of the Meat: - strain it through a sieve into a clean and dry stone pan, and set it in the coldest place you have.

This is the foundation for all sorts of Soups and Sauces, brown or white."

A helping of stew from the cauldron above, served on an 18th century Delft plate.

"HUNGER IS THE BEST SAUCE"
To a hungry man everything tastes good.
Proverbial saying, early 16th century.

Recipes and Quotes

Pease Pudding

"Put a quart of split pease into a clean cloth; do not tie them up too close, but leave a little room for them to swell; put them on to boil in cold water, slowly till they are tender: if they are good pease, they will be boiled enough in about two hours and a half; rub them through a sieve into a deep dish, adding to them an egg or two, an ounce of butter, and some pepper and salt; beat them well together for about ten minutes, when these ingredients are well incorporated together; then flour the cloth well, put the pudding in, and tie it up as tight as possible, and boil it an hour longer. It is as good with boiled Beef as it is with boiled Pork; and why not with roasted Pork?"

"Rost Bef with Sauce Aliper

To mak sauce aliper for rostid bef take brown bred and stepe it in venygar and toiste it and streyne it and stampe garlic and put ther to powder of pepper and salt it and boile it a litill and serue it."

"Stekys of Bef

Take Venyson or Bef, & leche & gredyl it up brown; then take Vynegre & a litel verious (juice of unripe fruit), & a litel Wyne, & putte pouder perpir ther-on y-now, and pouder Gyngere, & atte the dressoure straw on pouder Canelle (cinnamon) y-now, that the stekys be al y-helid ther-wyth, & but a litel Sawce; & than serue it forth".

"Sole Fryid

...Or elles take sole, and do a-wey the hede; drawe him, and scalde him, and pryk him with a knife in diuerse places for brekyng of the skeyn; And fry it in oyle, or elles in pured buttur."

"Apple muse

Take Appelys an seethe hem, an Serge hem thorwe a Sese in-to a potte; thane take Almaunde Mylke & Hony, an caste ther-to, an gratid Brede, Safroun, Saunderys, & Salt a lytil, & caste all in the potte & lete hem sethe; & loke that thou stere it wyl, & serue it forth."

"Fretoure

Take whete Floure, Ale, yest, Safroun, & Salt, & bete alle togederys as thikke as though schuldyst make other bature in fleyssche tyme, & than take fayre Applys, & kut hem in maner of Fretourys, & wete hem in the bature up on downne, & frye hem in fayre Oyle, & caste hem in a dyssche, & caste Sugre ther-on & serue forth."

From "The Cook's Oracle" 1823:

"Indigestion will sometimes overtake the most experienced Epicure; when the gustatory nerves are in good humour, hunger and savoury Viands will sometimes seduce the Tongue of a "Grand Gourmand" to betray the interests of his Stomach, in spite of his Brains.
On such an unfortunate occasion, when the Stomach sends forth eructant signals of distress, for help, the Peristaltic Persuaders are as agreeable and effectual assistance as can be offered; and for delicate Constitutions, and those that are impaired by Age or Intemperance, are a valuable Panacea."

"A Cook must be as particular to proportion her Fire to the business she has to do, as a chemist, the degree of heat most desirable for dressing the different sorts of foods ought to be attended to with the utmost precision."

Chacun a son Gout from "The Cook's Oracle" 1823

"Our Italian neighbours regale themselves with Macaroni and Parmesan, and eat some things, which we call Carrion.
Whilst the Englishman boasts of his Roast Beef, Plum Pudding and Porter,
the Frenchman feeds on his favourite Frog and Soupemaigre, the Tartar feasts on Horse-flesh,
the Chinaman on Dogs, the Greenlander preys on Garbage and Train Oil, and each "blesses his stars and thinks it luxury."

The great English moralist Dr Samuel Johnson was, we are told, a man who talked of eating and his stomach with great satisfaction. "People" he said, "have a foolish way of not minding, or pretending not to mind, what they eat. For my part I mind my Belly very studiously and carefully, and look upon it, that he who does not mind his Belly, hardly minds anything else."!!

The cook was a very highly regarded person in early society; William the Conqueror even gave his cook a manor, so says the Domesday Book

One very interesting quote makes the point that "servants are more likely to be praised into good conduct than scolded only of bad. Always commend them when they do well, and to cherish the desire of pleasing in them you must show them that you are pleased.
  Be to their faults a little blind,
  And to their virtues very kind."
This could apply to many children these days...

"THE BELLY HAS NO EARS"
A hungry man will not listen to advice or argument.

Roasting

Quails roasting on a lark spit.

Roasting

Roasting, probably the most emotive word used in cooking. The smell of a joint of beef roasting on the hearth (or these days cooking in the oven) must be one of the greatest delights in life.

Centuries ago people roasted their meat out in the open on a wooden spit over a fire. The secret of spit roasting was to cook the meat through without burning it and ensure it did not dry out by basting it frequently with oil or fat flavoured with herbs. This method of cooking certainly had its tribulations, one being maintaining a constant heat. The only way to control this was by moving the meat nearer to, or away from the fire: too near and the meat would burn, too far away and the meat would be undercooked.

The image above conjures up the joy of roasting - six quail on a larkspit, and delicious too.

"TO ROAST A PERSON"
To banter with him unmercifully, to give him a wigging.

Old English pork chop cooking on an adjustable bargrate fish toasting trivet or meat fork.

Old English Pork Chop

Pork was the most important meat in the past and even town dwellers often kept a pig in a sty adjacent to the house. The pig in those days was a different beast from the modern, slim, minimal-fat animal we know today. It grew to vast proportions and produced a very fat carcase; fat in the diet was good for a life of hard manual labour but not the sedentary lives we lead now. A valuable by-product of the pig was the excess fat for cooking and making rushlights, as well as other domestic uses. The pork chop illustrated came from such a pig, a rare thing not often seen these days.

Cooked chop on a pewter plate.

"TO SAVE ONE'S BACON"
To save oneself from injury, to escape loss. The allusion may be to the care taken by our forefathers to save the bacon which was laid up for winter, from the numerous dogs that frequented their houses.

Spit Roast Suckling Pig

A suckling pig roasting on a hand turned spit.

To Roast a Suckling Pig

"After the pig has been scalded and prepared for the spit, wipe it as dry as possible, and put into the body about half a pint of fine breadcrumbs, mixed with three heaped teaspoonsful of sage, minced very small, three ounces of good butter, a large salt spoonful of salt, and two thirds as much of pepper, or some cayenne. Sew it up with soft, but strong cotton, truss it as a hare, with the fore legs skewered back, and the hind ones forward; lay it to a strong, clear fire, but keep it at a moderate distance, as it would quickly blister or scorch, if placed too near. So soon as it has become warm, rub it with a bit of butter, tied in a fold of muslin, or of thin cloth, and repeat this process constantly while it is roasting. When the juice begins to drop from it, put basins, or small deep tureens under to catch it in. As soon as the pig is of a fine light amber brown, and the steam draws strongly towards the fire, wipe it quite dry with a clean cloth, and rub a bit of cold butter over it. When it is half done, a pig iron, or in lieu of this, a large flat iron should be hung in the centre of the grate, or the middle of the pig will be done long before the ends."

From The Cook's Oracle

"The larger the joint of meat, the further it must be kept from the fire."

"As beef requires a sound fire, mutton must have a fresh one."

"If your roasts are a little underdone, with the assistance of a stew pan, the gridiron or the Dutch oven, you may soon rectify the mistake made with the spit or the pot."

"BARTHOLOMEW PIG"
A very fat person. One of the chief attractions at Bartholomew's Fair, a whole roast pig sold piping hot.

Spit Roast Lamb

Rolled joint of lamb cooking on a spit.

"Cover the joint well with cold water, bring it gradually to the boil, and let it simmer gently for half an hour; then lift it out, put it immediately on to the spit, and roast it for an hour and a quarter to an hour and a half, according to its weight. This mode of dressing the joint renders it remarkably juicy and tender, but there be no delay in putting it on the spit after it is lifted from the water. A mild ragout of garlic may be served with it, or it may be garnished with roast tomatoes. Boiled; half hour; roast; one and a quarter to one and a half hours."

Leg of lamb in a slipware dish.

A steak cooked on a flesh fork over the embers of a fire.

Steak cooking on a rare 18th century cast iron downhearth baking iron on legs.

Game & Poultry

Here is a wonderful paragraph from 'Modern Cookery', an early 19th century cook book:
"Pheasant and partridges and other game may be chosen by nearly the same tester (test) as poultry: by opening the bill and the staleness will be detected easily if they have been too long kept. With few exceptions game depends almost entirely for its fine flavour and tenderness of its flesh, on the time which it is allowed to hang before being cooked; and it does not follow that it should be sent to the table in a really offensive state, for this is agreeable to few eaters and disgusting to many. Nothing should at any time be served of which the appearance or the odour may destroy the appetite of any person present"

In former times pheasants were often hung by their tail feathers, and when they fell they were judged fit to eat! But these old customs are rapidly being consigned to history as Health and Safety obsess our modern society.

17th/18th century Swiss / French bronze pheasant cooking pot . The interior was tinned.

"FIRST CATCH YOUR HARE"
Said to be a quote from Mrs Glasse (pen-name of Dr John Hill, 1716 – 1765).
However, in "The Art of Cookery" the exact words are "take your hare when it is cased (skinned), and make a pudding…etc".

Game & Poultry

A mixed bag of tradtional English game .

Pigeon, patridge & woodcock plucked ready to cook on the spit.

(below) 19th century French clockwork spit jack cooking two pigeons.

A duck roasting on a Continental spring-driven spit jack.

Cooked quail on a pewter plate.

Toasting

19th century downhearth toaster.

Toasting

Bread was a very important part of man's diet in former times. When meat became too expensive or was unavailable due to seasonal fluctuations, bread was the staple diet. It lasted longer than bread does today, and regularly used to be "revived" or toasted for meals.

The basic method of toasting was with a toasting fork; two are shown below: a utilitarian example (below top) and a more sophisticated one made of silver (below bottom) for the lady of the house.

A profusion of toasters, both downhearth and bar-grate, still exists today, and a small selection of what used to be available in the past is illustrated. One of these revolves, enabling the bread to be toasted on both sides without being taken from the fire. The more basic models were used by poorer families, and the more sophisticated ones by the wealthy.

"CHEESE-TOASTER"
A sword, also called a "toasting fork". "Put up thy sword bettime;
Or I'll so maul you and your toasting-iron
That you shall think the devil is come from hell."
Shakespeare, King John, IV, 3.

Toasting

Late 17th century downhearth bread toaster.

18th century downhearth bread toaster.

Two 18th century wrought iron harnens.

18th century revolving downhearth bread toasters.

―――――※―――――

"AS SHORT AS MARCHINGTON WAKE-CAKE" (Staffordshire)
Marchington was famous for a crumbling short cake, hence the saying that one of crusty temper is "as short as …"

18th century harnen.

Toasting

18th century harnen.

19th century downhearth toaster.

Downhearth toasters are very varied in shape and design, some with simple prongs to hold the bread, some with hoops and some that revolve so the bread can be toasted both sides without having to touch it.

"YOU CANNOT EAT YOUR CAKE AND HAVE IT TOO"
You cannot spend your money and yet keep it.

Toasting

(above & below) 19th century adjustable bargrate cooking fork.

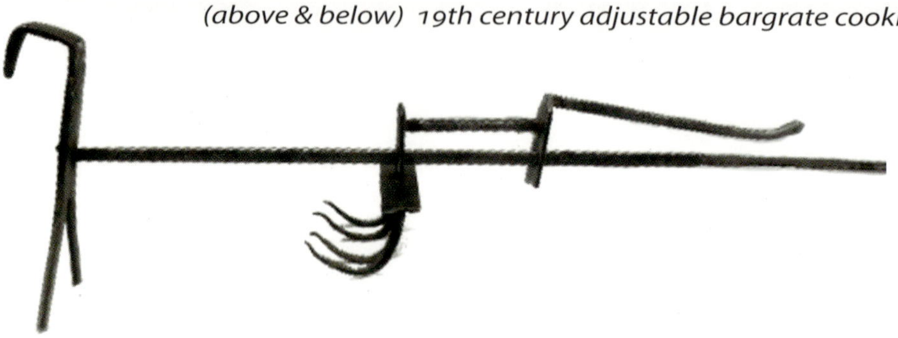

18th century rare iron harnen and cob iron combination with spit hooks.

19th century harnen.

Rare 18th century steel revolving bargrate toaster.

"SAD BREAD"
Heavy bread or bread that has not risen. Shakespeare calls it "distressful bread".

Toasting

18th century iron bargrate lark spit with trivet for fat catching pan.

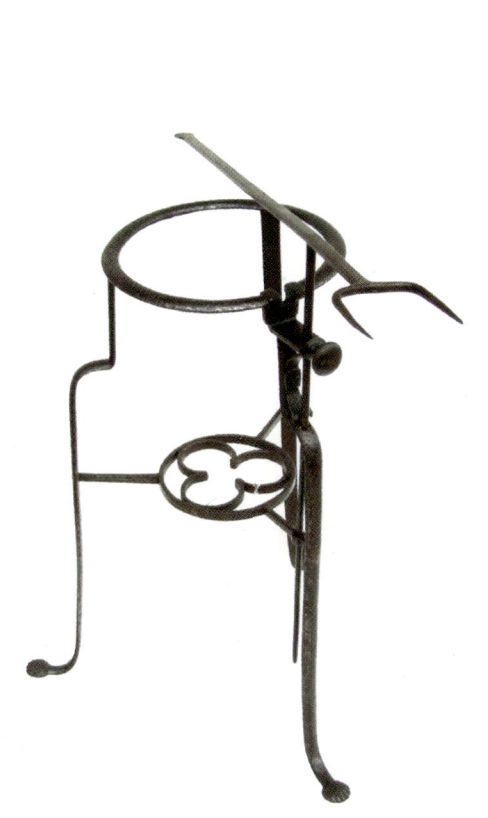

18th century wrought iron toasting trivet.

18th /19th century iron bargrate lark spit.

Early 19th century combination bargrate lark spit.

Early 19th century iron bargrate lark spit.

Rare 19th century iron and brass bargrate lark spit.

"CHAWBACON"
A contemptuous name for an uncouth rustic supposed to eat no meat but bacon.

Toasting

18th century rare bargrate revolving toaster.

19th century bargrate revolving toaster.

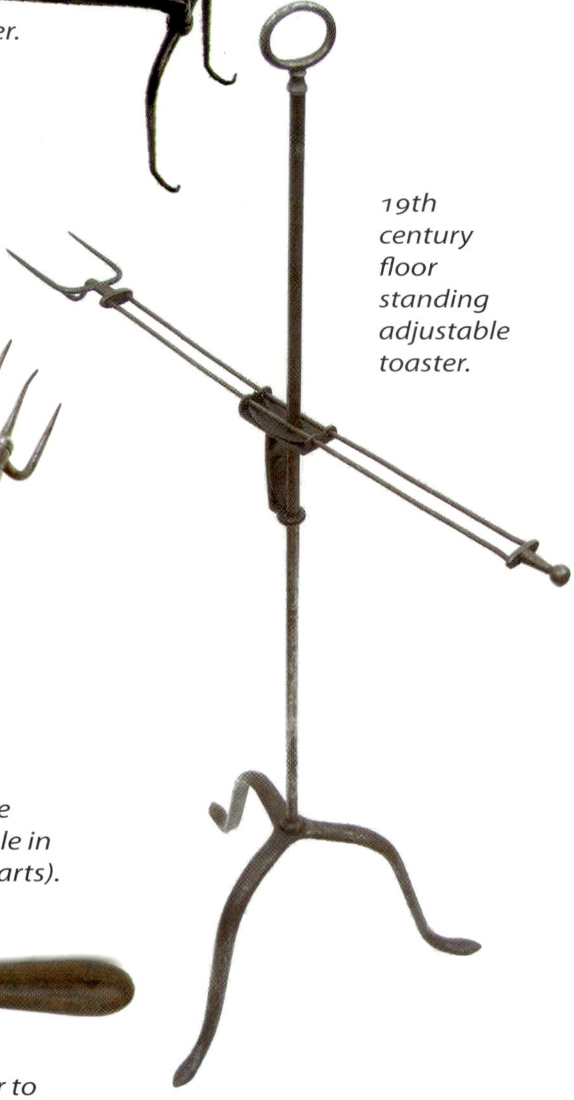

19th century floor standing adjustable toaster.

Late 19th century bargrate toaster.

18th / 19th century horseshoe meat toasting trivet adjustable in 3 ways (made from re-used parts).

19th century bargrate toaster to clip onto a trivet.

18th century revolving bargrate toaster.

Fish & Shellfish

A selection of shellfish and sea fish on a pewter platter.

Sea Fish

All the seafood shown above, whelks, cockles, oysters, mussels, winkles and scallops, together with gurnard, sea trout, plaice, mackerel, sea bass, red mullet and dabs, would have been sourced locally in the past by coastal dwellers.

A lot of shellfish like whelks, cockles or mussels, were gathered from the rocks at low tide along with various kinds of edible seaweed. Samphire grew on salt marshes and was regularly eaten locally.

Cockles in a treen bowl.

Samphire on a treen chopping board.

Spider crabs are now found in our coastal waters as far north as Wales. Their range would have fluctuated throughout history according to changes in sea temperature.

Spider crab on a treen chopping board.

"YOU MUST NOT MAKE FISH OF ONE AND FLESH OF THE OTHER"
You must treat both alike. Fish is an inferior sort of animal food to flesh.

Sea Fish

Fish awaiting preparation.

Red Herrings

"Red Herrings and other Dried Fish should be cooked in the same manner now practised by the Poor in Scotland. They soak them in water until they become pretty fresh; they are then hung up in the Sun and Wind, on a stick through their Eyes to dry; and then boiled or broiled. In this way, they eat almost as well as if they were new caught"

Lamprey Pie

"To make a lamprey pie take your Lamprey and gut him, and take away the black string in the back, wash him very well, and dry him, and season him with Nutmeg, Pepper and Salt, then lay him into your Pie in pieces with Butter in the bottom, and some Shelots and Bay Leaves and more Butter, so close it and bake it, and fill it up with melted Butter, and keep it cold, and serve it in with some Mustard and Sugar."

According to legend, King Henry 1 of England died in 1135 of food poisoning caused by eating "a surfeit of lampreys", of which he was excessively fond.

Here is a wonderful little quote from "Modern Cooking", an early 19th century cook book by Eliza Acton:

"To sweeten tainted fish

The application of the pynoligneous acid will effect this when the taint is slight. A wineglassful mixed with two of water may be poured over the fish, rubbed on the parts more particularly requiring it; it must then be left for some minutes untouched, and afterwards washed in several waters and soaked until the smell of the acid is no longer perceptible. The chloride of soda from its powerful anti putrescent properties will have more effect when the fish is in worse state. It should be applied in the same manner, and will not at all injure the flavour of the fish, which is not fit for food when it cannot be perfectly purified by either of these means. The chloride may be diluted more or less as occasion may require". Not to be recommended!!!

"I HAVE OTHER FISH TO FRY"
I am busy and cannot attend to anything else just now. I have more important matters in hand.

Fish Kettles

Various sea fish.

The most common way to cook fish was to steam it in a fish kettle; an 18th century hanging example is shown opposite cooking in the hearth and a Victorian copper one is below. The turbot, often known as the "king of fish", had the distinction of having its own cooking vessel, the turbot kettle (see below) which was also used for cooking ham.

A Victorian fish kettle with lifting liner.

19th century tin fish kettle with brass manufacturer's coat of arms.

18th century copper fish kettle.

19th century copper turbot kettle.

"A PRETTY KETTLE OF FISH"
An old Border name for a picnic by the riverside in which newly caught salmon is the chief dish. The discomfort of this sort of picnic probably gave rise to the phrase, meaning an awkward state of affairs, a mess, or a muddle.

18th century hanging fish kettle cooking fish and fennel, with sardines in a hanging frying pan.

Fish kettle and cauldron cooking simultaneously.

Cooked fish on pewter plates.

A selection of sea fish.

Mackerel on a pewter plate with a bargrate cooking fork
(below) Smoked kippers (herrings) on a Staffordshire willow pattern plate.

"WITH AN EYE TO THE LOAVES AND FISHES"
With a view to the material benefits to be derived. The allusion is to the Gospel story of the crowd following Christ, not for the spiritual doctrines He taught, but for the loaves and fishes distributed by Him amongst them.

Mackerel cooking on a bargrate adjustable cooking fork.

Eel

Eel.

To Fry Eels

"In season all the year, but not so well conditioned in April and May as in other months.

First kill, then skin, empty, and wash them as clean as possible; cut them into four-inch lengths, and dry them well in a soft cloth. Season them with fine salt, and white pepper, or cayenne, flour them thickly, and fry them a fine brown in boiling lard; drain and dry them and send them to table with plain melted butter and a lemon, or the sauce-cruets. Eels are sometimes dipped into batter and then fried; or into egg and fine bread-crumbs (mixed with minced parsley or not, at pleasure), and served with plenty of crisped parsley round, and on them.

It is an improvement for these modes of dressing the fish to open them entirely and remove the bones: the smaller parts should be thrown into the pan a minute or two later than the thicker portions of the bodies or they will not be equally done."

Sea trout on treen platter.

"TO SKIN AN EEL BY THE TAIL"
To do things the wrong way.

Fresh Water Fish

I clearly remember my father introducing me, in the 1950s, to an elderly man who was the last freshwater fisherman on Otmoor near Oxford. He earned his living soley by catching and selling freshwater fish, in the Covered Market in Oxford.

Here is a quote from "Food in England" by Dorothy Hartley: Clear Stream versus Muddy Pond
"Muddy-bottom fish has to be specially cooked or it will taste muddy. The skill was taught to me by an old fisherman of the Fens, where I first cooked bream. In detail he showed why all muddy-bottom fish have special overlapping and fringe scales, these keep the mud clear from the fish's skin while the fish is full, and swims against the stream; but once the fish is limp, and the scales are disturbed, the mud gets under them, and touches the absorbent skin of the fish. Therefore pond fish must never be washed, or even moved, more than can be avoided. Take the fish by the head, and smooth it down lightly towards the tail in clay or paste, and bake it quite flat without turning. For this reason you must roast it, raised up on a grid, or a handful of twigs, anything that will allow the underside of the fish to cook dryly. When done, this crust can be broken off, skin and all, and the fish will be clean tasting and of very fine quality".

Fresh caught pike; this was an important source of food in the 17th, 18th & 19th centuries.

Baked Pike

"To bake pike pour warm water over the outside of the fish, and wipe it very clean with a coarse cloth drawn from the head downwards, that the scales may not be disturbed; then wash it well in cold water, empty, and clean the inside with the greatest nicety, fill it with common forcemeat, sew it up, fasten the tail to the mouth, give it a slight dredging of flour, stick small bits of butter thickly over it, and bake it from half to three quarters of an hour, should it be of moderate size, and upwards of an hour, if it be large. Should there not be sufficient sauce with it in the dish, plain melted butter, and a lemon, or anchovy sauce may be sent to the table with it. When more convenient, the forcemeat may be omitted, and a little fine salt and cayenne, with some bits of butter, put into the inside of the fish, which will then require rather less baking. A buttered paper should always be laid over it in the oven, should the outside appear likely to become too highly coloured, or too dry, before the fish is done; and it is better to wrap quite small pike in buttered paper at once, before they are sent to the oven.
Moderate-sized pike, 30 to 45 minutes; large pike, 1 to one and a quarter hour."

"HE EATS NO FISH"
An Elizabethan way of saying that he is an honest man and one to be trusted because he is not a Papist. Roman Catholics were naturally opposed to the Government and Protestants. To show their loyalty they refused to adopt the ritual custom of eating fish on Fridays.

Carp

Carp (Cyprinus carpio) were introduced to England between c1450 and 1500, and were still only maintained on a small scale by fish-keepers by 1531.

In England, the first large-scale building of artificial fishponds was undertaken by the members of the Norman secular aristocracy to enhance their status. The earliest monastic fishponds were frequently granted as already existing entities by wealthy secular patrons. The monastic contribution was generally later in date, and on a smaller scale than that of the laity. Freshwater pond fish, as luxury food, were rarely consumed during Lent by ordinary monks. As Lent was a time of penance it was mainly salted sea fish that was eaten for much of the time, with freshwater fish reserved for special feasts, and the entertainment of important guests. A number of early grants of ready-made ponds to newly founded houses make it a specific condition of the grant that the fish should be reserved for special occasions.

Examination of detailed accounts of aristocratic homes with fish ponds before 1350 seems to indicate that little attempt was made to realise their full potential in terms of yields. In many cases they were seen as a conspicuous luxury. A good example of this is the 400 acres of ponds maintained by the bishops of Winchester, where barely a tenth of their potential was exploited. Despite extensive research, no evidence has been found of carp being kept in ponds in England before circa 1350. The most popular freshwater fish before this date were bream and pike, particularly on the royal table, where it is thought contemporary trends would be mirrored.

Common carp.

Carp Recipe

"Hops and Turkeys, Carps and Beer, Came into England all in a year." Traditional English saying.

Izaak Walton's Recipe for Cooking a Carp

"Take a carp, alive if possible, scour him and rub him clean with water and salt, but scale him not; then open him, and put him, with his blood and liver, which you must save when you open him, into a small pot or kettle; then take sweet marjoram, thyme, and parsley, of each a handful, a sprig of rosemary, and another of savoury, bind them into two or three small bundles, and put them to your carp, with four or five whole onions, twenty pickled oysters, and three anchovies. Then pour upon your carp as much claret wine as will only cover him, and season your claret well with salt, cloves and mace, and the rinds of oranges and lemons; that done, cover your pot and set it on a quick fire, till it be sufficiently boiled; then take out the carp, and lay it with the broth into a dish, and pour upon it a quarter of a pound of the best fresh butter, melted and beaten with half a dozen spoonfuls of the broth, the yolks of two or three eggs, and some of the herbs shred; garnish your dish with lemons, and so serve it up, and much good do you."

"NEITHER FISH, FLESH NOR FOWL"

Suitable to no class of people, fit for neither one thing nor another. Not fish (food for the monk), not flesh (food for the people generally), nor food for paupers (red herrings.)

Trout

Wild trout being cooked on a wooden spit over an open fire.

Cooked trout on an elm board with a sprig of fennel.

Shell Fish

Lobster, crab and langoustine.

Scallops, oysters, mussels, clams, whelks and winkle with samphire and seaweed.

Oysters on a chopping board.

Spider crab and shellfish on a chopping board.

Mussels

Unusual 18th century hanging pan cooking mussels.

Like all shell fish, mussels have been eaten by our coastal dwelling ancestors since time began. One pound of mussels seasoned and boiled in water till the shells open is a delicious dish. Those in the photograph were cooked in a hanging skillet rather like a miniature cauldron or a downhearth pan without the long handle.

Clean and wash the mussels thoroughly, discarding any that are open. Put them in a skillet with plenty of herbs, and cook them gently in enough stock to cover them for about twenty minutes.

"THE SAUCE WAS BETTER THAN THE FISH"
The accessories were better than the main part.

Fish stock for cooking mussels & cooked mussels in slipware dish.

A venison pie on a wooden platter having been cooked in the bread oven.

Raised Pies

Venison Pie

The venison was cooked with olive oil and herbs on a hanging frying pan. The pastry was rolled out, and with the use of a sycamore wood pie mould, was shaped into a coffin case and filled with the cooked meat. The pastry lid was put on and decorated with pastry "leaves" and the pie was then ready to be put into the bread oven (already hot from baking the bread) where it cooked for 35 minutes.

Game Pie

The raised pie was made with hot water pastry which was moulded round a pie mould to produce a coffin case. This was filled with cooked pork, breast of chicken and various kinds of game including pheasant and partridge. A pastry lid was put on top and the pie was put in the bread oven after the first batch of bread had been baked. The oven door was shut and the pie was left to cook for 35 minutes.

It was traditional to bake pies and pastries after the bread was cooked, but before the oven had cooled down completely.

18th century flour dredger.

18th century yew wood rolling pin.

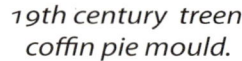

19th century treen coffin pie mould.

"TO HAVE A FINGER IN THE PIE"
To assist or interfere officiously in any matter, said usually in contempt or censoriously.

Rolling Pins

Treen yew wood rolling pin.

19th century French baguette rolling pin.

18th/19th century Scottish crushing roller.

19th century Bristol blue glass rolling pin.

19th century Scottish oat crusher rolling pin.

19th century brass rolling pin.

19th century wooden rolling pin.

Bristol Blue

Glass rolling pins were made of strong clear glass with a cork or bung at one end. They would have been filled with iced water, so the pastry would not stick to the roller, particularly important for biscuit making. The coloured glass "Bristol" rolling pins, were made originally at Nailsea, near Bristol, between 1788-1868. Some were sealed, some were closed with a cork at one end, and it is known that these were used to evade the 'Excise men' in the smuggling of liquor. These glass rolling pins were often given by Bristol sailors to their wives or sweethearts as love tokens.

Rolling pins

A variety of different rolling pins is illustrated. Early examples were made of wood, with many regional differences. They were also used for many different purposes - apart from beating a wayward husband over the head! For example there were Scottish oat crushers, glass bottle rolling pins which could be filled with cold water and used when making pastry and the butter worker for rolling the water out of butter (p.223). There were also brass rolling pins and blue glass rolling pins, many beautifully decorated, that were used in the 18th and 19th centuries.

"A HOLY ROLLER".
A derogatory term for a member of any evangelical sect who expresses religious fervour in an extrovert physical way.

The marble surface being floured with the dredger. The marble topped table used in this sequence of photographs is not a kitchen table.

Pie making; rolling out the pastry.

Building the coffin case for the pie.

Preparing the coffin case for the venison filling.

Venison for the pie being floured before cooking.

Venison for the pie cooking in a 19th century hanging frying pan, with chicken cooking on a spit.

The pie has been filled and the lid is ready to be put on; the pie will then be baked in the bread oven.

Finished venison pie on wooden platter. The result was most satisfactory and enjoyed by all.

"TO EAT HUMBLE PIE"

To come down from a position you have assumed. Here "humble" is a pun on "umble", the heart, liver and entrails of the deer, the huntsman's perquisites. When the lord and his household dined, the venison pie was served on the dais, but the umbles were made into a pie for the huntsman and his fellows who took the lower seats.

Downhearth Pie Baker

Apple pie in an 18th century sheet brass pie baker with iron handles and legs.

Apple Pie

The apple pie was cooked in a sheet brass pie baker dating from the second half of the 18th century.
The dish was lined with pastry and the apple filling put in. The pastry top was added and the brass lid was put on. The pie baker has three short legs so it can stand in the hearth, and the best result was obtained when it was placed in some good red embers for about 45 minutes.
The various stages in the making of the pie are illustrated opposite.

Recipe

Ingredients: pastry, 1½ lbs cooking apples, 4oz sugar, 8 cloves
Method: the shortcrust pastry was rolled out on a cold marble slab. The pie baker was lined with pastry and filled with the sliced apples, sugar and cloves; then a pastry lid was put on and sealed with beaten egg yolk to give it a wonderful golden colour when cooked. The lid was put on the pie baker which was placed in the embers of the fire to bake for about 45 minutes. It was important to ensure that a constant temperature was maintained - all part of the art of downhearth cooking.

"TO DINE WITH MOHOMET"
To die and dine in Paradise.

Apple Pie

The pastry base ready for filling.

The pie filled with apple, and the pastry lid on top.

The pie in a downhearth baker and the brass lid.

Downhearth pie baker assembled.

The pie being baked in the embers.

The pie turned out upside down on a pewter plate.

18th century brass and iron downhearth pie baker.

"MINCE PIES"
These originated from the Crusades when knights brought back spices like cinnamon, nutmeg or ginger, to name but a few. These were mixed with chopped meat and seasoned with salt and pepper to make mince pies.

The bread oven being heated with gorse and bundles of wood. Once the oven was hot enough the embers and ashes were raked out.

A well earned tipple!

Baking

Different types of bread cooked in the bread oven.

Bread

Bread making has been of paramount importance since Biblical times. Bread is still being baked in communal ovens in the Middle East as it was in Christ's time.
The baker was an important member of society in Britain. There were strict laws governing bread making, and the punishments for adulterating flour or producing under-weight loaves were dire: the baker could be towed through the streets strapped to a hurdle, and if caught a second time, driven out of society altogether.
In Britain bread was baked in the home in a bread oven and later people started to use a special pot called a yetling (right). Many bread ovens survive in rural houses today. A fire of faggots was lit in the bread oven and when it was hot enough the oven was raked out and wiped, then the dough was placed inside with a peel. The door was closed until the bread was baked. When it was finished and taken out, pies and pastries that did not need so much heat, were put to cook in what was then a cooler oven.

"Crusts of Bread for Cheese &c.

It is not uncommon to see both in private families and at Taverns a loaf entirely spoiled – by paring off the crust to eat with cheese; - to supply this – and to eat with Soups, &c. – pull lightly into small pieces, the crumb of a new loaf, put them on a tin plate or in a baking dish, set it in a tolerably brisk oven till they are crisp and nicely browned or do them in a Dutch oven."

Cast iron yetling.

"THE UPPER CRUST"
At one time the part of the loaf placed before the most honoured guests, the aristocracy. Bread was sliced horizontally in those days as the base of the loaf was likely to be hard and not very clean.

Milling Flour

Both parts of a 17th century English stone quern.

Both parts of a late 18th century Continental iron and wood grinding mill.

19th century French hand operated grain mill.

"BRING GRIST TO THE MILL"
To be a source of profit.

204

Sieves & Scoops

Horse hair and wire sieves.

Three 19th century grain scoops, the middle one is French.

"TO PUT THE MILLER'S EYE OUT"
To make broth or pudding so thin that even a miller's eye would be hard put to find the flour.

Measures

A collection of wooden measures, riddle sieves and other treen.

A measure and a miller's grain bucket.

Wooden grain and flour measures.

"I WISH MY CAKE WERE DOUGH AGAIN"
I wish I had never married.

Bread and Baking

Bread making using the floor standing dough trough.

Two balls of dough ready for 'proving'.

"To make bread take 1lb 2oz of flour – preferably a half-and-half mixture of unbleached white and 85 per cent wheatmeal; half oz of yeast; 2 egg whites; half pint to 12 oz of milk and water mixed, allowing for a rather larger proportion of water than milk, say six parts of water to four of milk; and half oz of salt.

Warm the flour and salt; pour in the yeast creamed with a little of the warmed milk and water mixture. Add the egg whites, beaten in a small bowl until they are just beginning to froth. Pour in the remaining milk and water. Mix as for ordinary bread dough. Leave to rise until spongy and light. This will take 45 minutes to 1 hour, depending on the temperature of the ingredients when the dough was mixed. Break down the dough, divide it and shape it into two round loaves – or long rolls if you prefer. Put them upside down on a floured wooden tray, board or flat earthenware platter. Cover with a light cloth and leave them to recover volume. About 30 minutes should be long enough.

Turn the proved loaves right side up onto a baking sheet. Slash the tops with one slanting cut, rather off centre, or leave them uncut if you prefer. These days this bread is baked on the centre shelf of a hot oven for the first 15 minutes. Then, to prevent the crust getting too hard, the loaves are covered with bowls; (for this reason it is easier to make the loaves round rather than long, unless you have a large oval casserole which can be used as a cover). In another 15 minutes the loaves should be sufficiently baked."

" BAKER'S DOZEN"

Thirteen for twelve. "To give one a baker's dozen" (slang phraseology) is to give him a sound drubbing i.e. all he deserves and one stroke more. A heavy penalty was given to bakers who gave short weight bread, so bakers gave an extra loaf.

Pastry Jiggers

17th & 18th century iron jiggers.

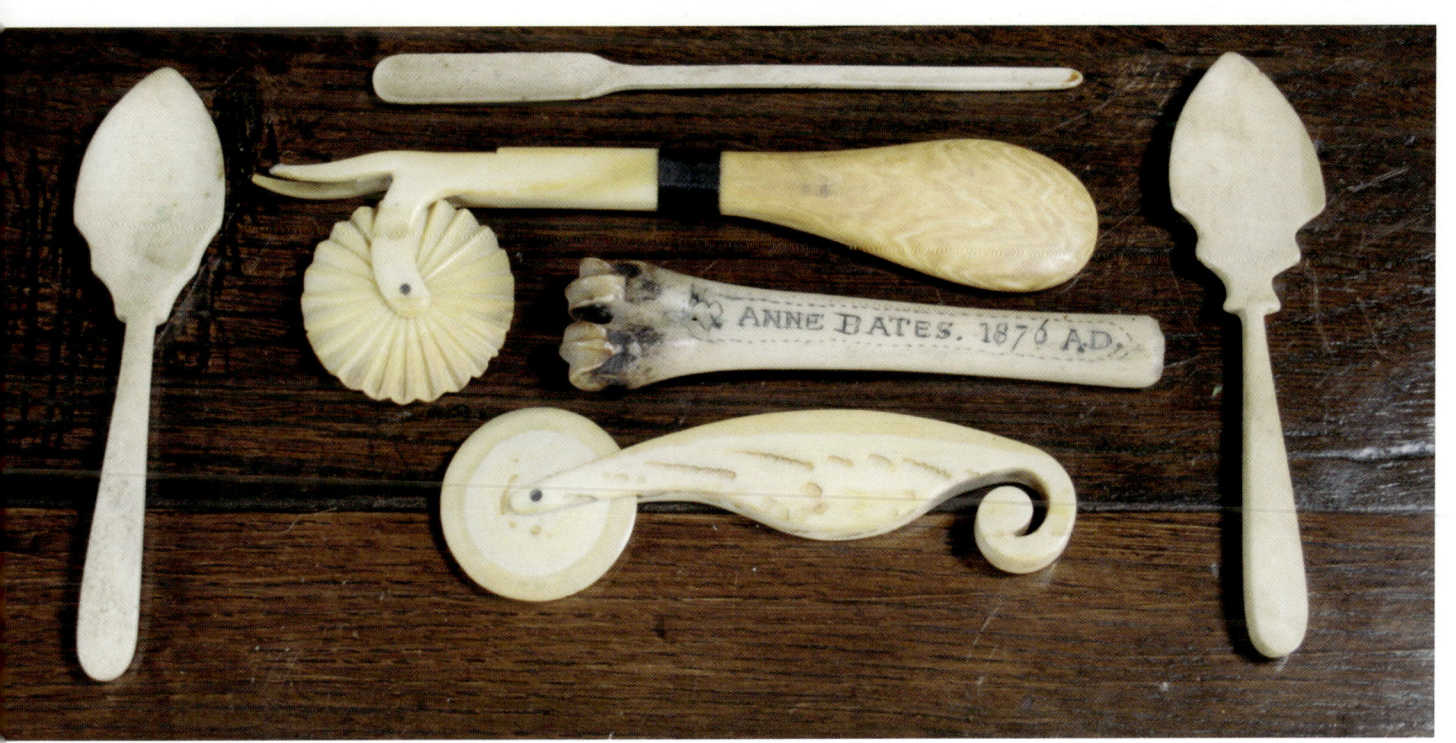

A bone pastry jigger and a selection of small bone utensils.

"TO GIBBET THE BREAD" (Lincolnshire)
When bread turns out ropey and is supposed to be bewitched, the good dame runs a stick through it and hangs it in the cupboard.

17th century Continental grinding 'mill' incorporating a hardwood stand and stone quern.

The bread oven being heated for baking.

Bread Ovens

Rare English wrought iron bread oven door, dated 1706.

19th century cast iron and brass bread oven door.

Rare 18th century copper and iron bread oven door.

"HALF BAKED"
Of weak mind. The allusion is to half baked food.

Cloam Oven

A cloam bread oven, used mainly in the West Country; they were usually made in Bideford. This example is displayed in the The Somerset Rural Life Museum, Glastonbury.

Trenchers

Trenchers were originally thickly sliced coarse slabs of bread which were used like plates. Loaves of bread were cut horizontally as against vertically nowadays. The bottom part of the loaf often contained a little ash and debris from the oven and tended to be rather hard. This made a good plate. Meat in the form of stews was served on the trencher which helped to soak up the juices; used trenchers given as alms to the poor. Sometimes several trenchers were used during a meal but this was only in grander households. The saying "he is a good trencherman" means the person likes his food.

Trenchers were replaced by wooden plates / platters; the earlier ones were square, later ones were round. A selection of these is illustrated in the Yeoman's Table chapter.

"HE THAT WAITS FOR ANOTHER'S TRENCHER EATS MANY A LATE DINNER"
He who is dependent on others must wait and wait and wait, happy if after waiting he gets anything at all.

Bread being taken from the bread oven using a wooden peel.

"HALF A LOAF IS BETTER THAN NO BREAD"
If you can't get all you want, try to be content with what you do get.

212

Different kinds of bread and a pie that have been cooked in the bread oven.

"NEVER TURN A LOAF IN THE PRESENCE OF A MONTEITH"

An old Scottish saying. The reference is to Sir John Stewart de Menteith (sic) who betrayed Wallace to the English. When he turned a loaf set on the table, his guests were to rush upon the Scottish patriot and secure him.

Recipes

Late 19th century Continental bread chopping board.

Havercakes

These were traditionally baked to be ready for hay making, and were eaten in the fields with a special white cheese and home brewed beer. They were light and sustaining and men could work long hours on them, without a lagging of strength.

Ingredients:
1lb fresh oatmeal, a piece of fat as big as a walnut, salt to taste.

Method:
Mix all the ingredients together, adding enough warm water to make the meal into a dough by kneading in a circular movement. When you get a firm paste that hangs well together, sprinkle a little oatmeal onto a pastry board and roll out a portion as thin as a sixpence and as large as a dinner plate, and bake on the girdle until a pale colour both sides.

Singing Hinnies

These came from Tyneside and were the "birthday cakes" of the past; a threepenny piece, a little thimble and a pearl button were hidden in the cakes, and the person who got the coin was to be wealthy, the button meant bachelorhood and the thimble foretold a "single blessedness" or a thrifty wife.

Ingredients:
1lb flour
A little salt
8oz lard
Cold water to mix
1 heaped tablespoon baking powder

Method:
Rub the lard into the flour until the mixture is as fine as meal. Add the baking powder and salt, stir well together and make quickly into a dough with cold water – not too stiff. Turn out onto the floured board and roll out into a large round about ½ an inch thick. Have the girdle heating over a slow fire and rub it clean with a damp dishcloth, then lay the cake onto it and leave until the side on the girdle is a delicious brown (about 10 minutes). Turn the cake so that the other side can cook on the girdle until it is the same colour, then when it is done cut it into pieces. It is delicious eaten hot or cold, with or without butter, and some people add a little sugar.

Bannocks

These are quick and easy to cook and were ideal to offer to guests who turned up unexpectedly.

Ingredients:
Pinch of bicarbonate of soda
4oz oatmeal
Pinch of salt
Boiling water to mix
1 teaspoonful melted dripping

Method:
Put soda, salt and dripping into a well in the oatmeal and mix to a stiff dough with hot water, knead on a board, roll out thin, bake on a hot girdle on both sides or toast the second side in front of a fire. Eat the bannocks well buttered or instead of bread with meat. They can also be baked in the oven.

"WHEN BREAD IS WANTED OATEN CAKES ARE EXCELLENT"
Those really hungry are not particular about what they eat and are by no means dainty.

A salamander and a hanging yetling.

Dairy

Dairy

Milk production has always been a very important part of agricultural life. I remember getting up at five o'clock in the morning to bring the cows in for milking, sitting on a stool to wash the udders and milking into a bucket. All this was quickly superseded by milking machines, bulk milk tankers and pipelines to take the milk straight from the dairy to the tanker, resulting in the demise of the milk churn, an "iconic" symbol of dairy farming as it used to be.

Dairy products have always been integral to our lives: we drink milk, we use cream to garnish our food, butter to spread on our bread and cheese for cooking and enjoying at the end of a meal.

The House Cow

It was fairly common for rural people in medieval times to have one or two house cows. Families in those days were usually quite large, with often three generations living under the same roof, along with the maids and other workers.

The house cow was an essential source of food, thus her well-being was important to everyone and she was treated almost as part of the family, often given a nice traditional name like Daisy or Buttercup.

She was milked twice a day in the cowshed or out in the field during the summer months. A simple three-legged stool was used as three legs are better than four, being stable on uneven ground. Some people used a one-legged stool that could be strapped with a leather belt onto the milker's bottom. The milk was carried to the house in pails which were often suspended from a yoke.

Some homes had a dedicated area like a larder or dairy for storing milk and milk products. Here the milk would be sieved to remove any impurities then poured

This is Elaine; she is seven years old and belongs to Mr Nott, whose family have been "yeoman" farmers for generations. Until a recent TB cull, Mr Nott kept cows as old as 17 or 18 years, all with names. A cow's udder becomes very pendulous the older she is, and in the past udders were strapped up to prevent them dragging on the ground.

"NO MILK IN THE COCONUT"
Half daft, barmy, crazed.

Yokes & Milking Stools

into glazed earthenware jugs or bowls; later, large settling pans made of tinned, enamelled metal, glass or pottery were used to separate the milk from the cream, which rose to the top and was then taken off with a skimmer. Cream was used in many recipes and was either whipped to thicken it or was heated to make clotted cream.

Butter was made by churning cream to remove the buttermilk. Butter churns came in various shapes and sizes, and ranged from simple plunger ones and smaller table box churns to larger barrel and end-over-end models. The buttermilk was normally fed to the house pig.

When the butter was ready it was scraped out and worked with either a pair of wooden bats called Scotch hands or on a board with a special roller called a butter worker; this was to ensure that every last drop of moisture was squeezed out. Salt was sometimes added at this stage.

If the butter was destined for the market it was usually marked with the farmer's individual design by means of a wooden butter stamp or mould. Many of these were very attractive and can still be found today.

Cheeses, both hard and soft, were made using animal and vegetable rennet in a variety of different procedures that resulted in an enormous array of different types of cheese: vegetable dyes, herbs, spices and even nuts were sometimes added to the mixture. Moisture was squeezed out during the final stages of production by means of cheese presses and chissets before the cheese was left to mature.

Early excavated medieval iron yoke.

19th century fruit wood or ash yoke.

Two 18th/19th century traditional milking stools.

"CRYING OVER SPILT MILK"
Lamenting something that cannot be altered.

Milk Buckets, Cans & Measure

19th century brass-bound coopered wooden milk pail with floating dolly to prevent milk spilling whilst being carried.

19th century iron-bound coopered wooden piggin or handle-piece pail.

Two small 19th century tin and brass milk cans, left with measure.

"FRESH AS GREEN CHEESE"
As fresh as cream cheese which is eaten fresh.

Milk Settlers & Skimmers

Late 19th century coopered milk settler.

Brass cream skimmer.

19th century treen cream settling bowl.

Treen skimmer.

"THE MILK OF HUMAN KINDNESS"
Care and compassion for others.

Butter & Plunger Churns

Miniature glass butter churn with a bigger family-sized one. Late examples from the early 20th century.

19th century wooden box table standing butter churn.

Two views of a 19th century table standing butter churn, showing the paddles inside (right).

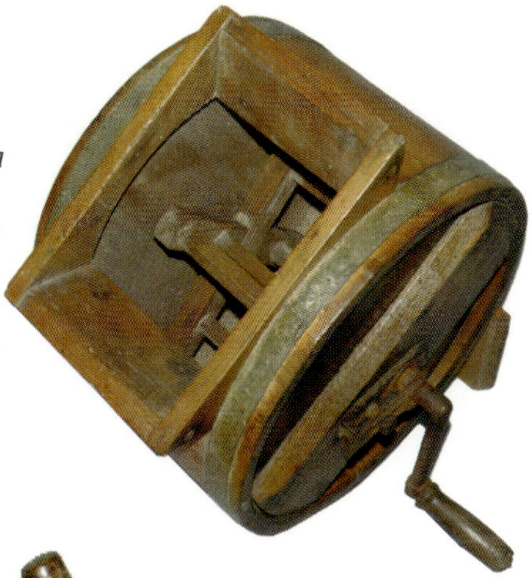

Three 19th century butter churns, one showing the plunger.

"BUTTERED ALE"
A beverage made of ale or beer mixed with butter, sugar, and cinnamon.

Assorted dairy utensils.

Butter Workers

19th century Scotch hands.

19th century butter pats.

19th century butter worker.

19th century table mounted manual butter worker.

"TO QUARREL WITH ONE'S BREAD AND BUTTER"
To act contrary to one's best interest.

Butter Stamps

18th/19th century sycamore wood butter stamps.

"SOFT WORDS BUTTER NO PARSNIPS"
Mere words will not find salt to our porridge, or butter to our parsnips.

Butter Stamps, Curlers & Knife

19th century wooden butter stamp.

19th century hinged wooden butter mould.

19th century wooden butter curler.

Early 20th century brass butter curler.

Butter curls in a bowl.

19th century wooden butter curlers.

19th century wooden butter knife.

"BUTTER FINGERS"
A person who lets things fall out of his hand. His fingers are slippery as if greased with butter.

Cheese Chissets, Corers & Scoops

Stone cheese press.

Scottish glazed chisset with dug out elm board for cheese press.

17th century treen weight for a cheese press.

Scoops for serving Stilton.

Two 19th century cheese corers for sampling the quality of the cheese.

Cheese Corers & Scoops

Corers were used to test the cheese in the dairy where it was made. Scoops were used to scoop out a portion of Stilton at the dining table and add a little port. Most of them date from the 19th century.

"HARD CHEESE"
Rotten luck.

Cheese Boards & Grater

Cheese board and Staffordshire cover - the plaited forelock on the bull's head forms the handle of the cover.

19th century brass grater.

Treen cheese board and early 19th century French knife with pewter and horn handle.

"CHEESE PARER"
A skinflint. A man chose his wife from three sisters by the way they ate their cheese: one pared it (she was mean), one cut the rind off extravagantly thickly, the third sliced it off in a medium way, and there his choice fell.

Romance in the Dairy

Two views of a rare handmade butter scoop, possibly given as a love token, dated 1746. The circular handle has broken away.

The dairy had a crucial part to play in the life of Sir Harry Fetherstonhaugh (pronounced Fanshaw) of Uppark in Sussex. He had always been something of a reprobate, counting Emma Hart among his conquests. (She became Lady Hamilton who went on to captivate Lord Nelson.)

In 1824 he was still unmarried at the age of seventy. One day while walking at Uppark he heard someone singing in the dairy. When he asked the housekeeper who it was, he was told it was Mary Ann Bullock who was helping out in the dairy.

When the old dairy maid retired Mary Ann took over and Sir Harry's visits became more frequent, until one day he arrived at the dairy and asked her to marry him. Mary Ann was apparently speechless but Sir Harry reputedly told her not to say anything immediately, but if her answer was "yes", to cut a slice out of the leg of mutton that would be coming up for his dinner that day. When the mutton arrived, the slice had indeed been cut out, much to the mortification of the cook.

At the age of just twenty-one Mary Ann was sent to Paris to be educated and in September 1825 she was married to Sir Harry who was exactly fifty years her senior. They lived happily together until his death at the ripe old age of ninety-two and Mary Ann stayed in possession of Uppark (below) until her death in 1875.

Uppark.

"TO BUTTER ONE'S BREAD ON BOTH SIDES"
To be wastefully extravagant and luxurious.

A collection of ice cream making equipment.

Moulds

19th century copper lion mould shown with the first attempt at using it – not as easy as you might think!

Moulds

Moulds had a great variety of uses in the kitchen of the past. Treen wood moulds were used for gingerbread and biscuits, (see pages 235, 236, 238). Terracotta moulds were used for cakes and puddings (see below), and porcelain, usually white, came into use in the late 18th century. A beech wood chocolate mould is illustrated on page 237.

Ice cream moulds were usually made of a pewter alloy and are illustrated on page 238. Copper jelly moulds, "iconic" pieces of kitchenware today, came in a bewildering variety of shapes and sizes, and a few are shown on pages 233, 234. They have become very collectable in recent years: rare shapes, a hedgehog for example, can fetch vast sums at auction.

19th century tinned copper mould of a chicken.

Two early 19th century French terracotta moulds.

"TO BREAK THE MOULD"

To change one's usual habits. In the past an artist would break the mould of a high quality cast so that it could not be copied by others.

Terrines

The terrine illustrated was made from my adaption of an old recipe and was delicious!

The meat used was as follows: pheasant, pigeon, woodcock breasts, thinly sliced venison steak and loin of rabbit.

Remaining ingredients: streaky bacon, forcemeat, chicken and pheasant livers, breadcrumbs, eggs, parsley, a tablespoonful of brandy, black pepper, garlic, thyme, salt and a small glass of red wine.

Method: the game meat was cooked first in a frying pan till nicely brown. The forcemeat was mixed with the rest of the ingredients, and the bacon rashers, with rind removed, were used to line the base of the terrine. This was then filled with alternate layers of forcemeat and cooked game to create a marbled effect. It was finally covered with more streaky bacon rashers and cooked for approximately 2 hours.

Terracotta Continental mould.

"TO PULL BACON"
To spread the fingers out after having placed one's thumb on the nose.

Moulds

19th century copper jelly, aspic and blancmange moulds.

"HUNGRY DOGS WILL EAT DIRTY PUDDING"
If a man is hungry enough he will eat anything.

Moulds

19th century copper jelly mould.

19th century copper topped tin ware mould.

19th century copper topped tin ware mould.

"Good Common Blamange or Blanc Manger"

"Infuse for an hour in a pint and three quarters of new milk the very thin rind of one small, or of half a large lemon and eight bitter almonds, blanched and bruised; then add two ounces of sugar, or rather more for persons who like the blamange very sweet, and an ounce and a half of isinglass. Boil them gently over a clear fire, stirring them often until this last is dissolved; take off the scum, stir in half a pint of rich cream, and strain the blamange into a bowl: it should be moved gently with a spoon until nearly cold to prevent the cream from settling on the surface. Before it is moulded, mix with it by degrees a wineglassful of brandy.

New milk, one and three quarter pint; rind of lemon, half large or whole small 1; bitter almonds, 8; infuse 1 hour. Sugar, 2 to 3 ozs; isinglass, one and a half oz.: 10 minutes. Cream, half pint; brandy, 1 wineglassful."

"LAMB ALE"
Given to the farmer when his lambing was over.

Gingerbread Moulds

Ginger

The ginger plant, Zingiber officinale, was first discovered in southern Asia and is now grown throughout the Tropics. The root or rhizome is the part of the plant that is eaten. Ginger has long been one of the most important cooking ingredients in the Tropics and its use is now very widespread. It was imported from India into Ancient Rome but became very expensive when the Arabs gained control of the trade after the fall of the Roman Empire. It was used in western countries as early as the 11th century, but was made popular by Queen Elizabeth 1st, in the 16th century; she was known to enjoy court jokes or jests and it amused her to have ginger biscuits or cakes made in the likeness of her courtiers as a treat at Christmas. These biscuits subsequently came to be called gingerbread men.

Ginger was often used to flavour wine, beer and coffee as well as being popular in cooking; it also had valuable medicinal properties and was used to aid the digestion and sooth feelings of nausea.

"Good Common Gingerbread"

"Work very smoothly six ounces of fresh butter (or some that has been well washed from the salt, and wrung dry in a cloth) into one pound of flour, and mix with them thoroughly an ounce of ginger in fine powder, four ounces of brown sugar, and half a teaspoonful of beaten cloves and mace. Wet these with three quarters of a pound of cold treacle, or rather more if needful; roll out the paste, cut the cakes with a round tin cutter, lay them on a floured or buttered baking tin, and cook them in the bread oven, making sure it is not too hot. Lemon-grate or candied peel can be added, when it is liked.

Flour, 1lb; butter, 6ozs; sugar, quarter of a pound; ginger, 1oz; cloves and mace, half teaspoonful; treacle, three quarters of a pound; half to three quarters of an hour."

18th century boxwood gingerbread mould (24" x 9", 61 x 23cm approx) of a bishop blessing three children.

Root ginger.

"GINGERBREAD"

Brummagem (Birmingham) wares, showy but worthless. The allusion is to the gingerbread cakes fashioned like men, animals etc. and profusely decorated with gold leaf or Dutch leaf which looked like gold, commonly sold at fairs up to the middle of the 19th Century.

Gingerbread Moulds

Two late 18th / early 19th century carved boxwood gingerbread moulds.
(left 22" x 8", 56 x 20cm, right 29" x 9", 74 x 23cm)

"TO TAKE THE GILT OFF THE GINGERBREAD"
To destroy the illusion.

Chocolate

Chocolate originated in Mexico and was first introduced into Europe by the Spanish in the 16th century and arrived in England about 1650.

Chocolate comes from the cacao tree which grows 20 degrees either side of the Equator. The tree produces large seed pods which are cut down and placed in piles to ferment. When ripe, the beans are extracted and dried in the sun. They are then transported to the factory where the shells are removed and the beans are processed into cocoa solids and cocoa butter. Chocolate as we know it is a blend of cocoa butter, cocoa liquor and sugar.

"To Make Chocolate"

"An ounce of chocolate, if good, will be sufficient for one person. Rasp, and then boil it from five to ten minutes with about four tablespoonsful of water; when it is extremely smooth add nearly a pint of new milk, give it another boil, stir it well or mill it, and serve it directly.

For water-chocolate use three quarters of a pint of water instead of the milk, and send rich hot cream to table with it. The taste must decide whether it shall be made thicker or thinner.

Chocolate, 2ozs.; water, quarter-pint, or rather more; milk, one and three quarter pint: half a minute."

Cocoa pods growing on a tree.

18th century brass and iron Continental chocolate pot with twizzle stick.

18th century two-part chocolate mould of a soldier.

"CUP"

A mixture of strong ale with sugar, spice and a lemon, properly served up hot in a silver cup. If wine is added the cup is called "Bishop", if brandy is added the beverage is called "Cardinal".

Ice Cream & Biscuit Moulds

Various examples of 19th century pewter and copper ice cream moulds.

19th century biscuit mould.

Detail of 18th century biscuit mould shown below.

"THE LAND OF CAKES"
Scotland, famous for its oatmeal cakes

Preserving & Spices

Traditional storeroom at the Weald and Downland Museum, Sussex.

Preserving

With no freezers, artificial preservatives or pre-packed food, how did people manage in earlier centuries? The answer is that they salted, smoked and bottled in order to keep food through the long cold months of winter. In those days the women of the house spent far more time working in the kitchen than they do now: they were salting meat or fish, storing vegetables (carrots in sand or peat for example) and drying herbs, apples and mushrooms.

Many early households kept a pig. When it had been slaughtered the animal was butchered into joints. The sides of bacon would be salted and hung in a bacon settle (p.121) or suspended in a hanging wooden frame as illustrated (p.245). Most pork was smoked in a smoke box which was located in the chimney, over a wood fire (never coal).

"TO CRACK A BOTTLE"
To open one. The allusion is to drunken frolics where bottles and glasses were broken.

The Yeoman's Pig

Gloucester Old Spot pigs.

The pig would be fed on vegetable peelings, waste leaves and any other edible residue from the kitchen; this was either cooked and mixed with corn mash or fed raw. The pig was duly fattened then the travelling slaughter-man would be sent for. The pig was loaded onto a litter, its throat was cut and the carcase was bled, a most important part of the process when preparing the meat for consumption, salting or smoking etc. The carcase was then carried to a fire of burning straw where the hide was singed before being scraped and then scrubbed in very hot water to remove the hair. The carcase was butchered and the offal was usually consumed first. Every part of the pig (except the squeak!) was utilised: sausages and brawn were made and bacon and hams were cured in salt and smoked and all this was done at home. I can still remember the squeal of the pig and the smell of burnt hair as a carcase was singed at my home in Oxfordshire.

Gloucester Old Spot bacon on treen platter.

19th century pig litter.

"FAT AS A PIG"

The pig was kept as fat as possible before being killed and salted for winter consumption. Unlike today, fat was regarded as a good nutritious food and used for many things.

Iron bound chopping block on stick legs with chopper & tenderiser.

Salting

Salting

As illustrated, the terracotta salting pot was used to salt a small leg of pork or ham. The salt, with a small pinch of saltpetre, was rubbed into the meat and packed well into the tunnel that held the bone. It was checked regularly and topped up if necessary for 4 weeks. The joint was then removed and soaked in fresh cold water for 36 hours to desalinate it. Once this was done it was dried and hung to smoke in the smoking chamber of the chimney for another week before being boiled in a cauldron. When it was sampled, the ham still tasted rather salty although it was quite edible, but apparently, according to several old books, that was often the case!

"IF SALT HAVE (sic) LOST ITS SAVOUR WHERE SHALL IT BE SALTED"
If men fall from grace how shall they be restored. The reference is to rock salt which loses its saltiness if exposed to the hot sun.

Salting

19th century terra-cotta salting pot curing a leg of pork.

Cured ham and hungry cat with empty salting pot.

Curing

Oak bacon rack of Somerset origin dated 1672.

18th century treen salting dish.

"I'LL COOK YOUR GOOSE"

I'll pay you out. It is said that when Eric, King of Sweden, came to a town with very few soldiers, the enemy, in mockery, hung out a goose for him to shoot at. Finding however, that the King meant business, and that it would be no laughing matter for them, they sent heralds to ask him what he wanted. "To cook your goose for you" he facetiously replied.

Sides of trout being smoked in the smokebox. View looking up the chimney through the smokebox to the sky above.

Smoking

In a good many houses a smoking chamber or box was installed in the chimney; this consisted of a rectangular or square chamber high enough up for the smoke to have cooled, because the object of the exercise was to smoke not cook the meat or fish. Joints were hung on iron rails in the chamber for the required amount of time until they were cured. As already mentioned, smoking and salting were the main ways of preserving food in centuries gone by; without this, winter would have been a very cold lean period indeed with no fresh meat or very little, due to the shortage of winter fodder. Cattle, sheep and pigs were all slaughtered in October or November and only the breeding stock was kept through the dark days of winter.

The trout illustrated above was caught and gutted, washed and salted then hung in the smoking chamber. After 4 days smoking it was cured and tasted good when eaten.

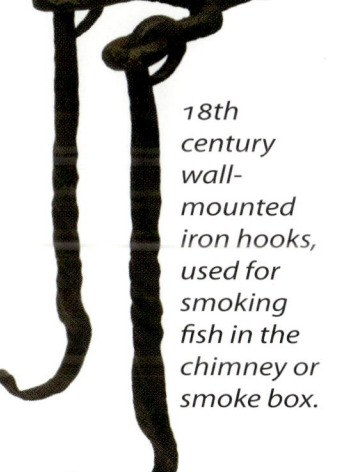

18th century wall-mounted iron hooks, used for smoking fish in the chimney or smoke box.

"TO BE WORTH ONE'S SALT"
Roman soldiers received some of their pay in the form of a portion of salt.

Jam & Preserving

A selection of 19th century storage containers.

Jam & Preserving

Fruit was grown in the garden and stoned fruit could be preserved quite successfully; soft fruit posed more of a problem and usually ended up being made into jam. This became common practice at the beginning of the 18th century.

19th century brass preserve pan with iron handle.

Pig's trotters, these were boiled up to produce gelatine.

"MONEY FOR JAM"
Money (or money's worth) for nothing. An unexpected bit of luck.

Earthenware

Preserving

In the past all manner of produce would have been preserved by pickling or bottling; nothing was wasted. Kilner jars have been used for preserving since 1842. (above) Kilner jars containing apricots, carrots and plums. (below) Garden produce for preserving or storing.

Presses

19th century tongue press.

Late 19th century juice press.

19th century fruit press.

19th century brass preserve pan with iron handle.

"BULL"

A name given to a drink made from the swillings of empty spirit-casks. "Bulling the barrel" – pouring water into a rum cask, when nearly empty, to prevent it leaking. The impregnated water was frequently drunk: called bull. Seamen talk of "bulling" the teapot/coffee pot (making a second brew.)

Spices

Spices were an essential ingredient in early cooking as they were used to mask the taste of rancid, stale or badly cured meat or salt bacon. They also added colour to a dish, further enhancing the appeal. Saffron is the spice that obviously springs to mind. Some spices would have been shipped from the Orient, while others probably started their journey on horse or camel back via the Spice Route, a famous and well travelled route to Europe used regularly in the Middle Ages. The length of time and the distances involved in these journeys meant that spices were extremely valuable commodities that would have been stored in locked cabinets once they reached their destinations. The lady of the house would have had sole responsibility for the key to avoid any petty pilfering taking place.

From the Cook's Oracle, 1823
"A Cook without Spice, would be as much at a loss as a Confectioner without Sugar…"

Spices from the East were brought to Britain by the Romans who were quite accustomed to using them in their meals and banquets. After the fall of the Roman Empire, the trade in spices was dominated by the Venetians and Genoese. Because of the high prices of spices, payments were sometimes made in peppercorns; this trade was tightly regulated by institutions like the Pepperers' Company which existed as far back as the 11th century. Spices included allspice, cloves, cayenne, cinnamon, ginger, nutmeg, mace and pepper.

18th century yew wood spice tray with a selection of spices that would have been used at the time.

This spice tray has a handle at each end, and then individual pots are shown above.

19th century spice box containing spices of the time. The central section holds a grater and has a hasp on the front for a padlock.

"FETTLED ALE"
Ale warmed and spiced – mulled. It is from a principally North Country dialect.

Spices

19th century nutmeg grater with nutmegs.

17th century spice box containg drawers and a lockable door.

Inlaid tea caddie with lock, circa 1800.

Tea

Tea was as valuable as spices, an expensive item in most households which was also locked up safely in tea caddies or teapoys. There are many tales of servants drying out used tea leaves and selling them on to unscrupulous merchants; these men would then rejuvenate them with dangerous dyes which sometimes had fatal consequences for unsuspecting customers.

Early 19th century china caddie with measure lid. A pair of these would have been kept in a lockable wooden case.

18th century blue & white teapot with swan knob.

"CAT-LAP"
A contemptuous name for tea or other "soft" drink such as a cat could swallow, a non-alcoholic liquor.

Apples

Rare early 19th century wrought iron apple baker and two apple corers.

The apple baker is a simple implement for cooking apples. They rested on the iron bars and the only adjustment necessary was raising or lowering them above the heat. The apple corer on the left in the photograph is made of ivory and is a fine 17th century example of a high quality implement. The 19th century corer on the right is made from a sheep shank bone and is much more utilitarian. It is engraved with initials, dated 1876 and would have been given as a love token.

Apples grew easily in many parts of the country and were a useful source of food throughout the year. As well as being eaten fresh or cooked, they could be stored for many months or dried; this was done by slicing them into rings, threading them onto string and hanging them up in the warmth of the kitchen. They kept for a long time like this and could be reconstituted by soaking in liquid prior to use.

Dried fruit in 19th century earthenware bowl.

"LAMB'S WOOL"
A beverage consisting of the juice of apples roasted with spiced ale.

Apples baking on the fire.

"AS YOU BREW, SO YOU WILL BAKE"
As you begin so you will go on. You must take the consequences of your actions.

On the cricket table are a baker loaded with apples, a late 19th century iron apple corer, an ivory and a bone apple corer and a wooden platter containing dried apple rings.

The Yeoman's Table

A 19th century yeoman's table setting.

The Yeoman's Table

The yeoman has been taken as the standard reference in this book, because generally he was neither rich nor poor. There are many examples of stately homes still extant, but few yeomens' houses remain intact. The Weald and Downland Museum, Sussex, and the Rural Life Museum, Cardiff, contain reconstructed settings of medieval life.

Ordinary people in the past would have used treen (wooden) items all the time; there was an enormous variety of timber available in the 16th and 17th centuries: oak for furniture, ash for handles and furniture, sycamore for platters.

Illustrated are items that would have been on a typical yeoman family's table; most average homes would have accumulated a mixture of things of different periods, types and styles over the generations, and this is reflected in some of the photographs. It was also demonstrated in the Will and Inventory of one of my ancestors, written at the beginning of the 18th century, which gives a good idea of what was in the average house of that period. (A copy of the Will and Inventory can be found at the end of the Yeoman's Kitchen chapter.)

"EAT, DRINK AND BE MERRY"

Eulenspiegel being asked for alms by twelve blind men, said, "Go to the Inn; eat, drink and be merry, my men; and here are twenty florins to pay the bill". The blind men thanked him; each supposing one of the others had received the money. Reaching the Inn, they told the landlord of their luck, and were at once provided with food and drink to the amount of twenty florins. On being asked for payment, they all said "Let him who received the money pay for dinner" but none had received a penny.

256

Treen Platters & Boards

A selection of 18th/19th century treen platters & boards made from sycamore, oak, pine, ash, fruit wood and sorbus.

"TO BREAK ONE'S FAST"
To take food after long abstinence; to eat one's breakfast after the night's fast.

Treen Bowls

Sycamore bowl.

Spanish olive wood bowl.

English stained turned burr wood bowl.

English turned burr wood bowl.

Spanish / Continental turned bowl with handle.

Sycamore bowl.

Scottish quaich.

18th century English bowl.

"SAVE YOUR BREATH TO COOL YOUR PORRIDGE"
Don't talk to me, it is only wasting your breath.

A treen table setting.

Knives & Forks

17th century horn and silver handled knife & fork.

Early 18th century brass handled steel boxed travelling cutlery set.

18th century knife and fork.

19th century bone handled steel cutlery.

261

"HE IS A CAPITAL KNIFE AND FORK"
A good trencherman.

Knives & Forks

Knives are an important subject in their own right. Most knives were used until they were completely worn out and were then thrown away. As a result very few early examples survive, although a number of excavated knives are shown in various books and periodicals. The ones illustrated in this book are mainly from the 19th century with one or two examples from earlier periods.

Forks came to be used in England rather later than on the Continent. Most people carried their knives with them to be used at mealtimes, and it was not really until the late 17th century that proper cutlery started to be generally used. The man who "introduced" the fork, Thomas Coryat was subject to ridicule by the average Englishman of the period, but the seeds he sowed eventually took root, and the knife and fork became generally accepted as the appropriate tools to use when eating a meal.

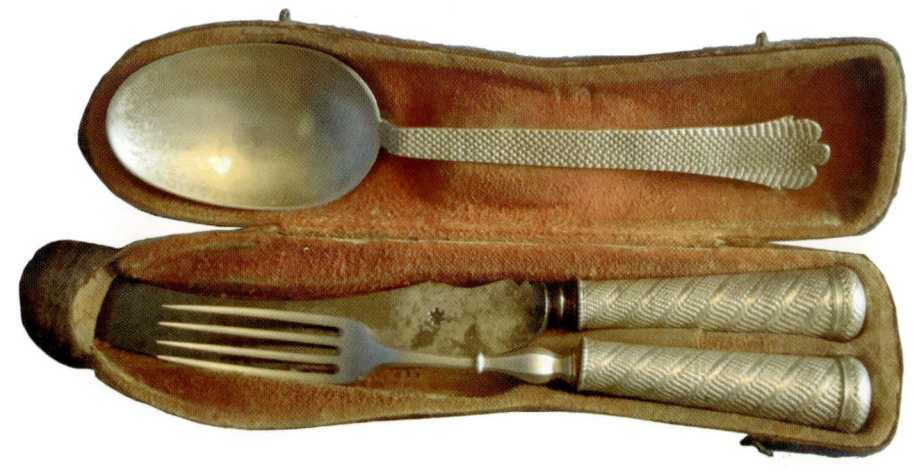

People often carried their own cutlery with them. This boxed set of silver handled German cutlery was made around 1700.

Early 19th century French travelling knife & fork with pewter and horn handles. Shown opening and open.

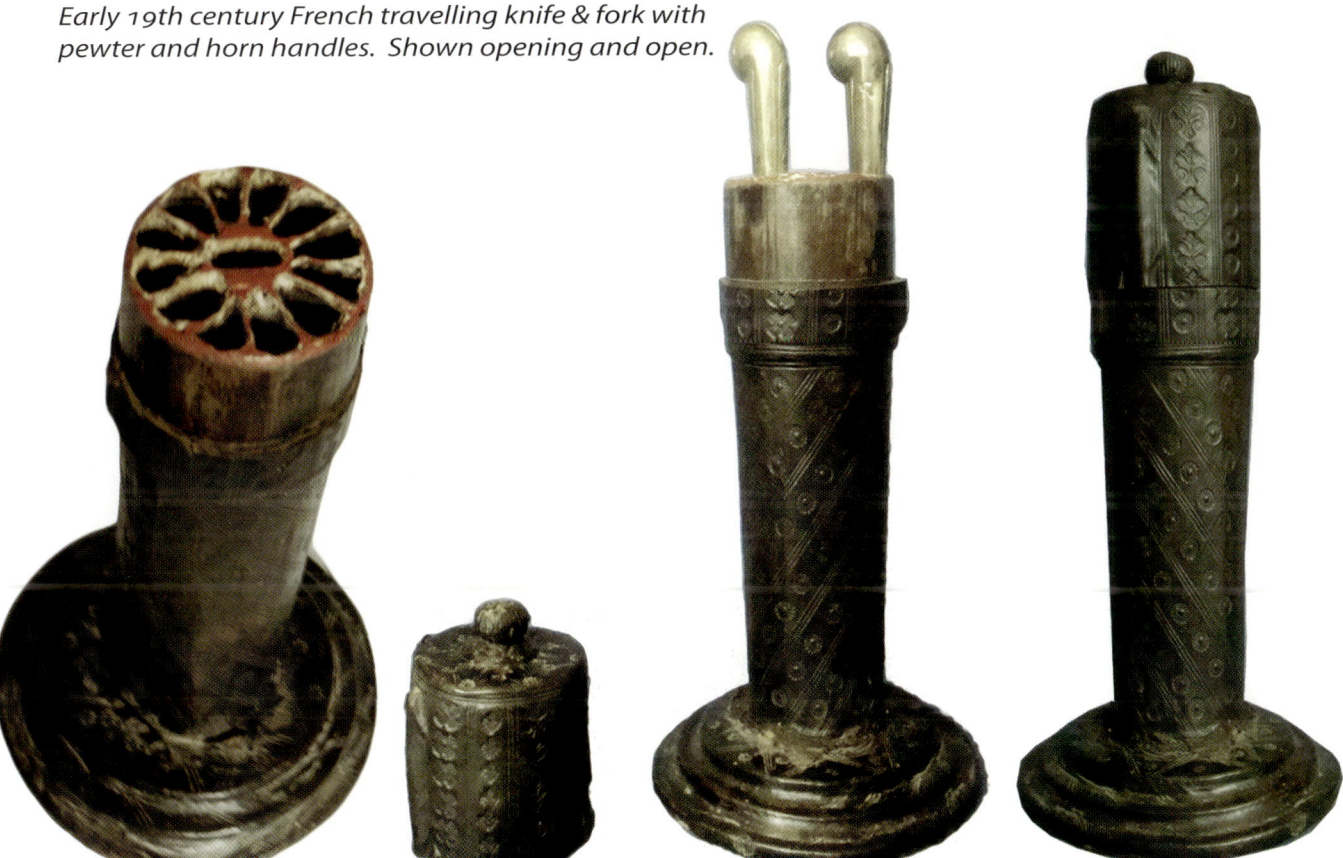

Late 17th century upright leather covered wooden knife case for 12 knives and one fork.

"FINGERS WERE MADE BEFORE FORKS"
Our natural gifts or advantages are of more value to us than artificial ones.

Cutlery

18th century steel knives. Note the upturned end of the blade, typical of the period.

19th century walnut knifebox.

17th century English brass spoons.

19th century French brass spoons.

"BORN WITH A SILVER SPOON IN ONE'S MOUTH"
Born to good luck. The reference is to the usual gift of a silver spoon by the godfather or godmother of a child. The lucky child does not need to wait for the gift, for it is born with it in its mouth or inherits it at birth.

Salt Pots & Spoons

18th century yew wood salt.

18th century faience salt.

18th century marble salt.

18th century silver salt with gilded well.

19th century copper-bladed ice or salt saw.

Three 19th century mother-of-pearl salt spoons.

"A COVENANT OF SALT"
A covenant which could not be broken, as salt was a symbol of incorruption.

A table setting with delft plates.

265

"BANQUET"
From the Italian "banco": a bench or table.

Continental Faience.

"AS IF HE HASN'T GOT ENOUGH ON HIS PLATE"
He already has enough troubles of his own without adding to them.

Horn

A selection of horn tableware. Horn was a cheap and readily available material for kitchen use in poor and some better-off homes.

Traditional 18th & 19th century horn beakers.

Two early 19th century horn beakers, one engraved with a verse, the other with a hunting scene.

"COBBLER'S PUNCH"
Gin and water with a little treacle and vinegar.

Mugs

Stoneware mug circa 1450-1550.

18th century seamed copper mug.

19th century seamed copper tavern mug often "pinched" and taken home.

19th century French pottery mug.

19th century pottery transfer printed mug.

19th century pottery transfer printed mug.

"ONE MUST DRINK AS ONE BREWS"
One must take the consequences of one's actions.

Tankards, Measures & Mugs

Late 18th century copper bound staved mug.

18th century silver mounted tankard of staved construction.

Late 18th century copper bound staved mug.

Early 18th century bronze 'Winchester' measure.

19th century brass rimmed pewter measure.

An 18th century seamed copper tankard. It was given to the author at the age of 7 - the first item in his collection.

When a customer bought the barmaid a drink in one of these tankards, he was paying for a full pint instead of the half that she drank. She stayed sober, he kept buying her drinks, and she pocketed the price of the missing halves. Everyone was happy.

19th century copper 'Barmaid's friend' tankard with false bottom.

"COOL TANKARD" or "COOL CUP"
A drink made of wine and water, with lemon, sugar and borage, sometimes also slices of cucumber.

Treen Goblets

18th /19th century treen goblets.

"ALEBERRY"
A corruption of ale-bree, a drink made of hot ale, spice, sugar and toast.

A collection of pewter tableware, platters and table salt, mostly 19th century Continental.

A table setting containing pewter.

"CREATURE COMFORTS"
Food and other things necessary for the comfort of the body.

Jugs

13th century English pottery jug.

14th century north European bronze jug.

Late 15th century Continental brass jug.

Late 16th century Italian cast bronze wine ewer.

Copper water jug.

16th century stoneware jug.

17th century seamed brass "Helmet" form jug.

Early 19th century seamed copper ale jug.

English West Country pottery jug.

"COMET WINE"

A term denoting wine of a superior quality. A notion prevailed that the grapes of "comet years" i.e. years in which remarkable comets appeared, were better in flavour than those of other years.

Measure from the "Mary Rose"

16th century pewter measure recovered from the 'Mary Rose', King Henry VIII's flagship which sank in 1545.

"DAGGER ALE"
The ale of the 'Dagger', a low class gambling house in Holborn, famous in Elizabethan times for its strong drink, formerly, and meat pies.

Jugs

Large slipware jug, probably from North Devon, dated 1799. Photo courtesy Roderick Butler.

The jug dates from 1880 and was probably made in Exeter, Devon.

"Come fill me full with liqours sweet
For that is good when friends do meet
But pray take care dont let me fall
Lest you lost your liqour jug and all"

---

275   "AT AFT-MEALS WHO SHALL PAY FOR THE WINE?"
THYNNE: c.1608

Treen table setting.

"TO TURN THE TABLES"

In the past tables only had one finished side; the other less expensive side was rougher. When the family was alone they ate on the rougher side, when company came the top of the table was lifted off and turned to the good side.

Glassware

English decanters and glasses from the 18th and 19th centuries.

"TO DRINK LIKE A FISH"
To drink abundantly or excessively.

Bottles

English wine bottles from the 17th to 19th centuries.

"CORKED"
The wine tastes of the cork i.e. is spoiled.

Corkscrews

Early 19th century bone handled steel two pillar corkscrew; continuous winding removes the cork.

19th century Champagne 'tap' used to draw off single glasses of champers without losing the fizz.

Early 19th century all steel 'wing nut' two pillar corkscrew.

Early 19th century all steel two pillar corkscrew.

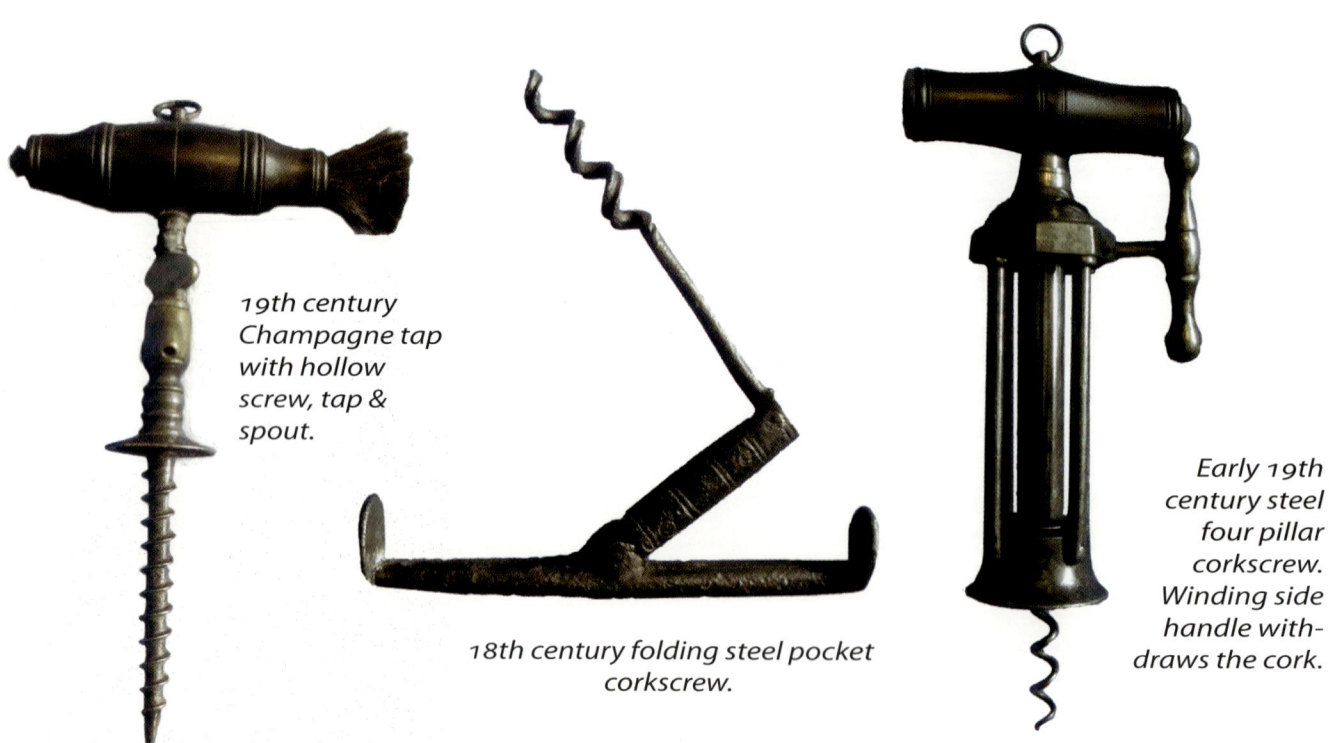

19th century Champagne tap with hollow screw, tap & spout.

18th century folding steel pocket corkscrew.

Early 19th century steel four pillar corkscrew. Winding side handle withdraws the cork.

"TO DRAW THE CORK"
To give one a bloody nose.

Nutcrackers

Bowl of nuts with 18th and 19th century nutcrackers.

Rare 18th century ivory screw nutcracker.

Rare 18th century brass and iron screw nutcracker.

Rare 18th century iron screw nutcracker.

19th century Swiss carved wood nutcracker.

Rare 18th century steel screw nutcracker.

Nutcrackers on a treen platter with cob nuts.

18th century Dutch brass nutcracker.

18th century English steel nutcracker.

"TO MAKE TWO BITES OF A CHERRY"
To divide something too small to be worth dividing.

Alms Dishes

Since medieval times, giving food to the poor was considered by the better off to be a duty and an honour. God fearing households gave away a proportion of their meals, presented in a large metal basin or alms dish. One or more of these dishes was displayed on a sideboard, next to the table where meals were eaten, as a constant reminder of duty and honour.

The tradition of giving food at the "back door" was well established by the 12th century. The earliest dishes were probably of silver, used by very wealthy families, and as the practice was taken up by more and more people throughout society, brass dishes became popular. Of course the more dishes one displayed on the sideboard when entertaining, and the larger and more decorative each dish was, the more generous the hosts would appear to their guests in this life and to God in the next!

Dishes of various materials and different sizes were made all over Europe, mostly for fairly local use but sometimes for export. In Italy repoussé copper dishes with fabulous beasts, the green man and foliage were made with the arms of the owner in the middle; specialist brass manufacturers in Nuremburg produced deeply repoussé dishes with designs showing the Annunciation, Adam and Eve, and St Christopher. These and other worthy images were popular for many years, and were sold all over Europe. Pewter dishes with enamelled brass bosses in the centre, often depicting the Royal coat of arms, were popular in England.

The tradition of distributing food from the tables of the wealthy to the poor continued right through the 19th century, and the designs of the dishes slowly changed and evolved as they continued to be made. Old dishes were often given to the local church where many can still be seen today.

17th century Swiss copper dish.

Nuremburg brass dish circa 1500.

Adam & Eve brass dish circa 1500.

"ALMS-DRINK"
Liquor left over from a feast and sent to the alms people.

The Aspiring Yeoman

Early 19th century Tolware monteith for cooling / rinsing glasses.

19th century wine cooler.

"BON VIVANT"
A free liver, one who indulges in "the good things of the table."

282

Lighting

Lighting

In the past the primary source of light in the kitchen was usually the fire itself. The other sources of light included rushlights (p.284, 285) wall sconces, candlesticks and oil lamps. Chandeliers were used in larger wealthier establishments - it must be remembered that the government of the day had introduced a tax on candles in England.

Wall sconces (p.291) usually had one or more candle holders mounted on extending arms; some could be driven into beams, some having a hook could be hung from a nail on a beam which allowed the limited light to be concentrated where it was needed. Many antique pieces of furniture bear the burn marks from candles being hung on them, especially the backs or arms of kitchen chairs.

At the end of the 19th century a great advance in kitchen lighting came with the use of gas. Although at first it was somewhat dangerous and the supply was irregular, before the invention of electricity, it provided a relatively clean, smell-free and, most importantly, an easy and wonderfully attendance-free bright light.

Constant improvements in lighting technology and fuels throughout this period led to increased safety, easier maintenance and brighter, more reliable light in the kitchen. One less thing for the busy cook to worry about!

18th century iron sconce for driving into a wall or beam.

"ANCIENT LIGHTS"
The right of access to light of a property, recorded from the mid 18th century. The sign "Ancient Lights" was often placed on a house adjacent to a site where a high building might be erected.

Making Rushlights

Cut some rushes as close to the ground as possible because you need the solid pith from the lower part of the plant. Put the rushes, cut ends down, in some water until you are ready to peel them carefully with a knife; leave a strip of the skin on one side to support the peeled stalk. When this is done, place your pith stalks somewhere warm to dry out; to stop them curling you can put them together in a bundle with some lengths of wood to keep them straight and tie them gently in a few places along their length.

Melt some animal fat (tallow) and when your rushes are dry, draw them through the fat in the grisset to coat them; lay them on paper keeping them well apart, or hang them up to dry. They will be ready to use when the fat has set solid. On average, a 12 inch long rush will burn for about 20 minutes.

Juncas rushes growing and (left) picked and in a jug of water ready to be prepared for use.

Animal fat for rendering in a grisset.

17th century iron grisset with dried rushlights.

A storage box and rushlights.

"RUSH-BEARING"
An annual ceremony in northern districts of carrying rushes and garlands to the church and strewing the floor or decorating the walls with them; normally a general holiday. Early 17th century.

Rushlight Holders

18th century Welsh rushlight holder with turned wooden base.

18th century treen based rushlight holder with candle sconce.

Tallow dipped rushes were stored in a box hung on the wall safe from rodents and away from the heat of the fire. The earliest holders were just crude cleft sticks stuck in the earthen floor. There is very little evidence of metal rushlight holders before the early 18th century. Cleft stick holders would have been used in poor households and not listed in inventories. Wealthier homes would have burned candles. (Occasionally v shaped fittings are found on medieval candlesticks which may have been for "emergency" use of rushes in wealthier homes)

In 1709 things changed when the government introduced a tax on candles sold by chandlers or made in the home. Harsh punishments for infringements of the candle tax meant that rushlights, which were excluded from the tax to help the very poor, suddenly became popular with the thrifty middle class who were evading the tax. Of course they didn't want cleft sticks in their homes so iron, brass and wood holders were made. Some finely turned wooden based holders (and some not so finely turned) were also made.

When a rush was held in the middle by a rushlight holder, more light could be had by lighting it at both ends. This was the origin of the phrase burning the "candle" at both ends (twice the light but for half the time!) As with all lighting equipment there was something for every taste and pocket.

Early 19th century Welsh cast brass based rushlight holder with iron stem and sprung jaws.

Rare early 18th century Welsh rushlight and candle holder.

Rushlight holders vary greatly according to regional style and date of manufacture. The wood bases were often replaced during long, hard lives. The candle tax wasn't repealed until 1831, and rushlight holders were still being made and used in rural areas in the 20th century.

Splint holders used in Scotland, and on the Continent, were a form of holder similar to a rushlight holder but they burned a splint of resinous wood instead.

(far left) Early 19th century sprung rushlight holder with exaggerated thumb piece. (left) Mid 19th century cast iron based wrought iron rushlight holder with weighted arm.

"BURN THE CANDLE AT BOTH ENDS"

Nowadays this phrase refers to a life that is lived frenetically and unsustainably. It was first coined in the 18th century; in those days, when both ends of the rushlight were burning, there was twice the light for half the time.

Early Candlesticks

15th/16th century very rare simple form, wrought iron candlestick.

Late 17th century rare form of mid drip pan wrought iron candlestick with adjustable height.

Late 17th century turned wood candlestick.

Mid 17th century cast brass, mid drip pan, Dutch 'Heemskirk' candlestick.

18th century Continental wrought iron spiral candlestick with a maker's mark. The candle can be raised as it burns down, by winding the tab up the spiral. (In England the problem of burning the last little bit of expensive candles was solved using various forms of a cunning device, known as a saveall.)

18th/19th century iron 'cage' candlestick. The height of the candle could be adjusted.

"HE CANNOT HOLD A CANDLE TO..."

To compare badly to an known authority - to be unfit even to hold a subordinate position. Apprentices used to be expected to hold the candle so that more experienced workmen were able to see what they were doing. Someone unable even to do that would be of low status indeed.

Brass Candlesticks

Candlesticks were the ideal option in the kitchen. They could easily be carried around and placed on any flat surface. Those made specifically for kitchen use were usually of iron; one type was known as a "hogscraper" because of its resemblance to a tool used to remove hair from a pig's skin. (This was a task usually done in the kitchen.) Brass candlesticks were also common in kitchens and were often described in inventories as being "old". This was probably because, as fashions in candlestick design changed in the dining room where they were seen by the guests, old fashioned candlesticks were relegated to the kitchen. Once there, brass candlesticks had a hard life as shown by their many dents and well polished finish.

17th & 18th century English brass candlesticks.

19th century brass chamber stick.

Savealls

Candles were so expensive that small devices called savealls were used. They often consisted of a little tray with a fitting underneath which sat in the candlestick socket. A screw was fixed upright on the tray, and the candle stub that had been taken from the candlestick could be screwed down onto it and burned to the end. Alternatively, three little upright rods were mounted on the tray and the candle stub was pushed down between them and held securely while it burned. One added advantage was that a single saveall could be used in almost any candlestick - all very ingenious and thrifty.

"THE BUTCHER, THE BAKER, THE CANDLESTICK MAKER"
People of all trades, from the nursery rhyme "Rub-a-dub-dub, Three men in a tub."

Candle Holders

18th century hanging adjustable wrought iron candle holders.

"TO SELL BY THE CANDLE"
A form of auction sale. A pin is thrust into the candle near the top and bidding goes on until the candle burns down to the pin. When the pin drops out, the last bidder is declared the purchaser.

Tinder Boxes & Pistols

18th century brass and steel 'strike a light'.

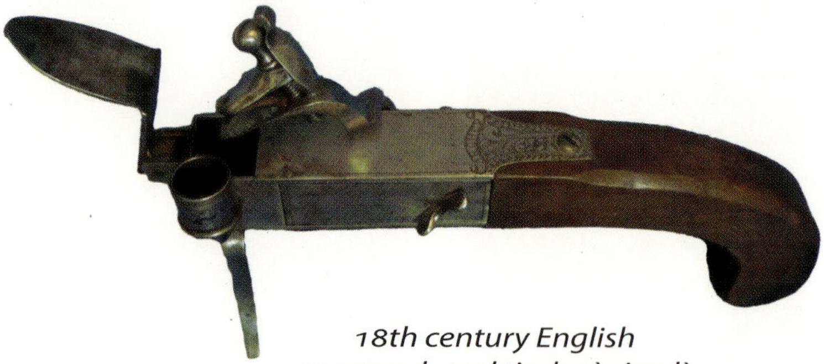

18th century English engraved steel tinder `pistol` signed ARCHER. The side opens and contains tinder and a spare flint.

Small, pocket tinder box with an integral steel striker down one side.

Three fire steels or strikers.

19th century brass tinderbox incorporating a candle holder and a some flints.

Early 19th century tinware tinder box with a candle socket on the lid. The box contains fire steel, flint, tinder and damper.

"STRIKE A LIGHT!"
An exclamation of surprise.

Mechanical Candle Snuffers

Scissor action candle snuffers were originally simply scissors with wide blades, to prevent cut wicks from dropping to the floor. Examples are known from the 15th century. Their style developed slowly until the mid 18th century; there was then a hundred year period of innovation with many different forms of snuffer produced. Often their designs were registered or their ingenious mechanisms patented. Simple forms of snuffer were made right through to the end of the 19th century but their styles were subject to the fashions of the times.

Candle snuffers were not intended for extinguishing the candle flame; they were for trimming the curled over burnt wick which caused guttering, resulting in wasted wax running down the side of the candle. Thus the snuffer kept the candle burning brighter for longer, but the trimming had to be done every 15 minutes or so. This need lessened as candle wicks improved around 1840.

The spike at the front of the snuffer was to lift up the wick before trimming it. The box contained the smouldering cut wicks, which were extinguished when the box was closed. If the user cut the wick too low the candle was "snuffed out". If the intention was to put out the candle a conical extinguisher, or a pair of doubters were used. Doubters were of scissor form with two discs, rather than blades, which "pinched out" the flame like a "mechanical finger and thumb"!

Rare English upright brass snuffer stand, circa 1730.

(far left) a conical extinguisher, (above) a rare brass pair of combined snuffer/doubters, (left) pair of English 19th century steel doubters.

"OUT LIKE A LIGHT"
To fall asleep suddenly like a candle that has had its flame extinguished.

Candles

18th century wall hanging primitive Welsh candle box.

18th century wall mounted wrought iron candle holder.

19th century tin candle mould.

Early 19th century hanging candle box.

19th century hanging tin candle sconce.

"CANDLEMAS DAY"
"If Candlemas Day be dry and fair, The half o' winter's come and mair;
If Candlemas Day be wet and foul, The half o' winter was gone at Youl."

"THE DEVIL'S CANDLESTICK"
The common stinkhorn fungus, also called the devil's horn and the devil's stinkpot.

Lanterns

Rare 17th century brass mounted sheet iron hand lantern with a pane of horn and wicker covered handle.

Tin and horn lantern. These were made over a long period.

Standard tin ware hand lantern with horn panes from the early 19th century. Examples with glass panes were used right through the century.

Late 19th century poche de nuit, small folding pocket candle holder.

Late 19th century brass oil lantern.

"THE FRIAR'S LANTERN"
A name for the Ignis fatuus or will-o'-the-wisp.

Oil Lamps

Wrought iron cruise (crusie) lamps were generally used in coastal regions where fish, seal or sea bird oil was easily accessible. The cruise usually consisted of two hanging, open topped pans, one above the other. The top held the wick in oil, and the lower caught the drips which were poured back into the top pan for re-use. These open top cruises could be dangerous if knocked and the oil spilled. Continental oil lamps were often enclosed. Of course the government had to have their say, so the use of cruises was prohibited unless the oil came from fish caught by British fishermen!

18th century Scottish wrought iron cruise lamp with removable upper pan.

17th century German wrought iron oil lamp.

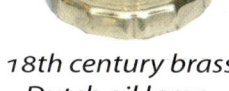

18th century brass crusie lamp.

18th century brass Dutch oil lamp.

Illustrated (above & right) are four rare examples of oil lamps from the late 19th century, used probably to light a nursery or a children's bedroom.

In the 19th century many forms of table oil lamp were invented for the dining room, a number of which would eventually have "found their way" to the kitchen. Some were modified for use outside the house, on boats for instance. Many were complex and difficult to keep in working order. But one great advance was in the supply of better oils. There was no need to use smelly products anymore - just imagine the cook's relief at not having to burn rancid fish oil! Even the alternative tallow candles must have produced an awful stench whilst cooking; beeswax candles smelled good but were expensive.

"LAMPS"
"The stars that Nature hung in heaven, and filled their lamps with everlasting oil to give due light…" Milton (Comus).

The Kitchen Garden

The Kitchen Garden

Gardens originally evolved from the early monastic traditions of the medieval religious orders. Abbeys and monasteries all had large gardens to cater for the people living and working within their walls, so monks really created gardens as we know them today. Grand gardens became fashionable in the Renaissance period, and their development culminated in the prodigious gardens of the Victorian era with their surrounding walls and glass houses; they epitomized gardening on a grand scale when labour was not a serious issue.

Of course it is important to realise that, unlike today, what you grew was what you ate! It was a question of survival and certainly not a fashion or a hobby, and the small strip or allotment was essential to provide sustenance and ensure survival in earlier times.

Probably the most famous kitchen garden is Villandry in the Loire district of France; this is gardening on a very grand scale, but the yeoman's kitchen garden was completely different, being a functional productive household necessity.

A traditional basket used to gather vegetables from the kitchen garden.

"CRAMBE BIS COCTA"
Literally, cabbage boiled twice. Figuratively, a well worn subject, a subject talked out.

This garden belonged to Robert Deeley. It is likely that vegetables have been grown on this plot for 500 years.

Herbs

Herbs had many uses in the home: there were culinary herbs, medicinal herbs, and those used for perfume, dyes and insect repellents.

Culinary herbs were many and would have included, among a multitude of others, basil, borage, endive, fennel, garlic, jack-by-the-hedge, mint, parsley, rosemary, sage, sorrel, savoury, tansy, thyme and violets.

Among the medicinal herbs there would have been aniseed, betony, cumin, lovage, liquorice, poppy, rue, rhubarb, stitchwort and valerian.

Herbs and plants used for their scent, and to keep the flea population in check would have included rosemary and lavender, and meadowsweet for strewing on the floor with the rushes, as well as sweet marjoram and rose petals used to add fragrance to the linen when it was washed.

Dye plants included agrimony, sorrel, marigold, madder and woad.

"FOOD FOR THOUGHT"
Something to ponder or mull over, especially something instructive.

Honey & Bee Keeping

Skep in bole, Devon.

When the Romans settled in England they noted that the people gathered honey from two sources, their own hives and wild bees' nests; those who collected the wild honey were called Mellitarios.

Some old houses in this country have "bee boles" incorporated into their outside walls; these are niches or alcoves in which bee skeps used to be kept. The boles were usually positioned at waist height or above and normally face east to south; they were 2 to 3ft high and about 18 to 24 inches wide. Skeps were made of straw which was coiled and stitched into a dome shape to make a simple bee hive. They were put in the alcoves to gain protection from the weather, and sat on wooden platforms to prevent the straw from rotting. Honey was gathered from the combs inside the skep, and smoke was used to stupefy the bees during this process.

It is thought that the Romans brought their own bees to England, and one of the reasons why the boles were incorporated into buildings was to provide the Mediterranean bees with warmth and protection from the vagaries of the English weather.

(left) Skep in alcove or bole. (above) Brass smoker for pacifying bees. Smoke was produced by burning rags. (right) Bees on honeycomb.

"HONEYMOON"
Mead, which was once our national drink, was drunk by newly weds after the moon was up following the marriage ceremony.

Brockhampton Estate, Hertfordshire, National Trust. A house fit for an aspiring yeoman.

INDEX

A

Adjustable ratchet 82
Ale muller 109
Alms dish 281
Andirons, see Firedogs, 10, 24
Ants 123
Apple baker 253-255
Apple corer 253, 255
Apple peeler 143
Ark (grain) 117, 123
Ash (wood) 126
Aspic mould 233
Axe (sugar) 115, 116

B

Bacon cooker 9
Bacon rack 245
Bacon settle 121, 239
Bain-Marie 111
Baker 203
Baker (apple) 253-255
Baking 203, 207, 215
Baking iron 215
Balance 142
Balance (spring) 141
Bargrate 4, 37, 39-42, 47, 51, 167
Bargrate fish toaster, 45, 171, 182, 183
Bargrate lark spit 172
Bargrate toaster 45, 46, 141, 170
Bargrate toasting fork, 171, 173, 183
Bargrate trivet 45, 46, 78
Barmaid's friend 269
Barrel 123
Basket 296
Basket (fire) 4, 37
Basket spit, 26, 53, 56, 165, 166
Basting 85, 87, 102
Basting pot 111
Beaker (horn) 267
Bee bole 299
Beeswax candle 294
Beetles 123
Bellows 36
Bench 93
Bins 123
Bird cooking fork 30
Biscuit mould 238
Blacksmith 93
Blancmange mould 233, 234
Block (chopping) 241
Blow pipe 36
Board (cheese) 228
Bone utensils 208
Book (recipe) 120
Bottle (glass) 278
Bottle (wood) 110
Bottle jack, 39, 54, 62, 85, 88-90
Bottled fruit 249
Bottlejack (Salter) 54
Bottling 239, 249
Bowl 258
Bowl (settling) 221
Bowl (sugar) 116
Box (candle) 291
Box (knife) 263
Box (salt) 108
Box (smoke) 239, 242, 246
Box (string) 108
Box (tinder) 289
Boy (turnspit) 52
Brandeth (hanging) 18
Brandreth 16, 104, 147
Brazier 48
Bread 167, 203, 207, 211
Bread board 94
Bread knife 94
Bread oven 3, 7, 201, 203, 210, 212, 213
Bread oven door 210
Bread peel 212
Bread proving bowl, 107
Bread toasting fork 27, 31, 33, 34
Broody coop 114
Bucket 125, 206, 220
Butter 219
Butter bowl 226
Butter churn 219, 222
Butter curler 226
Butter knife 226
Butter mould 226
Butter scales 142
Butter stamp 225, 226
Butter worker 224
Buttermilk 219

C

Caddy (tea) 252
Caius (Dr.) 52
Can (milk) 220
Candle (beeswax) 294
Candle (tallow) 294
Candle box 291
Candle mould 291
Candle tax 283
Candlestick 283, 286-289, 291, 292
Candle holder (hanging) 283, 288
Carcase 154, 240
Carving set 95
Cat (plate warmer) 48
Cat (rodent control officer) 123, 124, 133, 244
Cauldron, 7, 10-15, 38, 41, 81, 83, 84, 102, 104, 126, 147-150, 190, 242
Cauldron scraper 140
Cave 3
Central fireplace 3, 11
Central hearth 3
Chafing dish 48, 50
Chain 147
Chamber (smoking) 246
Chamber stick 283, 287
Chandelier 283
Charcoal 48
Cheese 219
Cheese board 228
Cheese press 219, 227
Cheese scoop 227
Chest 123
Chestnut roaster 113
Chimenee (porte de) 25
Chimney 55, 70, 239, 246
Chimney crane, 81, 82, 84, 147
Chisset 227
Chloride of lime 123
Chocolate 237
Chocolate mould 237
Chocolate pot 237
Chop 158
Chopper 94, 131, 139, 241
Chopping block 241
Chopping board 94, 214
Churn (butter) 219, 222
Churn (milk) 218
Churn (plunger) 222
Cider 123
Cistern (hot water) 75
Cleaning 126
Cloam oven 211
Clockwork spit 54, 69
Coal 4, 14
Cob irons 26, 84
Cockroach 123
Cockroach trap 123
Coffee bean roaster, 113
Coffee grinder 137, 138
Coffin pie mould, 193, 195, 196, 198
Colander 107
Conical extinguisher 290
Cooker (bacon) 9
Cooking pot 7, 163
Cooler (wine) 282
Coop (broody) 114
Cooper 93
Copper (for heating water) 3, 127
Corer (apple) 253, 255
Corer (cheese) 227
Corkscrew 279
Costrel 110
Cow (house) 218
Crackers (nut) 280
Cream skimmer 221
Crown (Dutch) 117
Cruise/crusie lamp 294
Cup (egg) 114
Cupboard (hanging food) 117
Curfew 26, 35
Curler (butter) 226
Cutlery 261-263

D

Dairy 218-230
Dangle spit 52, 54, 61
Dangle spit 52, 54, 61
Deeley inventory 129, 130
Delft 265, 266
Dippper 102
Dish (alms) 281
Dish (chafing) 48, 50
Dish (salting) 245
Dish (slipware) 92, 160, 197
Distilled 126
Dog 123
Dog (spit) 52, 102
Dog (toasting) 57
Dog (turnspit) 52, 71-74
Dog wheel 52, 71-74
Doubters 290
Doubters 290
Dough trough 207
Dovecote 146
Downhearth 3-5, 38
Downhearth fruit pan, 19
Downhearth pan 4, 7
Downhearth pie baker, 199, 200
Downhearth saucepan, 14
Downhearth settle 121

Downhearth toaster, 11, 167, 168, 170
Dr Caius 52
Dredger (flour) 107, 193, 195
Dried fruit 253, 255
Drip tray/fat catcher, 14, 21, 38, 52, 53, 57, 84, 86, 88, 153, 158, 163, 164, 166
Dry measure 206
Dutch crown 117
Dutch oven, 39, 54, 85, 87-89, 91,

E

Earthenware 123, 218, 248
Egg cup 114
Egg poacher 114
Ember shovel 36
Ember tongs 36
Embers 5, 155
Enamel 104-106, 218

F

Faggot 104
Faience 265, 266
Fat 157, 158
Fat catcher 4, 21, 38, 52, 53, 57, 75, 84, 86, 88, 153, 158, 163, 164, 166
Fender 40
Fire 1-5, 7, 11, 39, 48, 52, 54, 55, 59, 72, 121, 150
Fire (wood) 2, 3
Fire back 43, 44
Fire basket 4, 37
Fire grate 4
Fire guard 36
Fire irons 35, 36
Fire keep 26, 35
Fire screen 59
Firedogs see andirons, 10, 24, 53
Fireplace 3, 11
Fireplace (central) 11
Fish 175-187
Fish cooking fork 30
Fish kettle 177, 178
Fish pond 186
Fish slice 101
Fish smoking hooks, 246
Fish toaster (bargrate) 45, 171, 182, 183
Flask (powder) 123
Flask (shot) 123
Flesh fork / hook 11, 15, 27, 28, 104
Flies 1, 123, 154
Flintlock 123
Flour dredger 107, 193, 195
Flour measure 206
Food cupboard (mural) 117
Footman trivet 17
Fork (and knife) 261-263,
Fork (cooking) 30-34
Fork (flesh) 11-13, 27, 28, 104
Fork (log) 36
Fork (toasting) 27, 29, 31-

INDEX

34, 167
Founders 104
Fruit 247, 249
Fruit (bottled) 249
Fruit dried 253, 255
Fruit pan (downhearth) 19, 128
Fruit press 250
Frying pan 18-20
Frying pan (hanging) 178, 197

G

Game 8, 123, 163
Garden (kitchen) 296-300
Garlic 151
Geese (turnspit) 52, 72
Gingerbread mould 231, 235, 236
Glass 277
Glaze kettle 111
Goblet 270
Grain ark 117
Grain measure 206
Grain mill 204
Grain scoop 205
Grate (basket) 37
Grate (fire) 4
Grater 228, 252
Grease 126
Griddle 21, 22
Griddle plate 215
Gridiron 21, 22
Grinder (coffee) 137, 138
Grinding 135, 137
Grinding mill 204
Grisset 7, 9, 21, 284
Grocer's ledger 119
Guard (fire) 36
Guttering 290

H

Half kettle 78, 80
Ham 242, 244
Hand spit 52
Hands (Scotch) 219, 224
Hanging brandreth 18
Hanging candle holder, 288
Hanging food cupboard, 117
Hanging frying pan, 178, 197
Hanging pan 190, 191
Hangols 11, 14, 41
Harnen 168-171
Hastener 48, 85, 88, 89, 91
Hearth (central) 3
Hearth (stone) 5
Hedgehog 8
Herbs 135, 298
Hog scraper 287
Holder (rushlight) 285
Honey 299
Hook (meat) 86, 87
Hook (pot) 75, 81, 83
Horn beaker 267
Horn spoon 267
Horsehair sieve 205
Hot water cistern 75
Hour glass 108
House cow 218

Household Wants Indicator, 118
Hygiene 126

I

Ice cream 230, 231
Ice cream mould, 230, 231, 238
Ice saw 264
Implements 98, 99, 208
Inglenook fireplace 3
Intestine scraper 140
Inventory 129, 130
Iron (wafer) 216
Irons (baking) 215
Irons (cob) 26, 84
Irons (fire) 35, 36

J

Jack (bottle) 54, 85, 88, 90
Jack (smoke) 54
Jack (spit) / (spit engine) 23, 63-69
Jack (water) 70
Jack rack 62
Jack Veruvolver 68
Jam 123, 247
Jar 123
Jelly mould, 231, 233, 234
Jigger, (pastry crimper) 208
Jugs 273-275
Juice press 250

K

Keep (fire) 26, 35
Kettle 75-80, 84
Kettle (fish) 177, 178
Kettle (glaze) 111
Kettle (half) 78, 80
Kettle (turbot) 177
Kettle lifter 108
Kettle tilts 75, 76
Kettle trivet 17
Kitchen 93
Kitchen (fender) 40
Kitchen garden 296-300
Knife 94, 261-263
Knife (bread) 94
Knife (butter) 226
Knife and fork 261-263
Knife box 263
Knife case 262
Knife sharpener/steels, 95, 96

L

Ladle 15, 102, 103
Ladle (toddy) 102
Lamp 294
Lamp (cruise/crusie) 294
Lantern 293
Lantern clock 100
Larding needles 87
Lark spit 16, 57, 58, 145, 146, 153, 172
Lark spit (bargrate) 172
Ledger (grocer's) 119
Lifter (kettle) 108
Lighting 283-295

Lignum vitae wood 134, 137
Litter (pig) 240
Loaf (sugar) 115
Log fork 36
Love spoon 102
Love token 229

M

Malt bucket 125
Marrow bone 140
Marrow scoop 140
Masher 97
Measures 107, 206, 269
Meat cleaver 131
Meat hook 86, 87
Mechanical candle snuffer 290
Medecine 134
Merlin (Joseph) patent, 54
Mice 123, 124
Milk 218-223
Milk bucket 125, 220
Milk can 220
Milk churn 218
Milk pail 220
Milk settler 221
Mill (grain) 204
Mill (grinding) 204
Miller's grain bucket, 206
Milling 204
Mincer 137
Misericord 8
Monteith 282
Mortar (pestle and) 97, 108, 132-135
Mortar with cover 134
Mould 231
Mould (aspic) 233
Mould (biscuit) 238
Mould (blancmange) 231, 233, 234
Mould (butter) 226
Mould (candle) 291
Mould (chocolate) 237
Mould (coffin pie) 193, 195, 196, 198
Mould (gingerbread) 231, 235, 236
Mould (ice cream) 230, 231, 238
Mould (jelly) 231, 233, 234
Mould (sugar) 115
Mould (terracotta) 231
Mouse trap 124
Mug 268, 269
Muller (ale) 109
Mural food cupboard, 117
Mussels 190, 192

N

Needles (larding) 87
Nips (sugar) 115, 116
Nutcrackers 280
Nutmeg grater 252
Nuts 280

O

Oat crusher 194
Oil lamp 294
Olive oil 126
Oven (bread) 7, 201, 211, 212
Oven (cloam) 211
Oven (Dutch) 39, 54, 85, 89, 91

P

Pail (milk) 220
Pan 19, 20
Pan (downhearth) 7
Pan (hanging) 190, 191
Pan (preserve) 247, 250
Pan (saute) 20
Pan (warming) 112
Patent Joseph Merlin, 54
Peat 2
Peel 94, 99, 203, 212, 215
Peeler (apple) 143
Peppercorn 135, 251
Pestle and mortar, 108, 132-136
Pewter, 107, 158, 166, 175, 179, 180, 182, 200, 230, 231, 271,
Pheasant cooking pot, 163
Pie baker (downhearth) 199, 200
Pies 193, 195-200
Pig 158, 240
Pig litter 240
Pig's squeak 240
Pigeon 151
Piggin 220
Pipe (blow) 36
Pistol (tinder) 289
Plate, 128, 151, 211, 266, 271
Plate (griddle) 215
Plate warmer 47, 48, 49
Platter 156, 256, 257, 259
Plunger churn 222
Poacher (egg) 114
Pole screen 59
Pomander 126
Pond (fish) 186
Porringer 107
Porte de chimenee 25
Posnet 6, 14
Pot (basting) 111
Pot (chocolate) 237
Pot (salt) 242-244
Pot hook 14, 75, 81, 83
Pot stick 11, 13, 104
Pot-pourri 126
Potato 1, 5, 7,
Potato baker 7
Potato rake 7
Poultry 123, 163
Powder flask 123
Preparation 131, 134
Preserve pan 247, 250
Preserving 239, 247
Presses 227, 250
Proving 207

Q

Quern 204, 209
Quick fire 11

302

INDEX

R

Rack (bacon) 245
Rack (jack) 62
Rack (skewer) 60
Rack (spit) 56
Range 4
Ratchet (adjustable) 82
Rats 123
Recipe book 120
Reflector oven, see Dutch oven 39, 54, 85, 86, 88, 89, 91
Repairs 128
Roaster (chestnut) 113
Roaster (coffee bean) 113
Roasting 2, 153, 155
Roberval scales 142
Rolling pin 193, 194
Romance 229
Rushlight holder 285
Rushlights 7, 157, 283-285

S

Salamander 101, 215, 217
Salt 135, 219, 264
Salt box 108
Salt pot 242-244
Salt saw 264
Salt spoon 264
Salting 239, 242
Salting dish 245
Sauce 151
Saute pan 20
Saveall 286, 287
Saw (ice) 264
Scales 141, 142
Sconce (wall) 283
Scoop (grain) 205
Scoop (marrow) 140
Scotch hands 224
Scourer (twig) 126
Scraper (cauldron) 140
Scraper (intestine) 140
Screen (fire) 59
Screen (pole) 59
Scummer 11, 12, 104-106
Serving spoon 107
Settle 121
Settle (bacon) 121, 239
Settle (downhearth) 121
Settler (milk) 221
Settling bowl 221
Sharpener (knife)(Steels) 95, 96
Shellfish 188-192
Shot flask 123
Sieve 205
Silver fish 123
Simmering 11, 14, 147
Skewer 54, 55, 60, 87, 92
Skewer rack 60
Skillet 6, 7, 14, 128
Skimmer 104-106, 221
Slice 99
Slice (fish) 101
Slipware dish 92, 160, 197
Smoke box 239, 246
Smoke jack 70
Smoking 239, 246
Smoking chamber 3, 246

Snippets 104
Snuffer (candle) 290
Soap 126
Soap wort 126
Soft fire 11
Soup 151
Spice 115, 123, 251, 252
Spice box 251, 252
Spice tray 251
Spit, 52-55, 57, 58, 72-4, 85, 91, 126, 159, 187
Spit (basket) 26, 53, 56, 165, 166
Spit (clockwork) 54, 69
Spit (dangle) 52, 54, 61
Spit (hand) 2, 52, 159
Spit (lark) 16, 57, 58, 145, 146, 153, 172
Spit (wooden) 152, 155, 156
Spit dogs 52, 71, 74
Spit engine (spit jack) 23, 63-69, 166
Spit jack 52, 53, 63-69
Spit rack 56
Splint 285
Spoon (horn) 267
Spoon (love) 102
Spoon (straining) 102
Spoons 97, 98, 107, 262-264
Spring balance 141
Spurtle 97
Squirrels 8
Stamp (butter) 225, 226
Standing toasting fork, 173
Steels 95, 96
Steelyard 141
Stick (pot) 104
Stilton scoop 227
Stool 23, 218, 219
Storage 117
Storage containers 247
Straining spoon 102
Striker 289
String box 108
Suckling pig 2, 159
Sugar 115, 116, 135, 237
Sugar axe 115, 116
Sugar bowl 116
Sugar loaf 115
Sugar mould 115
Sugar nips 115, 116
Sulgrave Manor 129

T

Table (yeoman's) 256
Table setting 259, 260, 265, 272, 276
Tallow 126, 284, 285
Tankard 268, 269
Tansy 123
Tax (candle) 285
Tea caddy 252
Tea pot 252
Tenderiser 241
Terracotta mould 231, 232
Terrine 232
Tidy 126
Tidy (kitchen) 126

Tilt (kettle) 75, 76
Tinder 289
Tinder box 289
Tinder lighter 289
Tinder pistol 289
Toast stand (cat) 48
Toast trivet 17
Toaster (bargrate) 45, 171-174
Toaster (downhearth) 11, 167, 168, 170
Toasting 167-174
Toasting dog 57
Toasting fork 31-34, 167
Toasting fork (bargrate) 41, 171, 173
Toasting fork (bird) 28, 30
Toasting fork (fish) 30
Toasting fork (hand) 28-34
Toasting fork (standing) 41, 173
Toasting stand 48
Toasting trivet 172
Toddy ladle 102
Tolware (Tinware) 282
Tongs (ember) 36
Tongue press 250
Traps 123, 124
Tray (drip) 14, 38, 52
Tray (spice) 251
Treen 97, 98, 137, 138, 144, 184, 221-229, 256-260, 270, 276
Trencher 211
Trivets 17, 45, 46
Trough (dough) 207
Trough (water) 126
Turbot kettle 177
Turnspit boy 52
Turnspit dog 72-74
Turnspit geese 52, 72
Twig scourers 126

U

Utensils (bone) 208
Utensils (kitchen) 107

V

Vegetables 147, 148, 249, 297
Venison 1, 29, 154-156
Vermin 123, 124
Veruvolver Economic Roasting-Jack 68

W

Wafer iron 216
Waffle iron 216
Wall sconce 283
Warmer (plate) 47-49
Warming pan 112
Washing 127
Wasp trap 123
Water jack 70
Water trough 126
Weevils 123
Wheel (dog) 52, 71-74
Whisk 107
Wine bottle 278

Wine cooler 282
Wire mouse trap 124
Wire sieve 205
Wood ash 126
Wood bowl 258
Wood fire 2, 3
Woodcock 8, 164, 165
Wooden plate 211
Wooden spit 52, 155, 156
Worker (butter) 223, 224

Y

Yeoman 93, 256, 282, 300
Yeoman's pig 240
Yeoman's table 256
Yetling 203, 217
Yoke 219

INDEX
FOOD, DRINk & RECIPES

Apples	143, 253-255	Pheasant	52, 157, 164
Beef	21	Pies	193
Bread	203	Pig	2, 159, 247
Capon	55	Pigeon	146, 165
Chestnut	113	Pork	140, 157, 158
Chicken	55, 132	Porridge (sweet chestnut)	113
Coffee	113	Potatoes	1, 5, 7
Dairy	218	Pyramidis Cream	11
Deer	1	Quail	8, 57, 153, 166
Duck	166	Salt	242
Eggs	114	Soup	102
Fish	175-192	Spice	115, 126, 251, 252
Fruit	247, 249	Squirrel	8
Gravy	102	Sugar	115, 116
Hedgehog	8	Tea	252
Herbs	135, 298	Teal	8, 164
Honey	299	Toast	167, 169, 171, 173, 174
Lamb	85-88, 92, 160	Trout	54, 187, 246
Milk	104, 218-221, 223	Venison	1, 29, 154-156, 193
Nuts	139, 280	Woodcock	8, 157, 158, 164, 165
Partridge	8, 164		

Apple Muse	152	Old English pork chop,	158
Apple pie	199	Oxtail Stew	149
Baked Pike	185	Pease Pudding	152
Bannocks	214	Red Herrings	176
Beef Broth	151	Rost Bef with Sauce Aliper	152
Carp	186	Sausages	140
Chacun a son Gout	152	Singing Hinnies	214
Crusts of Bread for Cheese,	203	Sole Fryid	152
Fish	175	Spit Roast Suckling Pig,	159
Fretoure	152	Stekys of Bef	152
Game pie	193	Stewed Pigeon (Peiouns ystewed)	151
Good Common Blamange or Blanc Manger	234	To Boil a Chine of Mutton	104
Good Common Gingerbread,	235	To Fry Eels	184
Havercakes	214	To Make Bread	207
Lamprey Pie	176	To Make Chocolate	237
Marrow bone	140	To Sweeten Tainted Fish	176
Meat Terrine	232	Venison pie	193
Milk Punch	105	Waffles	216
Mussels	190		

Part of Robert Deeley's extensive collection.

BIBLIOGRAPHY

"English Bronze Cooking Vessels and Their Founders, 1350-1830" by Roderick Butler and Christopher Green. (Acanthus Press, Wellington, Somerset)
"Iron and Brass Implements of the English House" by Lindsay Seymour. (Tiranti 1970)
"The Book of Copper and Brass" by Geoffrey Wills. (Country Life Books)
"Food in England" by Dorothy Hartley. (Macdonald 1975)
"Living and Dining in Medieval Paris" by Nicole Crossley Holland. (Cardiff University of Wales Press 1996)
"Mrs Groundes-Peace's Old Cookery Book". (David and Charles)
"Irons in the Fire" by Rachel Feild. (The CrowoodPress)
"Luttrell Psalter 1340". Mansell Collection
"Antique Iron" by Herbert, Peter and Nancy Schiffer. (Schiffer Publishing Ltd.)
"A Taste of History" by Maggie Black. (The British Museum Press)
"A Taste of the Fire", Hampton Court Palace.
"Modern Cookery in all its Branches" by Eliza Acton. (Longman Brown, Green and Longmans)
"Cook's Oracle". (A. Constable and Co. Edinburgh)
"Treen and Other Wooden Bygones" by Edward Pinto. (London G. Bell and Sons)
"Domestic Metalwork" by Rupert Gentle and Rachel Feild. (Antique Collectors' Club)
"The Old Devon Farmhouse" by Peter Brears. (Devon Books)
"Lost Crafts" by Una McGovern. (Chambers)
"Metal Work" by Hans-Ulrich Haedeke.
"English 18th Century Cookery" by Cecilia Ware. (Roy Bloom Ltd.)
"The Open-Hearth Cook Book, Recapturing the Flavor of Early America" by Suzanne Goldenson, Doris Simpson.
"Mrs Beeton's Everyday Cookery", (Ward Lock & Co.)
"Recipes From the Dairy" by Robin Weir, Caroline Liddell and Peter Brears. (National Trust)
"Making Fire and Light in the Home pre 1820" by John Caspall. (Antique Collectors' Club
"Cooking and Dining in Medieval England" by Peter Brears. (Prospect Books)
"The Antique Metalware Society Journal" 2009, 2010 & 2011, Tony Weston.
"The Forme of Cury" compiled by Richard II's master cooks about 1390
"The Brass Book" by Herbert, Peter and Nancy Schiffer. (Schiffer Publishing Ltd.)
"Collecting Antique Copper & Brass" by Peter Hornsby
"Pewter, Copper and Brass" by Peter Hornsby
"English Decorated Bronze Mortars and Their Makers" by Michael Finlay
"Treen for the Table" by Jonathan Levi (Antique Collectors' Club 1998)
"Domestic Utensils of Wood" Owen Evan-Thomas
"Collecting Antique Metalware" by Evan Perry (Country Life Books 1974)